Get a Grip

"Janie" —
Hope you enjoy!
♡ Ann Reed

ALSO BY ANNIE HANSEN

KELLY CLARK MYSTERY SERIES

GIVE ME CHOCOLATE
BEAN IN LOVE
TAKE THE DONUT
BACK FOR S'MORE

Get a Grip

Annie Hansen

|HF
Publishing

Get a Grip copyright © 2023 by Annie Hansen.
Published by HF Publishing
Cover design by Deborah C. Blanc

ISBN: 979-8-39252-640-6 (soft cover)

This book is a work of fiction. All names, characters, places and events are products of the author's imagination or are used fictitiously, and any resemblance to actual persons, living or dead, or to actual places or businesses, is entirely coincidental.

All rights reserved. In accordance with the U.S. Copyright Act of 1976, no part of this publication may be reproduced, distributed, or transmitted in any form or by any means, or stored in a database or retrieval system, without prior written permission of the publisher, HF Publishing.

This ebook is licensed for your personal enjoyment only. This ebook may not be re-sold or given away to other people. If you would like to share this book with another person, please purchase an additional copy for each recipient. If you're reading this book and did not purchase it, or it was not purchased for your use only, then please purchase your own copy. Thank you for respecting the hard work of this author.

Dedication

This book is dedicated to all the parents that went through Covid — those that homeschooled, isolated, sheltered in place. If you went a little crazy, this book is for you.

Lisa

"Did you hear that?" Petra asked, her head swinging wildly to the left. Her long legs, wrapped in very expensive camo-colored Lululemon leggings stopped dead in their tracks. Her black eyes bulged out like they wanted to burst from her head.

"What?" I asked, stopping just short of knocking into her. The hypervigilant tone of Petra's voice made me want to scream. I couldn't take anymore. The last thing I needed was more intensity. The level that we were functioning at for the last nine months was unbearable. And there seemed to be no end in sight. This run was supposed to be my break from the mania that was raining down on the world during this never-ending pandemic.

"Over there?" Janie pointed. "I heard it, too."

Janie reached up and pulled off her hat, a puff of blond hair bursting out while she bent over and put her hands on her knees. I tried to make eye contact with her, but she kept her eyes locked in the direction Petra was pointing.

"It sounded," Janie said, between winded breaths, "like an animal, right?"

"No, that was no animal," Petra said, putting her hands on her hips and starting to walk in the direction she had been pointing. I watched her tight butt sashay further away and thought, "Oh no. Not again."

"That was human," Petra said, looking back at us. "Someone in distress."

Ever the skeptic of the group, I did my best to keep my expression open, even though I hadn't heard anything. There was a little part of me that felt left out for being the only one to not have picked up on something. Was I slipping? I was normally so observant. But who would blame me if I was slipping? Especially based on what I was going through.

"Have you been watching too many of your true crime shows?" I asked Petra, keeping my tone respectful but light. I didn't want to insult Petra. Especially not now.

"That's Carrie's house," Petra said, ignoring my comment. "That's where it came from. Let's go ring the doorbell."

"Petra, it's five in the morning," I said, pulling out my phone and double checking the time. Was she serious? I selfishly began calculating the time it would take me to get home, showered and back to the hospital to start my shift. I didn't have time for any shenanigans this morning. "We can't go around ringing doorbells this early."

Petra didn't say anything but turned and gave me a look.

"So, we don't do anything?" she said, looking at me with those dark, sad eyes she'd been sporting for the past year. Seeing them made my selfish thoughts stop. It was all still there.

Janie and I snuck each other a look as if asking, "What do you think?" It was hard to say no to Petra. Almost impossible. She did have a good gut instinct, and we both respected her, but she had not been herself after the death in her family, and then there was Covid. The pandemic was just making her impossible situation worse.

"How well do you know Carrie?" Janie asked, standing back up to her full height. As a petite blond, she and I were both about 6-7 inches shorter than our statuesque friend. Petra could pass for a runway model, whereas Janie and I were both barely up to her chest.

"I only know her through school. Her daughter is in Shane's class," Petra said.

"Look," I point out, grabbing onto Petra's arm, relief running through me. "There! A coyote!"

A mangy-looking mutt ran through the field just twenty feet to the left of us, causing us to scream and grab onto each other. He turned to look at us with what could only be described as content. Like we were messing with his morning routine.

"Oh, for God's sakes," Janie said, laughing.

"They are getting bigger and bigger, I swear," Petra said, clearly sharing my relief based on the radiant smile she flashed me.

"And bolder. Look how close that thing was to us," I said, feeling better and freaked out at the same time.

"Now we know what the scream was," Janie said. "Now can we get going? I need to get home before the kids wake up."

"Are you satisfied, Petra?" I asked, glancing quickly at my watch and running through the day in my head. This was my life. Every minute, every second was important.

"Sure," Petra said, turning in the direction of her driveway, right next to Carrie's house.

Though she was "better," I noticed she didn't quite meet my eyes and hold them when she answered.

"Okay, girls, talk to you later today," Janie called out and continued to run past Petra's house, up the hill to her own driveway.

My old hand-me-down junk car sat in Petra's driveway, sad and pathetic, waiting for me. It looked out of place in this fancy-pants neighborhood. It was. And so was I now.

"Have a great day!" I called out to my friends, relieved when my car unlocked after I hit the button. Yesterday I was having trouble with my key fob. It seemed like every day there was something new with this old car. Ugh. My life.

My new home, still in the same suburb of Chicago but on the less desirable side, was a ten-minute drive but felt like a world away from the gargantuan mansions I was pulling away from. I waved goodbye to Petra and made a point to turn my head at the right moment so as to avoid seeing the one I used to live in with my family. It was too painful.

As sad as this all sounded, I was at the moment still feeling invigorated and happy. The way I always felt after our runs. Worth the hassle. Worth the super early wake up, the drive, the getting dressed in the pitch dark. These runs were my therapy and my guaranteed time with my friends.

Already spinning through my to-do list for the day, I barely noticed the pink streak of Petra's sweatshirt in my rearview mirror heading in the wrong direction but caught it at the last second before I turned. Was she trying to get my attention? Maybe I left something behind. Like a hubcap. I tapped the brakes and looked back to see what was going on.

But she wasn't looking for me at all. She seemed totally focused walking quickly, but not looking for me. I knew she had a shift today, too. I planned on seeing her at the hospital. She didn't have time to mess around. But sure as shit, there she was jogging down the block back in the direction we came from. Back to the place we stopped after we saw the coyote. Back toward Carrie's house.

Petra

"You're going to be late," my hunk of a husband said, placing a steaming cup of coffee on the white granite bathroom counter next to where I normally sat and did my make-up.

"You can take the kids?" I asked, already knowing the answer. We'd discussed this last night. And the night prior. We were always on top of our schedules. We had to be. Paul was phenomenal about having to keep the schedule.

"Of course," Paul said, leaning back against the counter and crossing his muscular arms. He had on his white, post-workout, muscle T-shirt he always wore in the morning and baggy sweatpants. I could feel him watching me in the shower, something I would have appreciated in the past, but with the way things were for us right now, I didn't like.

"Any chance of you coming home earlier?"

"I'm going to be later today, remember?" I said, stepping out of the shower and wrapping my body quickly in the towel Paul handed me. I could not handle him looking at me. Or the sad look he tries to hide that he gets when he looks at me.

His dark brown eyes pull away from my legs and meet my eyes, covering up what I know he's thinking by flashing his signature smile. The smile I fell in love with that is driving me crazy right now. He's still sexy as hell, twenty years into marriage, and I'm more attracted to him than ever. But, right now I'm hot in another way. Still mad.

"That's right, I remember," he said, turning and washing his hands. Is it so that he doesn't have to look at my damaged legs? I don't blame him. It's not easy to look at me. To look at my body and know it will never be the same. Meanwhile, he continued to keep building his perfect body-builders physique year after year.

A flash of anger attacks me and I do my best to battle it down. This was how it was now. I would be doing fine, moving on with my life and then the inferno would strike, building me up almost instantaneously to a level of anger that felt unbearable. I would become angry and filled with a desire to lash out, to yell, to accuse, to justify and finally to cry.

"Wednesday," I mumbled quietly to myself, doing my best to refocus and use the skills my therapist had given me so far.

"What?" Paul asked, turning back from the sink and running his hands over his bald head. He'd started losing his hair fairly early in our marriage and quickly decided to shave it, a move that made him even more attractive from my point of view. He looked nearly identical to Dwayne Johnson, also known as The Rock, and was often mistaken for him. A fact that we both got a kick out of.

When I didn't answer him, he moved a little closer and suddenly I was face to face with the extreme whiteness of his teeth. Had he recently had them bleached again? Had I not noticed?

"Nothing," I said, shaking my head and turning to walk into the bedroom, avoiding his approach completely. I took a moment to touch the top of the gray, silk cover over our down comforter, hear the sound of the duvet under my fingers, breathe in the fresh smell of the sheets washed in lavender, thanks to our new housekeeper, and then run my tongue around my mouth again to retaste the minty toothpaste I had used before jumping into the shower. I didn't have time to have a panic attack this morning. There was too much to do. I had a laundry list of things at work today. Wednesday. If I was going to have another panic attack, it needed to happen Wednesday. At my therapist's office. Within those walls. That was the only place I would allow myself to break down. To release my grief, my anger, my weaknesses.

"Baby, can we please talk?" Paul asked softly, coming up behind me for what felt like the millionth time. He was always asking for a moment. To explain himself. Perhaps to make his own guilt go away, so we could finally fix us. Too late. Or I should say, too little, too late.

"Paul, this is a bad time," I said, trying my best to keep my tone even and calm. "I have to go."

"Mommy, you said you would make pancakes with me," my five-year-old daughter, Ellie said, wandering into the room, her eyes still half-closed.

Her long, black hair, the exact match to my own color, ran all the way to her little round butt and not for the first time, I chastised myself for not taking her to a hair salon in the last ten months. She wanted her hair to look like mine, but at some point, it had way surpassed mine and then some. How had I not noticed? This was getting out of control.

"I can't do that today, sweetie. Today Mommy has to go to work, remember? It's a school day, too. We never make pancakes on school days," I said, quickly covering my body with the long-sleeve, floor-length robe I had laid out on my bed. Hopefully, she was still too half asleep to have seen anything. I didn't want her to see the scars or at least have as little exposure to them as possible.

"But I want to. You said we could make them," she whined, rubbing at her eyes.

"I'll make them with you this morning," Paul said, scooping her up into his massive arms.

"But Mommy never does anything with me. She is always at work," she whimpered, tucking her head into Paul's neck. Hearing that broke my heart. I worked really hard to maintain a balance, but these last few months of Covid had been nearly impossible to keep stability. Plus, when I was home, Ellie was probably registering that I wasn't all there mentally.

"Mommy has to help the sick people. Especially today," Paul said, covering for me. He always did. It made me feel supported but also shamed at the same time. Why did I think I could have it all? Paul ran a very lucrative business from home. His life seemed a lot healthier than mine in many ways. This was the year of regret for me. Had I chosen the right profession? It felt like the right thing for as long as I could remember, but this year had been soul-crushing.

"I promise you, Ellie, I will make them with you on the weekend," I said, moving in to hug her along with Paul.

She kept her face tucked in tight to his arm, pouting a bit, but he turned his shining eyes on me and embraced me tightly, the three of us locked close together. His familiar smell and his strong arms held me as he whispered in my ear.

"How about a date on Saturday night? Ellie is not the only one that misses you," he said, pulling me even closer. I thought back to the first time I met Paul at a friend's house. That first spark of attraction. That first moment when I thought, "How is a man this nice, so sexy? This is too good to be true."

As much as I wanted to accept his proposal for a date to talk things out, I stalled. It meant one-on-one talking. Talking meant picking and dissecting our problems. Dissecting once again what had happened. As much as I wanted to be close to my husband, physically and emotionally again, pulling away offered comfort as well. The wounds, the physical and emotional ones, were just starting to scab over a bit. Why ruin my progress?

Janie

"So, did you tell them?" my husband asked, before I even closed the back door upon returning from my run. I lived only one door down from Petra, so all I had to do was my usual goodbye wave and home was a matter of seconds away. It was such a great arrangement. We all knew we were individually spinning a million plates, so there was no need to explain the hurried goodbye. It was understood that the plates were calling.

I made a point to never miss my run with my friends. The time with them put me in the right head space to stay productive throughout the day. And if I was going to keep my spot as the number one realtor for my firm, I needed to stay focused. Real estate had launched into hyper speed during the pandemic. Great for my business, but also an incredibly hectic pace to keep. The city dwellers were fleeing for the suburbs, the very area I focused on. And sellers knew this was the time to make top buck.

"No," I said, letting out a big sigh. "I couldn't do it," I dropped my shoulders a bit and frowned. My husband laughed at my dramatics, passing me a coffee.

"You're offering them a weekend away at a spa, not a trip to the guillotine, Janie. Why won't you ask them?" Sam demanded, using his best persuasive lawyer voice to sway me. Even this early in the morning, still dressed in his pajamas, he looked lawyerly, his hair brushed and his robe neatly tied.

"I know, but there's so much to this, Sam. You don't understand," I said, glancing at the clock on the stove. My all-white, newly remodeled kitchen was spotless and smelled like it had just been buffed and polished. Sam was a clean freak to a fault. He used cleaning to destress, thank goodness, because I had no interest in it whatsoever. And even though the sun had not even risen, Sam had been up before I left for the run, working in his home office. My guess was he'd probably thrown some countertop scrubbing in while prepping the coffee just to relieve any tension he'd built from his early morning ritual of reviewing his firm's cases. At this point in his career, Sam had attorneys who worked for him, so he wasn't as involved in as much in regards to the day-to-day maintenance, but he was still a perfectionist. When he didn't like the way a case was going, he wanted to be ready to pounce at any minute.

"Here, sit down with me for a minute before the kids get up and talk to us," he said, pulling out a stool for me to sit next to him. I looked down at it and smiled, knowing I should listen to Lisa's nagging voice in my head that told me I needed to rehydrate after a run, not caffeinate up. Today, I would ignore it and indulge in a little coffee time with Sam.

"Sam, you don't understand. Moms are maxed out right now," I said. "Like, going to blow into a million pieces, maxed out. Moms were already at their limit and now we are expected to teach the kids, calm the family, and somehow keep working full-time while the world is on this roller coaster of Covid. It's an impossible situation. Haven't you heard that we are the great, what did they call it?" I asked, sitting down on a stool and enjoying the attention Sam was giving me.

"Shock absorbers," he said, running both hands through his white, thinning hair and smiling at me. "I remember. You told me about this last week," he said. "I know you're feeling all this, honey. That's why I'm pushing you to do this."

Although I appreciated his encouragement, I didn't think he really grasped the complexity of the situation. I checked in on the time again, already feeling the pressure building. I was hoping to shoot off a few emails before the kids woke up. Now I had to make a decision. Sit here and spend time with Sam, who appeared as though he really wanted to connect, or get those emails out.

"Hey," Sam said, reaching out and taking my hand. "My offer still stands about getting a live-in nanny. It feels like you could use more help."

As much as I appreciated his efforts, his hand felt a little bit like an anchor. A heavy one. Pulling me down. It felt like they were all pulling at me nonstop nowadays. At least he cared. I had to remind myself that. His insistence on checking in came from love. It was so much better this way than what I had before.

"No, I don't think we need that. Maybe. Let me think about it," I said, pushing back like I always did when he offered to hire me more help. Although we had sitters for the kids, I wasn't ready to pull the trigger on full-time, live-in help. That being said, I was probably in denial that I could keep going at this pace.

"Is there anything you want to talk about? You're still doing okay, right?" Sam asked, watching me with that critical eye I both appreciated and felt embarrassed about at the same time.

When I paused, he got off his stool and came toward me, his knees cracking a bit when his feet hit the floor. Even if I wasn't okay, I wouldn't tell him. I wouldn't put him through that again. It was just that one time. Never again. He had enough pressure as the head of his firm.

"Oh, Sam, honey, no, I'm fine," I said, reassuring him. "Totally fine. I'm great, in fact. I'm just worried about my friends," I said, stopping him before he cracked anymore body parts. "Sit down, sweetheart."

Sam was older than me. A fact I thought about every day. Especially now in this time where the over sixty-five population had been hit so hard by this virus. I wanted to lock him in a room and never let him out. But that was extreme. I was just scared for him. Thank God we were finally vaccinated.

"You can tell me," he said, taking my direction and sitting back down on the stool.

We'd met a few years after his wife had died in a tragic car accident, and I'd gone through a very contentious divorce. Meeting him had been like someone throwing me a lifeline. I'd finally been able to have the children I wanted, and the ones he was never able to have with his first wife. He encouraged me to pursue my dreams of selling real estate, and poured affection on me like I was the most important person in the world. My self-esteem that had been destroyed by my first marriage blossomed into a beautiful garden now. And the money. The security that the money brought certainly felt good. But it was truly his love. His generous love that made me so strong today.

Not to say that the weeds weren't still there sometimes. I had to watch those weeds. Always. Dark, spindly veins that crawled in and sucked the life out of my beautiful garden I had worked so hard developing.

"I promise, I would tell you," I told him, looking into his eyes and counting the wrinkles around them. I swear they multiplied on a daily basis.

No, I wouldn't, I thought to myself.

"Okay, good. I can see you are distracted, so go do what you have to do to maintain your lead at work. I'm so proud of you," he said, sitting back in his chair and flashing me a great big Sam smile.

I'm so ashamed, I thought silently for myself.

"No," I said aloud.

"What?" Sam asked, raising an eyebrow and placing his coffee cup down on the counter.

"Oh, I'm just talking to myself," I laughed off, getting up from the table. "I'm trying to decide if I should have more coffee. I'm watching you drink that cup and as much as I want more, I think a third cup may push me over the edge."

Sam said nothing but smiled and winked at me.

"I'm just going to hit the emails before any of the munchkins wake up," I said, leaning down to kiss him on the lips quickly. "I love you, honey. You are everything to me. And I am going to book this weekend with my friends. You're right. I need the stress relief," I said.

Sam and I had always been openly affectionate with each other. It was something I had established from day one in our relationship. There was no way I was going to risk wasting my life on someone who didn't show me they loved me, treasured me and respected me. I'd done that before. Never again.

"And you are everything to me, my love," he said, grabbing at my arm and pulling me back to him just as I had started to turn my body in the direction of the office.

"Janie," he said, pulling my face gently to look at him.

"Yes," I said, doing my best to not allow anything to come to the surface.

"Take this break for yourself. You deserve it. You need it," he said kindly. His voice was warm. Like warm milk poured into my cappuccino, trying to somewhat dilute my manic state.

"Okay" I whispered back, allowing for one moment the mask to slip a bit.

"Go," he smiled into our kiss.

He released me, and I reluctantly stepped away from his embrace. How simple would it be for me to just rely on him, let my whole business fold and allow him to take care of me, which I knew he wanted to do? But we also knew, both of us, what my success did for my self-esteem. It would be a mistake to walk away.

Sitting down in front of my computer in my large office off of the den, I took a deep breath in and started my day just as I'd been instructed to do. As I'd made sure to do in the last nine months of this pandemic.

"Lord, grant me the serenity," I began reciting quietly to myself. I closed my eyes, willing my mind to stop obsessing over the numbness I knew I could so easily get if I really wanted to.

Lisa

"I told you that I can't take you because I have to go to play practice. Just deal with it," Veronica hissed at her sister, Brenda.

"Why do you always have to be such a bitch?" Brenda shot back to her twin sister. The steam from her coffee cup wafted up in front of her face still half-comatose from sleep. Her eyes were barely open, yet she was able to attack her sister. I hated the way they could treat each other with such cruelty.

"You guys, please," I said, already feeling the endorphins I worked so hard to achieve start slipping away. So much for my morning run/therapy with my friends solving all of my problems for the day. "Don't fight. Mom can't take anymore."

I sat down on the worn chair we kept by the door and ripped off my running shoes, anxious to get the nastiness off. My feet were wet again this morning. A result of having shoes so old they were ripping. Sure enough, upon close inspection, I noticed I'd sprung another hole in the right shoe. It was time for a new pair. But with these shoes running a minimum of $150, there was not much chance of that. Could I somehow snag a used pair? This was how low I'd sunk. From living in one of the most luxurious neighborhoods in the Chicago suburbs to considering wearing other people's running shoes. And it happened in the blink of an eye.

"Mom, we really need another car. We can't keep doing this," Veronica whined, scooting up to sit on the counter and glare at me.

"Ha!" I simply barked out. "You really think that is an option, honey?" I asked, raising an eyebrow in her direction. "I can't even afford new shoes for myself right now."

As proof, I held up the well-battered shoe and laughed out loud. I wasn't hiding anything from the girls these days. I'd done enough of that. Enough of the smiling and pushing down. No, these girls were going to get the truth from now on. Avoiding it and hiding from it was how we ended up in the mess we were in.

"But Mom, how are we going to be in two different places at one time? It's impossible," Brenda said, joining forces with her sister to call out the never-ending laundry list of wants and needs.

"I agree. You can't be in two places at once," I said, moving over to the kitchen and pulling down a coffee mug from the shelf. "So, come up with a solution. Did you guys ever consider a carpool? Can't you ride with a friend?"

I poured myself a huge cup of coffee, noting that it would drain the entire pot I set to brew this morning. So, that meant the kids had almost the whole thing to themselves. Not fitting with the caffeine discussion we just had last week. "Keep them off caffeine. It's adding to their anxiety," their counselor had recommended in a condescending voice. Like it was that easy.

"But then that means we are driving all over town and dropping people off. That's too much time with all of our other work. Besides, they are really pushing us to not carpool. Prevent the spread of the virus," Veronica argued. A week ago, she had been volleying hard for a sleepover with three other friends. Where did that carefree child go?

"Well, you can call your father to see if he will buy you a car," I said, a sarcastic smile on my face.

Both girls stopped in their tracks and stared at me like deer in the headlights.

My mother always told me, don't use sarcasm when you're raising kids. They don't understand it, and they don't function well when it comes from the person raising them.

Well, so much for that, Mom. All of my efforts at doing things right went out the window a long time ago.

"That's not funny, Mom," Brenda said, her voice cracking a bit and her eyes locking on mine.

I sighed and took a sip of my coffee, reminding myself that I was the grown-up here and needed to act like one.

"No, it's not funny," I said, treading lightly. "But the bottom line is, we," I said, circling my fingers in front of me to indicate our little crew, "don't have the money for a new car. So, we're going to have to figure out a way to make it work with what we have."

Or, you can ask your dad's new girlfriend, Ms. Moneybags, to lend you the BMW SUV she's been gallivanting around town in. I decided best to keep that to myself. We didn't need any more animosity in this house. Clearly, I had enough for all three of us.

"Now I have to shower and get moving, or I'll be late for work and that is the last thing we need," I said, shoving back from the counter and standing up to my full height of 5'1. My beautiful daughters towered above me already, blessed by the height passed down to them from their father's side.

How gorgeous they were. Full lips, flowing hair, not a wrinkle in sight. They had the world at their fingertips, yet now I worried that I may have messed it all up. That we may have messed it up. No. Wait a minute. I wasn't going to do this anymore, I promised myself. HE had screwed it up. I had been a great wife. There was no reason to doubt myself constantly. This was not my fault, and no matter how he tried to spin it; his actions had taken us here, not mine.

"Are you okay, Mom?" Veronica asked kindly. For a moment, she wasn't the perpetually angry teenager I had gotten used to living with. Her tone stopped me in my tracks. How lovely to have someone concerned about me for once.

"I…" I stuttered, having a hard time meeting her eyes. If only I could open up to her. I needed a shoulder to cry on, but I was confused on what I should and should not do and how much I should say. Hadn't they been through enough with their father's infidelities, his lies, and his dismissal of not only me, but them?

I had questions I wanted to ask. Had he called them? Had he asked to see them? Had he extended any kind of olive branch? Anything? But the last time we all talked about this, they asked me to stop pestering them. Let them come to me. I was trying to honor what little control they had left in this situation.

"I just need to get ready. I can't be late," I mumbled instead, turning and heading out of the room.

"Mom, I need money for lunch," Brenda called out to me. "Remember you were going to give me cash this morning?"

I stopped in my tracks and balled my hands into fists, embarrassed that I had to tell her no.   To think of the life we once had; a gigantic home, beautiful cars, college funds, retirement funds. Now, I knew that the twenty I was going to hand her was my last until I got paid next.

"I'll leave it on my dresser," I called out. I knew I should tell her that we couldn't afford to buy lunch, but I just couldn't. We'd cut back so much and this twenty was part of a bargain I'd made with her for something else I wanted her to do, which at this moment, I couldn't even remember. When was this constant bargaining and negotiating over?

How was this my life? I sighed and continued on to my room in a huff. No need to search far for that answer. I knew how we got here. There was no denying who had done this to us. And that I was utterly alone now cleaning up the mess he had made.

"Mom, the washing machine is broken," I heard Veronica yell up the stairs. I chuckled quietly to myself at the irony. I didn't even have a working appliance that functioned well enough to clean up a mess.

Petra

"So, that's it. The numbers are actually looking slightly better. Not great, but better than where we were. HR is still working like crazy to fill these openings but there's just not a lot of movement. A large portion of our staff quit to stay home with young kids and aren't pounding on the door to come back. I don't blame them after what we all saw," Maggie, my head nurse manager said.

"Hmm," I said in reply, nodding my head and scrolling through my phone as she spoke. I didn't want her to see what I was looking at, so I carefully placed it at an angle where there was no way she could see.

"I do have an idea," she said.

"Okay," I said, keeping my eyes on the screen.

"How about male strippers?" she asked.

I nodded my head, acknowledging her contribution, but not fully registering what she had said. When it did finally click, I set the phone down and met her blue/green eyes, glistening with excitement behind her glasses lined in rainbow colors. Her entire face lit up when she smiled at me, her years on the job registering in her well-earned wrinkles. I couldn't have heard what I thought I just did.

"Wait, what?" I asked, meeting her smile.

"Finally, I got your attention," Maggie said, belly laughing and slapping the table. Her laugh was the sunshine of the ER unit and had been for years. She was known for bringing patients back from the brink just by using her greatest gifts-her sunny disposition and her mood-changing laugh. When she walked in the room, she changed the entire atmosphere.

"Did you say male strippers?" I asked, raising an eyebrow and smiling.

"Yes," Maggie laughed. "I needed to get you back to Earth, Petra. I knew you weren't listening to me. What's going on with you?"

"Nothing, I'm sorry," I said. "I'm paying attention now. Just spinning too many plates. And for the record, I hate when people look at screens when I'm trying to talk to them. And I was just doing that to you. I'm sorry," I said, crossing my legs and leaning forward in my chair to give her my full attention. If anyone deserved it, it was Maggie. I couldn't even imagine going through Covid without her. She'd saved countless lives and somehow kept the entire staff going, never showing signs of despair. She definitely did better than me.

"Seriously, are you okay?" Maggie asked. As my most senior staff member, Maggie served as a mother figure to so many of us. The younger nurses, especially. I relied on her to be a leader for the staff and she always came through.

"I am," I said, not wanting to get into it. Maybe later. Besides, the thing that's really bothering me seems a bit silly, considering all that is going on in the world. Or was it?

What took you so long?

The way he had said the words, his last, as it turned out, didn't come out of anger or spite. He had been truly confused, and that was what hit me so hard. He'd expected more from me, and I just didn't do enough. The guilt was killing me.

"Well, if we're serious about this, we have to get planning. It's a few short days away and with the Covid regulations, I need more time to figure out what is allowed and what isn't," Maggie was saying.

"For what?" I asked, still stuck hearing my brother's voice from the past. The flashbacks were keeping me from being able to concentrate. They were in control at all times. I just couldn't get a grip.

"Petra! Seriously, what is wrong?" Maggie asked, putting down the file folder she was holding and leaning in over the table. We did have our face shields on, so technically, she wasn't risking anything. And we'd both had our vaccine, so we were okay, but 2020 had programmed me to feel scared when someone got close.

"Nothing, I'm just having an off day," I said, pulling my wrist up to take a quick look at my watch.

"Is this a bad time to talk about the team-building party? I can come back later. I know you're under a lot of pressure," Maggie said kindly. "We don't have to do this now."

"Isn't that the point? We all are. This is important. I promise you have my undivided attention now," I said.

We were supposed to be planning a little event/party for the staff to raise morale, not swim around in my silly theories. Still, couldn't we do both? I could use someone to bounce my theory off of.

"And you have mine. Come on. What's really going on? Talk to me," Maggie said in that nurturing tone that worked so well with the rest of the staff. She set down her folder on the desk and sat back in her seat.

I sighed and tilted my head back to the ceiling for a second. I wanted to talk to her. I trusted her, but I was always worried about looking crazy to be honest.

"Should I close the door?" Maggie asked.

"It's just something silly," I said, trying to keep things light.

Today I wore my pink scrubs-my favorite ones. It worked well with my skin color and my dark hair. It was the first time in a long time that I put some effort into the way I looked. It had been a while since I cared. I used to love getting all dolled up with make-up and hair. Looking good on the outside always gave me confidence when I wasn't feeling so solid on the inside. My efforts didn't have quite the same effect anymore, but even the act of trying did a little bit.

Maggie got up anyway and closed the door, glancing at the clock.

"I've got a few minutes. Hit me," she said, plopping down in the chair in front of me. Seeing her sit down like that, I questioned once again how many good years I had left with Maggie. She was going to be sixty-two and still working this hectic pace. I didn't know how much longer she was going to keep it up.

"We should plan this party first," I said, feeling bad to be talking about this now.

"We have plenty of time to talk about that. And I promise, no strippers. I was just trying to shake you up. Now tell me," she said. "If you want to. I have a guess, by the way," she said in her all-knowing grandmotherly way.

"You do? What?"

"Are you having flashbacks again?" she asked, tilting her head.

Yes.

"No," I said, shutting that down. When she said the term flashbacks, she could have been referring to a number of things. We all saw way too much in this ER unit over the past year. Unimaginable, horrific scenes that we signed up for when we took these jobs. But I don't think we could have predicted that the nightmare scenes would all come at once. Working in the ER during Covid was like being hit by a tsunami. There was a period of time when it felt like the deaths would never slow down. So much was riding on this vaccine. Now it was a matter of getting the public to accept it.

"It would be perfectly normal if you were. My sister saw her daughter in that accident with the boat and she replays it all the time," Maggie started.

"No," I said, cutting her off, knowing she wasn't referring to the scenes here at the hospital. She was talking about a much more personal flashback. That awful day with my brother. "It's not what you think."

Maggie stopped talking and crossed her legs.

"Oh," she said simply. "I'm listening," her lips plumped out in the way they always did when you knew she was truly going to just be quiet and listen.

I hesitated on what to say. Maggie was the only one at work, besides Lisa, who knew the full story about my brother. I could trust her. I knew that. As a female doctor, there was so much pressure. My reputation here was very good, but I struggled constantly with showing people my weaknesses. I just didn't want to. With Maggie though, I could let the walls down a bit. She didn't judge and she didn't seem to change her opinion. And the best thing about her was that she didn't share. Maggie was a vault. When you told her something, it stayed with her and only her.

"I don't want to say. It's too crazy," I said. But even while I was speaking, I was pulling up what I was looking at on my phone earlier. I had to get someone's opinion on this.

Maggie was the first non-family member I called after the fire. She was at all three of the christening parties for my children and a confidante for me when I needed help with the PTSD I still struggled with. I knew where she hid the spare key to her house, where her children and grandchildren lived, and even about her recent cancer scare that turned out to be just that. We'd been through a lot in the fifteen years we'd worked together.

"Honey, I'm over sixty years old, with asthma, and I'm working in the ER during Covid. Nothing is going to scare me."

I couldn't help but laugh a little at that.

"Yeah, I guess not. I'm probably way overthinking this. Don't look at me like I'm nuts," I said, finding what I was originally looking for on my phone and glancing up at her to see if I could predict her reaction.

"You can trust me. Come on, lay it on me, girl," Maggie said.

She leaned forward and raised her eyebrows at me expectantly.

"Okay, you promise you'll hear me out?" I said, gripping my phone, ready to exhibit my first piece of evidence.

"You know it," Maggie said, uncrossing her legs and holding onto the sides of her chair. "Hit me."

Sighing, I placed my phone on the desk between us. My office was well-lit, and I'd also put effort into making it feel less corporate and more welcoming by adding in soft lamps and warm little accents like my essential oil diffuser that changed colors. Glancing quickly at my diffuser, I noticed the color was pink, my signature color. It was a sign.

"So, let me tell you what I'm looking at," I began.

Maggie glanced at the phone, then up at me. There was no mistaking the weariness there. Her shoulders were hunched over and her eyes crinkled in worry, looking between me and the phone.

"What am I looking at here?" she asked.

I took a breath and then pushed on.

"Do you see the woman in the picture? It's my neighbor," I said slowly.

Maggie nodded in encouragement, appearing as though she was holding her breath.

"Go on," she said. "I'm listening."

"Her name is Carrie. And I think…" I said, bouncing my knee up and down, my mind racing back to a year ago.

Examining the broken bones, I cringed thinking of the pain she must be in. This one looked bad. I made quick work of changing my face before turning to speak to her.

"It was an accident," she said through watery eyes.

"We're going to get some pain meds going immediately and get you cast," I said, running my hands along the rest of her body to look for any other obvious injuries. As her doctor, all that mattered to me was getting her physically well in that moment.

"I'm so embarrassed," she whispered, her husband outside of the door but nearby. This was my chance.

"Carrie, if someone did this to you," I said in a quiet, non-threatening voice. We were trained not to make eye contact when saying this. To keep the conversation as casual as possible.

"No," she said defiantly. "We have kids. He would never hurt me."

Her body betrayed her, though, as the tears kicked in, the answer so obvious to me. She had to say it, or I couldn't report it.

"It's okay. It happens and there are ways we can help you," I said. "You would be surprised how much I see this happen," I said, trying my best to keep this conversation casual and give her power. This was how I was successful with any patients suffering domestic abuse. Separate them from the abuser and give them options.

"We have someone here who can escort you to a safe house and help change your life," I said, running my fingers over the three distinct bruises on her upper arm that in my expert opinion were caused by a strong hand grip.

"No," she said sharply, pulling her broken arm away. "Petra, leave me alone," she demanded, then winced. That had to have hurt to try and move that arm.

She knew my first name. I had recognized her the minute she had walked in as my brand-new neighbor who I had not yet met. She certainly seemed to know me though. I hadn't given her my first name nor was it posted anywhere in the room. She had slammed a door in my face, so I backed down.

"Her name is Carrie and you think what?" Maggie pushed, pulling me back to the present.

"I think there is no Carrie anymore," I said, closing my eyes, unable to meet hers.

Janie

While in the car driving to my first showing of the day, my cellphone rang, pulling me out of my thoughts. I had been spiraling to a bad place about the same thing I always obsessed about. How to stay the number one agent on my team. As silly as that sounded, especially considering what the world was facing, I couldn't stop my mind from going there over and over. Especially when Frederick, the number two, was hot on my heels this month. And there was also the fact that I hated him with an intense passion.

He was so snide and condescending all the time, especially to women. The fact that he mansplained everything made my blood boil. He didn't have to come out and say it, but everything about him made it clear that he thought women were stupid and couldn't compete. And in the current political climate, this heated time in the United States, he was so tone-deaf. He flaunted his supremacy anyway he could. I just wanted to smack him and yell, "Wake up." If someone should be canceled, my vote was for Frederick.

That was why every month when our numbers rolled in, I took a personal victory. It had nothing to do with the money, though that was certainly exciting. It was that I could look over at him and shrug with a little smile.

I couldn't imagine being his wife. Having to deal with that at home 24/7? Terrible. Maybe his general attitude rubbed me so wrong because, in some ways, he reminded me of the man I used to be married to. I smiled to myself thinking how proud my therapist would be about me making that break through. I bet that was what she was trying to get me to see for a while now without coming right out and saying it. Maybe all this therapy really was working.

The phone rang again. Shutting down my racing thoughts, I hit accept even though I didn't recognize the number. I glanced in the rearview mirror, checking my lip gloss. I'd put extra effort in this morning to look good, mainly because I'd be showing my highest-priced home I'd listed thus far. I wanted to make a good impression on the couple I was meeting. They sounded great, and most of all, they'd mentioned that they were interested in buying one home for residence and one for rental. That was my favorite kind of customer. Two for one deal.

"Good morning, this is Janie Frank," I said, in my professional realtor voice.

"Janie, long time, no talk," I heard a booming voice say. Although it sounded familiar and friendly, I couldn't quite place it. Before my mind made the connection, my body did. I could feel my heart pump faster and my stomach turn a little.

I paused and took a second to collect myself. There was no way he was calling me. Rick the Dick had been off my radar for a bit now. It was shocking to hear from him.

"Hi," I said, trying to stall. "It's great to hear from you," I managed, not really feeling that way at all. Had I not made myself clear? Had he not seen me sitting next to her in court and holding her hand on the way out? I was not on his side. He got that, right?

"Listen, I'm sure you're a little surprised by my call. I am, too. I'm not an idiot. I know we're in a tough place with the divorce, but this is business. And you know what they say. Don't let silly things like emotions get in the way of business," he said with a smile in his voice.

Because I didn't know how to respond, I kept quiet and let him continue. My instinct told me to just hang up the phone.

"I need a realtor and you're the first person I thought of. I know you're the best, Janie. June has fallen in love with a home and wants to move as soon as possible. We'll sell our old place as well, so I'd love for you to take care of that. Would you do that for us?" Rick asked, really laying it on thick with his compliments.

My mouth dropped open. I had no choice but to put my turn signal on and pull into the parking lot of a Target. This was too big. I needed to not be driving while having this conversation.

"I'm shocked you thought of me," I said truthfully. My mouth was very dry, and I had to reach for my water bottle to replenish.

What I really wanted to say was how dare you call me? After you broke my best friend's heart? After you left her high and dry with barely enough money to keep a roof over the family that you supposedly loved so much. Now you were selling "your" place? You mean the place you moved into with your rich girlfriend while you were married with kids? The place you slid into while claiming foreclosure on the home you owned with your wife and stopped making payments on unbeknownst to her? The home you cashed all the money out of to court your new lady while your wife and kids were barely getting food on the table?

"Well, of course I did, Janie. I wouldn't work with anyone else. Like I said, you are the best," Rick said, really laying it on thick.

"And I'm hoping that we could not have our personal lives, well, my personal decisions, get in the way of our working relationship. I know you might not approve of, my, you know," he said, sounding the perfect mixture of contrite but also that confident, C-suite, dominant male who took no prisoners and never apologized for taking what he wanted. The kind of personality that men could so easily get away with but women were still unable to pull off without being labeled a bitch.

Just as I was opening my mouth to tell him I was going to refer him to my colleague, Frederick, because my plate was too full, he interrupted me.

"What I'm trying to say is that I'm looking to buy multiple properties, and I know who I want the commission to go to. You. You have access to a lot of the lots I'm looking at and I know you'll work hard to get me the best deal," he said.

I could picture him driving in his car in his custom suit, with those gigantic fake teeth Lisa made us laugh at the other night. He'd posted a new profile picture of himself on LinkedIn, looking smug and happy with his new teeth. I remember specifically the humiliating sound of Lisa trying to cover up her tears and sound like she was still laughing. Petra and I played along, so as not to make her pain any deeper.

"Yes, well, it's just that my time right now is so tight. I don't know that I could be of service to you," I said, trying to buy time. This was going to be quite a quandary for me based on what he said. I had a bad feeling I knew what properties he was talking about. This was just how the universe worked.

"My pretty little bride-to-be is looking at 765 Pearl Avenue," he sang as proud as a peacock, ignoring that I'd just suggested I was too busy.

I closed my eyes and put a hand up to my mouth to hold back the bloodcurdling scream I wanted to release.

"Oh," I managed.

He was talking about the home I was currently driving to. The diamond of the neighborhood. Just added to the market after the builders completed their work on the 8,000-square foot monstrosity, my most expensive listing, and the home that I watched being built on my daily runs with his discarded ex-wife, and my best friend, Lisa. For a second, I nearly burst into tears thinking of us stopping countless times to catch our breath and gaze in awe as the house made progress. Lisa loved that house. She had even been promised it once. As a stay-at-home mom for years, they had lived off of Rick's income from a start-up company that never lived up to what it was supposed to be. He never let Lisa in on that though. She lived off of his lies for years. Even believed him when he told her that due to the success they were about to have, they could build a new home. It had all been a lie. And now, he was moving into the dreamhouse. Without her.

Rick's new reality, or so it seemed, was newly minted boyfriend of a retired super model/news anchor/trust fund baby. And apparently, money was no object. What was untouchable real estate to most was accessible to him. Who knew with him, though? There was a big part of me that hoped this would blow up in his face as well. He didn't deserve this level of happiness after the way he treated my friend.

"I see you are listed as the agent in charge of selling it," Rick said. "Congratulations. That was quite a get."

I pondered my choices. I could just refuse to sell it to him. No, I couldn't. Who was I kidding? I was stuck and he knew it.

"Yes, I'm very excited to show it. I'm heading there right now," I said, doing my best to remain professional. There had to be a way to get out of this. I just needed more time to think.

"Oh, really?" Rick cooed. "Well, I better make a move then, huh?"

I should have known. Nothing was more appealing to Rick the Dick than the thought of whatever it was being off limits.

"Sure," I said, unable to come up with more.

"We can be there in an hour," he said, his tone suddenly a bit more serious.

The thought of seeing Rick made me gag. He was going to get away with it. All of it. Cheating on his wife, walking away from his kids, breaking up two marriages. He got everything he wanted. A new, young spouse with enough money to buy multiple luxury homes and by the sound of his voice, no guilt whatsoever. Who did this man think he was? And how was I ever going to face Lisa again?

Before I could respond, I realized he had hung up on me. Not even checking to see if that time worked for me.

"Dick," I said aloud, closing my eyes and shaking my head.

Lisa

Pulling up to the hospital, I noticed Petra's car was already there. Good. Maybe I could sneak in a few minutes with her. Even grab a coffee on our break. The fact that I could access my friend at work whenever I wanted was the highlight of this job. After staying home for over fifteen years raising my kids, I was left scrambling after Rick left me. Good old Petra had saved the day for me, and I was so grateful. Not only had she saved the day, she'd actually carved out my whole future. Now if only I could scrape together enough money to make it happen. Right now, it seemed nearly impossible, but if I could get my degree while working and put two other kids through school, there was nothing I couldn't do. And after going through my divorce and getting kicked out of my home during the middle of Covid, managing school actually seemed fairly doable.

"Good morning," my coworker, Betty, called out to me as I walked in the door.

"Morning," I called back, stomping my feet on the rug once inside the front door. On the way in, it had started to snow, and my boots were packed with slush. I made a beeline for the break room where I stored all my stuff, knowing I was cutting it close to clocking in on time.

Petra got me this job and was, for the most part, in charge of this place, but HR watched the clock. She wasn't technically my boss, due to the structuring, but everyone around here knew she was top bitch in charge.

The last thing I wanted to do was mess this opportunity up. For the first time in a long time, I was happy. Stressed beyond belief, but happy. At least I was a little bit in control for once. I'd always relied on Rick's income to support us, and when things started to go south in our marriage, I was so helpless. In all honesty, if I'd had the financial ability to, I probably would have left him a long time before he left me. I was just too unsure of how I would support the girls and myself. And, I always fancied myself still in love with him. The never-ending loops in our marriage made me nuts-a few years of good, a few years of bad. I guess I was planning to ride the roller coaster forever. It seemed like the right thing to do for so long.

In a way, I was grateful that Rick made the decision for me, for all of us really. I would never tell him that, though. He was such a shithead about the whole thing. He didn't have to publicly humiliate me the way he did and then basically pretend like he'd never known us at all.

"Hey," a voice said behind me, breaking me free of my negative thoughts.

"Hey, there," I said, happy to see my friend, Petra, standing in the break room in her light pink scrubs. She looked beautiful today, her light, buttery, cocoa skin glowing. She never seemed to get as dried out in the winter as I did. She looked the best I'd seen her in months at this moment. Maybe she was coming back.

"We have bagels and that speaker here this morning, remember?" Petra said, leaning back on the wall and watching me as I threw my boots and coat in the locker. I glanced at the clock on the wall and noted thirty seconds left to clock in on time.

"Yep," I said, pulling my shoes on and shutting the door. I raced over to the computer and clocked in using my badge, settling down only when I heard the satisfying beep.

"Are you going to go?" Petra asked.

"I'm going to do my rounds first and make sure everyone is good, and then I'll grab as much of the talk as I can. Are you?" I asked, checking out myself in the mirror and rubbing under my eyes. My mascara had smudged a little bit from the soft shower of snow I'd walked through to get into the hospital.

"Why?" Petra barked, startling me.

I whipped around, thrown off by her tone. She was watching me with eyes turned suddenly very intense. Her brows were pulled down a bit and she no longer leaned against the wall.

"What?" I asked softly, confused by her reaction. She must have read something in my response, because her face changed.

"Sorry," Petra said, turning her head over her shoulder and looking behind her. She moved closer to me.

Petra was kind of stuck here. Being the supervising doctor, she probably never felt like she could let her guard down. The team loved her here. It was because she was always strong, always kind. Even in the darkest days of Covid, I saw her lead everyone consistently and with grace, even a bit of humor. She really held up even in the most stressful times.

But I knew she was battling other demons. The death of her brother, which I knew she felt responsible for.

"I didn't mean to bite your head off. I know it's the right thing to do, but I'm just not looking forward to it," Petra said, stepping forward and looking around before whispering to me. "When I set up this PTSD speaker, it felt like the right thing to do for everyone here, considering all we've been through." She sat down on the bench and let her shoulders slump down. Then bounced back up as though she was afraid that she would be caught letting go a bit.

The words, "all we've been through" brought back images I'd been trying to forget. The body bags. The screaming. The panicked hunt for more iPads, so that the families could see their loved ones and say goodbye. It was still hard to believe that it had happened in the first place. And it wasn't over. Would it ever be over for the first responders? I know a lot of my coworkers were questioning if they could move on. If they could keep working in this line of work.

Petra had put in the longest hours, stepped in when staff became overwhelmed, was always first on the scene and made all the calls on what came next. I could only imagine the weight she carried. On top of the other stuff.

"If it doesn't feel right, Petra," I said, sitting down and leaning in very close to her. I could only get so close to her in our protective gear but managed to grab her hand in mine. "You don't have to attend. Didn't your therapist say do it all at your own pace? No one else could set it for you?"

Petra took in a breath and made eye contact with me through her face shield. For a second, I thought she was going to rip it off. I could tell she was fighting tears.

My job started here after this hospital had seen its worst. Things were starting to improve a bit by the time I walked into these halls. I could only imagine what Petra saw. She never really talked about it. On our runs and our girl's nights, she often referenced Covid, but she hardly ever went too much into details, and we didn't push her. And she never touched on her family's tragedy. Janie and I knew she would talk when she was ready.

"I have to," she whispered. "They're all watching me," she said, scratching at her leg.

"Who?" I asked, feeling like I needed to say the right thing here.

For a second, Petra just stared at me. I held my breath, thinking back to this morning and the run. For a second, I saw again in my mind, Petra turning and walking away from her home instead of going in after I had left her. What was going on?

Petra

Pulling into my driveway, I found myself wondering not for the first time, what made me stay in Chicago. It wasn't even five and it was pitch black. And thanks to a polar vortex that blasted down on us today, it was hovering right above zero with a "feels like" temperature of negative thirteen.

I released a sigh and hit the garage door opener. The sight of Paul's SUV in the garage sent a flurry of mixed emotions through me. On the one hand, I was relieved to know that he was here, caring for the kids and prepping dinner. He was reliable in so many ways, even more so now. He knew I was still mad and was probably going to be mad for some time.

I still found him incredibly attractive. There was no denying our chemistry. We had three kids to remind us of that. As the years passed, he'd only become more focused and driven in all things, especially his workouts. It had helped him focus at work and kept him happy. His clothes looked great, the accounts he managed looked great, his kids looked great. But all of that didn't really matter because guess what? His wife was still mad.

I closed my eyes and tried to focus on the skills my therapist had taught me. She was right. I was pinpointing way too much on a short time in our lives together. Really just a couple of months in what, for the most part, was a happy, long-term marriage. I was never going to get past that moment if I didn't do better at looking at the big picture. The whole picture.

I opened my eyes, letting out another sigh. Sometimes closing them did me no good. I kept seeing the tragedy. I was haunted.

The sound of a door closing to my left distracted me. What? That didn't make any sense. I turned the car off and just sat in silence for a second in my car, wondering what to do next. Carrie and Tom Watson had lived next door to us for only the past eighteen months. And even though she also had young kids at the same school my kids attended just a few blocks away, I hadn't connected with her really on a social level. I think she was too embarrassed. I wouldn't blame her. She'd looked pretty bad that time I saw her in the ER. Her story about falling down the stairs was shaky at best, but try as I might, there was no getting her to change it. She said she had tripped and that had been that. I'd cleaned her up and worked my magic on her broken bones, but there was something about that visit that never sat right with me. Thank goodness, there were no more. Unless, she had chosen to go elsewhere for care to hide from me, her nosy neighbor.

Thanks to my deep dive on Facebook this morning, it appeared as though they were all in Florida enjoying a warm, sunny vacation. She'd even said something like, "Escaping the pandemic," which didn't sound like her. I thought I heard that they were pretty much on lockdown in their home at least for the beginning of the pandemic. It seemed odd to me that they traveled at all, considering vaccines were not yet easily available to all. I'd been one of the first because of qualifying as a health care worker. If I learned one thing in this time though, it was that people were not consistent. The ones who were the most outspoken about the pandemic, tended to be the first ones breaking the rules, so I would believe anything at this point. Maybe they were whooping it up in Florida. I just didn't know.

They hadn't asked me to watch the house, move garbage cans, etc., yet still, as their next-door neighbor, I felt some level of responsibility. And after hearing that scream this morning, which I was still sure was human, even though the girls were convinced otherwise, I was even more spooked about what was going on next door.

When I'd walked over there this morning post run, I'd done a little bit of peeking in windows and after scaring the crap out of myself when I saw my own reflection in a huge mirror hanging on the opposite wall, I decided to throw in the towel. There was no one home. At least, I didn't think so. But something wasn't sitting right.

Carrie and Tom Watson were a quiet couple. They kept to themselves at school events, parties, etc. Their kids seemed sweet, and they were always there to support their kids, but something about Carrie always made me uneasy. Even before the hospital incident. I couldn't really put my finger on it. Normally, I would just say, "to each his own" but Carrie stuck with me. She looked well put together, always dressed in her conservative sweaters and pearls with expensive shoes and bags. Her hair was long and wavy, highlighted a pretty blond and always freshly cut. Her make-up was ever present and her skin dewy and fresh. She didn't look malnourished or mistreated in anyway, neither did her kids. But something in her eyes wasn't right. It was hard to describe. To me, she reminded me of a houseplant that was so beautiful you thought there was no way it was real. Then upon further inspection, only when you got really close and touched the plastic did you realize that your initial assumption was spot on.

I stepped out of the car and took a couple of steps toward her house. The cold air hit me like a ton of bricks, making me want to abandon my investigation. But that scream this morning. I couldn't let it go.

Taking a few steps in the direction of the side door attached to the garage, the first thing I noticed was that it looked like there was a light on now that I hadn't noticed before. Our properties sat about one hundred feet apart from each other on the gargantuan lots they were built on. When we first bought, that was one of the most appealing things. We were close, but not too close. Now, though, it felt so far to walk in this freezing weather just to get a better look. Maybe this was a mistake. Too far.

Wouldn't this have helped me though if I had followed this mantra? Listen to your gut. Maybe if I had, my brother would still be alive. I knew something was wrong and I had hesitated. Look what it had cost me. I scratched at my leg, a habit I'd picked up on as my scars continued to heal.

I took a deep breath and walked the steps needed to close the gap between our garages. The bulk of their property was on the other side of the garage, as was ours, guaranteeing the most amount of privacy for both of our families. Climbing the steps quietly to the side door that faced our house, I hesitated, fully expecting to see someone on the other side of the glass. Part of me wondered why they'd made this too easy. Paul was always on me about protecting anyone's view into our garage.

"*The windows into a garage tell you everything. Who is home, and who isn't. You should never have access to that type of information,*" he'd preached after coming home from a dinner with one of his best friends from college who'd worked as a detective for over fifteen years in the police force a few towns over. After that dinner, Paul had coverings for the two windows in our garage put in. Carrie's family apparently hadn't gotten that memo because here I was standing right next to her garage door with full visual access to all the inner workings.

From what I could tell, it held two out of the three cars I knew them to own. Tom's sports car, and one of the two SUVs they owned sat snuggled up next to each other in their three-car garage.

They must have driven the other SUV for their family trip and left the other two here. So, maybe no one really was here? But sure enough, that light I thought I'd noticed earlier was on right above the door leading into the house. Why would that be on? And had it been on when I'd inspected the house this morning? I couldn't remember. The devil was always in the details, right? I closed my eyes, trying to shake off the bad thoughts that raced over me.

"Well, maybe if you had acted on that thought earlier, he'd still be alive," my smug, know-it-all sister had said to me the morning after our brother's death from her cozy position as a VP of Sales in Paris for a marketing company. Her position had kept her from being able to fly in and help, of course, so she had the luxury of sitting back and judging what I had been able to do and how I should have done it better.

"Shut up," I mumbled to myself aloud.

Damn this PTSD.

I opened my eyes and took a deep breath. This wasn't helping anything. I needed to settle my

thoughts and focus. The only thing that really seemed to help me when I got stuck in the past like this was action. And I knew exactly what I had to do.

"What are you doing out here?" I heard a deep voice growl from behind me, making me freeze like an ice sculpture in place.

Janie

My phone rang while I was sitting in the Whole Foods parking lot waiting for my groceries to be delivered to my car. My heart began racing the second I saw her name appear. It was time. Here we go.

"Hello," I squeaked out, sounding like a frog. I cleared my throat, hoping to pull it together.

"I told you, I can't and that is the end of it. If I could afford it, you know I would," I heard Lisa saying to someone on the other end. I waited quietly knowing she'd address me when she could.

"Sorry," she said into the phone. "My kids are accosting me again. They want to go on some ridiculous spring break trip, as though I can afford it. Honest to God, Janie. They just don't get it. It's like they think nothing has changed and nothing ever happened," she said, sounding completely stressed out. Her voice was jumbled for a minute and then she got clear again.

"Okay, I'm hiding in my pantry, so I can talk to you in peace," she said.

For a second, I thought that this was going to be the moment. I thought she was going to finally take me up on the offer I had extended months ago to lend her some money. Petra and I had both, at the beginning, stepped up with offers and even tried to anonymously pay for things, but she had quickly put the kibosh on that. And after an epic fight that I thought would end our friendship, she made it clear that there were to be no donations.

Lisa was a proud woman and I respected that. But I'd been in Lisa's shoes before, and I knew that getting help had been beneficial for me. It was killing me that she wouldn't let me help her. At least Petra had figured out a way to help her by coordinating a job opportunity for her. I had yet to figure out my way, but I was determined to do so.

"I have to talk to you about Petra," Lisa whispered into the phone.

"Oh," I said, a bit thrown off by the direction the conversation was going.

"Something is wrong," Lisa said, still whispering.

At that moment, I made eye contact with the Whole Foods attendant rolling the humongous cart my way. I always felt bad for the people who took on this grueling work, especially now in this brutal cold.

"Hold on for one second," I said into the phone. "I'm just picking up groceries. Hold on, Lisa," I said.

"We're just checking in to see if you got a chance to review all the substitutions?" a young man asked me through his mask.

I scrambled to put mine on, feeling awful that I hadn't bothered to do it.

"Yes, they are all fine," I said, wanting to get back to Lisa as soon as possible. Her time was so limited. I knew that I only had her for a few minutes before I was going to get interrupted.

"Do you want these in the trunk?" he asked.

I nodded my head and pushed the button that automatically opened the trunk.

"Thank you," I said, rolling up the window as he struggled to wheel the big cart toward the back of my car.

"Sorry," I said, placing my ear bud back in.

"That's okay," Lisa said. "I told you, I'm not letting you do that. Do you know what they do to mothers who allow friends to sleep over during Covid restrictions? They burn them at the stake in the town's square. Now go away," I heard her say to one of her daughters.

My phone beeped, alerting me that I had received a text message.

Ready to make an offer. Call me when you get this.

We're going over asking price. Way over.

The text from Rick the Dick made my heart stop. This was going to go fast. I had to tell her.

"I said, no," I heard Lisa say again to one of the girls.

This poor woman. She was battling so many things and I was about to throw salt on the wound.

"Do you want to meet for a quick bite? Sam can watch the kids. I'll swing by and pick you up. We can talk live about Petra."

"Janie, that all sounds great, but I'm already running late for class, I have no dinner made and my girls are trying to eat me alive right now. Another night, I promise. Let me get this out quick before I get interrupted again," Lisa said. "Hold on a minute," she yelled at one of the girls.

"Seriously, don't let your kids reach their teenage years. They go nuts. Okay, I found another hiding place. I'm just saying this really fast and maybe we can talk more later. It's happening again, Lisa. I mean with Petra. We have to do something because it's happening again. Oh crap, I have to go," she said, hanging up on me.

I let out a long sigh and looked at my reflection in the mirror. I looked exactly like I felt. Guilty.

Lisa

"You can't keep us locked up forever, Mom," Veronica hissed at me after she'd whipped open the pantry door, exposing my hiding spot. I'd disconnected with Janie after I spotted her through the crack in the door coming at me like an angry red-wing blackbird. I knew I was busted.

"We are not prisoners here, you know," she said angrily.

These girls and their anger. I could only handle so much. I knew it was a direct result of being pulled through an ugly divorce and often times being smack dab in the middle of the fights I had with their dad, Rick. But couldn't they see that I had been a victim, too? I needed some tenderness and all my family offered me was constant hostility. There was only so much I could take.

"I'm not keeping you locked up. For the last time, how can I make you understand this better? You can't have people over right now. We're in a global pandemic. We are not supposed to be entertaining," I said, stepping out from my solitude in the closet. "I have a job in health care. Are you watching any news? Are you reading anything about what is happening in the world?"

"But Pauline's mother let her have friends over," Veronica huffed.

"Yes, I'm aware of that because Pauline's mother was publicly mutilated on Facebook when one of the kids got Covid and ended up giving it to the entire party. I'm surprised the local mothers' groups haven't banded together to have her children taken away from her. Do you have any idea how much judgment is going around right now on how people are dealing with their kids in this pandemic? Like I don't deal with that enough. The last thing I need is more judgment," I said angrily.

I was trying my best to stay calm, just like my therapist said I should with these kids. They were coming out of personal trauma. And, to make matters worse, they were coming out of personal trauma right at a time when the world was in the grips of a global trauma.

But these girls were on me all the time. It was starting to feel like the only way to fight fire was with fire. They simply didn't back off or seem to hear me unless I was yelling or upset. Of course, I knew that wasn't healthy, but my fuse with them was short. I needed them to step up, grow up, and help this family get through this. And right now, I needed them to let me go upstairs and get ready for my class.

"You are in charge of dinner and clean up tonight, so don't forget," I said, making my way up the stairs to change into something suitable for class. Or, truthfully, him.

Ahh, him. Besides my runs with my girlfriends in the morning, the young, hot, nursing student, Erik, with the phenomenal Shawn Mendes hair and the sexy muscles, was what kept me smiling these days. I felt like a pedophile even thinking about him the way I did. He had to be ten years younger than me, but that didn't stop me from gazing at him all through class with hungry eyes. If I was ever going to choose to be a cougar, this is when I would play that card. And yes, the fact that his name was so close to my ex-husband's name, Rick, was like the universe trying to make me laugh.

And here was the best part. Or the most ridiculous part. I hadn't even met him yet. Due to Covid, the entire first semester of classes had been spent on Zoom. Next week we were going to go in person for the first time to begin our clinicals. I couldn't wait. It had been five long months of interacting via Zoom class, stalking him on Instagram, and doing a deep dive on Facebook to learn everything I could about him, which was very little. He had a very small social media presence, which I kind of loved. A few pics of him skiing with friends in Colorado, a picture in the Bahamas, and a few pics of dogs. He didn't even have a LinkedIn profile, which made me nervous. But I guess I didn't either. I barely knew him, yet I felt like he was the highlight of my life in some ways. I had it bad.

The worst part was that I couldn't even tell my friends about it. My embarrassment about our age difference kept me from doing that. It was all so ridiculous.

"But I have to study for a final tonight," Veronica whined behind me. "I don't have time to clean up."

"Funny, so do I," I said, enjoying the fact that now that I was in school, I got to play the same card.

These girls needed compassion and sympathy from me. I knew that. I'd heard countless stories about kids suffering, young girls seemingly having it the hardest during the pandemic. The isolation was extremely detrimental for them. We'd all been through so much, but sometimes I had nothing left to give. I was doing my best.

My phone rang again in my hand. I accepted the call, seeing that it was Janie.

"Hello," I said, placing her on speaker phone and setting the phone on my dresser so that we could talk while I dressed.

"Hey, I'm sorry, I know you're busy, but I just wanted to double check on our run for tomorrow. Are we still meeting? Maybe we can talk more then?"

"Definitely," I said while pulling off my pants and stepping into a relatively clean pair of jeans. I picked up the phone and walked over to the closet to peruse through my tops. I was stuck now with all of these fancy clothes that once fit my lifestyle, but now made me stick out like a sore thumb. I wasn't going to wear a five-hundred-dollar silk top to my night class for nursing school. How ridiculous. On the other hand, once we started our clinical work, I would be in only scrubs, so if I was going to wear it, if I was going to catch the attention of that young, hot stud…

"So, I'll see you in the morning?" I heard Janie say from the other line.

"I'm sorry, I dazed out for a second there," I said, shaking my head, trying to get the image of Shawn Mendes singing to me about meeting in Japan out of my head.

"I was just saying I'll talk to you in the morning. Before I go, you have me all worried now. Is Petra okay?" Janie asked.

"Mom!!" One of the girls screamed my name from downstairs. What followed was a loud crash that told me the trauma must be something involving dinner cleanup. I imagined a huge mess I would have to deal with before heading to class. I quickly put the silk top I'd pulled out to look at back in my closet and picked a simple sweater. Who was I kidding? I didn't have time nor the bandwidth for romance.

"Let's talk later. I'm a hot mess right now. I'll see you for the run tomorrow. And wait, aren't we going over for girl's night at Petra's tomorrow?"

"That's right!" Janie said excitedly. "Okay, go kick butt on that final and we'll talk Petra tomorrow."

She hung up and I was left feeling bad that I didn't and couldn't even make time tonight to discuss what was worrying me about Petra. It just had to wait until tomorrow. I was running late and balancing too many things. And I had to concentrate. Tonight's test in my anatomy class was not going to be easy. Tomorrow. It just has to wait until tomorrow.

"Let's just hope it's not too late," I mumbled to my reflection as I fluffed my hair and applied a little gloss.

Petra

My husband's deep, authoritative voice stopped me in my tracks. My mind raced to come up with an explanation as to why I'd somehow ended up on the back porch of our neighbor's house, peering into their garage windows.

"I thought I heard something," I said, turning around to meet his angry, hooded eyes. He didn't have a coat on, just his thin button-down shirt and dress pants he wore while working from home most days. To me, it seemed unnecessary and uncomfortable to get that dressed up, but he always said it made him feel better and helped with his productivity. Plus, the Zoom calls required that he be dressed from the waist up, so why not complete the full package.

"Petra, get down from there," he said, motioning with his arm. "Come inside," he said, his voice softening. "What if they have cameras out here? We do," he said, his brows finally lifting a bit.

"I thought I…" I said, pausing and turning back one more time to see if the light by the door was still on. I watched for a few more seconds, convinced that someone would walk through the door.

"Do you know if they are home?" I asked, giving up and making my way carefully down the stairs. They were completely iced over, a detail I hadn't noticed on the way up. In fact, I barely remember getting to the top of the stairs. I was so determined just to get to the window.

"Honey, I have no idea. Why are you so concerned?" he asked, making his way closer to me and putting an arm around my shoulder. I almost told him to stop, but seeing him walk through the snow with his expensive dress shoes on, not caring that the snow splashed onto his perfect dress pants warmed my heart.

For a second, I stood speechless, allowing him to tuck me under his protective embrace.

"Come on, sweetie. I'm sure it's been a long day. Let's just get you inside. It scared me when I saw your car but couldn't find you," he said, pulling me toward him and our home. I didn't resist his overprotective tone this time. This is what he'd been trying to do for the past three months. Touch me, embrace me, hold me, comfort me. I'd been fighting him and resisting him. It felt good to allow this moment.

"You're worried about them?" Paul asked softly as we made our way back inside our garage. His breath smelled of mint and berry, a result of the gum he liked to chew on while working in his office.

"Yes," I said, feeling a little bit of defiance start to build. I knew where this was going.

"Give me your keys. I'll pull your car in. Why don't you go inside and change and we'll talk?"

The tone of his voice pushed me over the edge. Like he was helping set the crazy lady straight. Whether he meant to or not, to me he sounded condescending.

"Paul, I'm fine. I will pull my own car in," I said, gripping the keys in my hands tighter as though he would rip them away from me. I maneuvered my body away from him and met his stare with an edgy glare. "I don't need your help."

Instead of getting angry at my rejection, Paul put his hands on his hips and looked down at the ground.

"Petra, I'm trying to help you," he said softly. "I'm just trying…"

"I don't need your help now, Paul. I needed it back then. He died, Paul. And I knew it was coming. I told you it was coming. You weren't here," I said, releasing my pent-up anger. It felt good. We were under strict instruction by our marriage therapist to not have these conversations unless we were with her. She told us to try and take breaks from fighting. I could see where she was coming from. Things were still too volatile. I think the actual words she used were that "I" was too volatile. I hated when she said that. I hated to think of myself as being out of control. I was a doctor, in a pandemic. With a dead brother. Everyone just needed to back off.

But deep down, I knew she was right. I was bouncing back and forth still in the PTSD cycle from anger to denial to guilt to full depression. I was out of control. The idea that I could actually keep myself from lashing out at Paul was just impossible.

Paul's eyes met mine with the usual helplessness I saw when I got to this place.

"Petra, I didn't know," he said, putting his hands out in a gesture of, "I'm sorry."

"No, I'm not doing that, Paul. We're not doing the 'I didn't know thing.' You knew because I told you. You did know. You can't keep using that excuse. You did know. You weren't listening," I said, defiant and sure I was right.

"Honey, I couldn't handle it. Okay? Is that what you need to hear from me? Listen to me now. I keep telling you, I blew it. I should have gone there. I should have done more, but the kids, and work and," he stopped, yelling back at me now, which he so seldom did. "You didn't go over there either," he said, delivering a blow. His muscles were bulging out of his shirt now as though they were getting pumped up bigger as Paul let his own anger rip.

I stepped further away from him, my eyes instantly filling with tears. He immediately moved toward me, probably aware of the mistake he had made.

"Baby, I'm sorry. Please, let's call, Jackie. We can't fight like this in our garage. We need someone to help us. You need more help," he said, pleading his case with me. His deep, brown eyes looked so sad and defeated, but it felt like he had just slapped me by what he just said.

"The only one that needs help is you, Paul. You can't handle the guilt that when I needed you, you were a deadbeat husband," I yelled with a ferocity I didn't know existed inside me. We had never been physical with each other, but in that moment, I could have hit him. Hard. What was happening to me? My anger and physical reaction to the anger were scaring me.

Paul simply closed his eyes and looked back down to the ground, his strong, muscular body folding in defeat.

"What can I do?" he begged, his voice breaking. "How can I make this right?"

"You can start by not calling me or my hunches crazy anymore. I've had enough of you labeling me the crazy woman," I said, pointing my finger at Carrie's house and turning on my heel to get back in my car.

After firing up the engine, I made the decision to simply pull away. It wasn't healthy for me to be around Paul right now. I was so mad, there was no telling what else I would say.

As I put the car in reverse, I saw him look up and start walking toward my SUV. He called out my name, but I ignored him and continued peeling down the driveway, not caring if I was going too fast.

One last look in his direction before I turned, I contemplated flipping him the bird. Something stopped me, though. It was the sight of the wet snow stains that covered the bottom half of his dress pants.

Janie

Walking over to Petra's house in the dark, I tried my best to overcome the anxiety that filled me when I saw Lisa's older than dirt car pull up. The squeaking and rumbling of the engine made me want to turn around and go back home. I was a terrible person.

"Crap," I mumbled to myself, plastering a smile on my face and waving back at her. She was waving maniacally at me from the driver's side door as she parked at the bottom of Petra's driveway per her usual routine.

"Good morning," she said, her petite form popping out of the car. She turned and locked her door then quickly pulled on her gloves. I could tell just by her jumpy movements that she was in a good mood. I didn't want to ruin it with my bad news, but I had to tell her. And it had to be soon.

"Did you see the message from Petra?" Lisa asked, turning and walking down the driveway to me.

"No," I said. "What did she say?"

"She's out this morning. She didn't really give any explanation. Just said she'll see us tonight," Lisa said. "Are you ready?"

Lisa turned and started out on our path, past Carrie's house and toward the school.

"Are we doing five today?" she asked, turning back to glance at me. "It's pretty cold, but I could use the stress relief. That final was a killer last night, but I think I nailed it."

"Five sounds good," I said, looking back at Petra's house.

Her not being here meant I had the perfect opportunity to speak one on one with Lisa. I had to tell her. The more time that passed the worse it was. She was going to find out sooner or later.

"I'm kind of glad it's just us," Lisa said. "I really need to talk to you."

She knows, was all I could think. *She knows and she's pissed.*

Of course, she was pissed. I would be, too. She had every right to be. So why wasn't I seeing the anger in her? Why wasn't she shoving my face into a snow drift right now?

"Lisa, I'm…" I began, doing my best to keep up with her. My anxiety about her confronting me wasn't helping me keep up with Lisa the Speed Demon, our nickname for her. I was having trouble catching my breath. In general, the more heated she was on a topic, the faster she ran. At least if Petra were here, there would be two of us trying to set a slower pace.

"Not surprised?" she suggested. "Is that what you were going to say? I'm sure you've been picking up on clues as well. We have to do something. She's spinning out of control. Not that it's your fault, but I wish you never would have sold that house. I wish they would have just demolished it. Maybe that would have stopped all of this. She drives past it every day, you know."

I remained quiet, not knowing how to proceed. She was talking about Petra. She was talking about her brother's house I had to sell after the fire. She probably had no clue about her ex-husband's latest real estate venture. Though I knew he would jump at the earliest chance he got to rub it in her face somehow. Even though he had left her, he still seemed to be determined to show her how well he was doing without her. Probably because he saw how well she was doing without him, at least emotionally, since things had ended.

"Can we slow down a bit?" I managed, sucking air.

"I'm so sorry," she said, backing off of her frantic pace. "I'm really worked up. I barely slept last night worrying about Petra."

"We're going to figure out a way to help her. I know we can," I said, reassuring her.

"I know. Also, I'm still a bit jacked up from that ridiculously hard final I had to take. I don't know how I'm going to do this. Granted, it feels great. I feel more alive now than I've been over the last twenty years. I really love school," Lisa said, smiling back at me.

"I'm so proud of you," I said, a lightbulb going off in my brain. Why didn't I think of this earlier? Suddenly, I knew what I was going to do to make this right. There was no way I could legally stop the sale going through of her dream house, nor did I want to. Because I was going to give the commission to Lisa. It would be able to pay for a huge chunk of her classes. Petra had helped her get tuition reimbursement through work. There had to be a way she and I together could come up with a plan to make sure Lisa would accept the money I was offering her. Maybe it could be some kind of scholarship we "won." There had to be a way.

The commission would be huge, and in the end, I didn't really care about the money. I cared about how it affected my standing with the team of realtors in my company. It would be extremely difficult for Frederick to nudge me out of first place if I closed this deal.

"And if I tell you something, will you promise not to laugh at me?" Lisa said, pulling her hands up to her mouth, barely holding in a giggle.

"What?" I asked, giggling back at her. Her energy was helping calm me, despite my anxiety.

"I have a crush," she said, hiding her eyes from me.

"That's amazing," I said, feeling a wave of relief rush through me.

"Janie, I think he is at least ten years younger than me. Maybe more," she said, speeding up again. I put my arm on her sleeve to physically pull her back a bit. Her white ball on top of her pink snow cap bobbed back as I dragged her to a slower pace.

"Sorry, slower, I promise," she said.

"So what? I'm sorry, but seriously who gives a shit? My husband is almost twenty years older than me," I said. "And it works great. Don't think about that. Just think about making yourself happy. Seriously, you spent too long in absolute hell going through that divorce."

"I know, but you know there is still a stigma about men dating older women, not the other way around. I would still be considered a cougar and, oh my God, the girls. What would they say? For some reason, even in these 'modern times' it is much more accepted for women to date older men but not the other way around," Lisa said, though I couldn't help but notice she was still smiling.

"No, the new stigma is not letting people live the way they want to. Times are changing. No one would dare say anything to you in regards to your lifestyle choices in this current environment," I laughed. "They'll get canceled if they do."

"Yeah, you're right," Lisa chuckled. "Maybe this is the time to be a cougar."

This light, fun topic was distracting us from the ones we really needed to talk about, but I didn't care. This was a good one. Even though Lisa technically did not get divorced until last year, she'd been in a painful marriage for at least the last five. And that's just what she told us. We hadn't been as close to her until then. My guess was that she endured emotional abuse the majority of their marriage just to try and keep her family together. They'd gotten pregnant with twins right before they finished college then married quickly and settled down. She'd supported him through multiple start-ups, the last one blowing them up.

"Also, don't you think that the world may be a bit less likely to jump all over you because of Covid? Hopefully, we're all a little less concerned with each other's choices and just happy to be alive?"

Lisa laughed sarcastically and lifted her head to the sky.

"Well, you would think, but I'm just picturing me bringing my new friend into one of our school's events. Can you imagine those over-Botoxed, BMW-driving snobs taking that in? You really think they are going to give me a chance? They've already booted me from most of the social gatherings because I'm no longer in their income bracket."

"Honey, who cares. We don't want to hang around with those people anyway."

Lisa had a point. Unfortunately, once Lisa moved out of the neighborhood, most of the moms that we'd raised our kids with had cut her off or stopped inviting her to events. Some of it could be due to the fact that her kids were older now, but that shouldn't really matter. She didn't have a child at the neighborhood elementary school anymore, but she could still be invited to the happy hours and such.

It was hard to tell though what was Covid and what was really her getting cut. Social events came to a near standstill when the world shut down. And now, almost a year later, her kids were all out of the elementary school, and she lived clear on the other side of town. She was divorced and working full-time while going to school. She was a totally different person now.

No more leisure time for nails, coffees, and yoga classes, like she had in her old life.

"And you know that most of them would trade places with you in a heartbeat. Can you imagine Sexy Sally thinking she had a shot with your young man? She'd dump Humping Harry in a heartbeat," I laughed, causing both of us to stop running momentarily and double over in hysterics.

Sexy Sally was the fundraising chair for a local charity we had both been involved in a few years ago. She chased down donors relentlessly and always dressed a little more provocatively than what I felt was appropriate. Her cleavage was consistently on display, regardless of what the temperature was outside. Her husband was rumored to have had an incident where he danced inappropriately with a chair once when he got overserved at one of her charity events. None of us actually saw it live, but he was such a bully in his role as a volunteer soccer coach that the three of us enjoyed thinking it were possible. He owned some kind of software company and bragged constantly about his "wise investments." All of this while he screamed bloody murder at your six-year-old trying to kick a ball down the field with their uncoordinated legs. He also had a tendency to finish his rampages with extremely inappropriate name calling, even going so far as to call them, "little pussies."

"Alright, enough about this. Believe me, we'll talk about this ad nauseum when I'm ready. I just wanted to let you know that I'm a bit over the moon over someone I technically haven't met, just over Zoom so far. So, buckle up, it's going to be a lot of ridiculous stories coming from my end," Lisa said, her smile beaming back at me.

"Well, I am ready. This is so much better than watching you cry over Rick the Dick. I'll take crazy happy stories over crazy sad stories any day," I said, feeling true excitement for my friend. "And who cares if it's over Zoom. Can you imagine all of the romances that had to develop this way? People have had no choice. Love always wins. Even in a pandemic, it found a way."

"Well, I don't know if this is necessarily love yet," Lisa laughed. "Obsession, for sure. Maybe not love yet."

We laughed together for a bit at that before Lisa cut in.

"Okay, now on a serious note. Speaking of obsessions, we have to talk about Petra," Lisa said, her voice going low and dark.

"Oh no," I said, knowing exactly where this was going when she linked in the word, obsession.

"Is it starting again?" I asked. "That scream yesterday, right?"

"Yes, and that's the tip of the iceberg," Lisa said. "Brace yourself."

As Lisa dove into the full story, I knew this was not the right moment to bring up the sale of her dream home to her ex-husband and his new woman. We had bigger things to talk about right now.

After a good twenty-minute discussion on Petra and what we were seeing, we stopped to walk the last mile. I simply couldn't run any more, I was so overwhelmed.

"Do you think Paul knows?" I asked, feeling some old demons lurking.

"I don't think so," Lisa said, taking a deep breath.

"Do we tell him?" I asked, knowing that it would be the right thing but possibly a betrayal of girl code.

"I don't think so," Lisa said. "Maybe."

"You're not sure?" I asked.

"I don't want Petra to feel like we don't believe her. She and Paul are already struggling. I'm just not really sure how to help Petra, you know? What's the right thing here?" Lisa asked.

"Do we know for a fact that she's still seeing her therapist?" I asked, trying to problem solve.

Lisa shrugged. "She says yes, but who knows. Only Petra knows that."

"And, we have to ask ourselves this. Is there any way she could be right?" I sprinkled in, having to play devil's advocate, just so we were looking at this from all angles.

Lisa shrugged again.

"I can honestly say, I have no idea. Logic tells me no. But it's Petra, my rock-solid, doctor friend who put herself through school after immigrating with her family and barely even speaking the language before starting high school. She's amazing," Lisa said.

"For sure she is. There's no doubting that. But even those kinds of people break down. She's been through too much this past year. Her brother dying in the fire, her injuries, then going straight into having to lead her team at the hospital through the pandemic while raising young kids and struggling in her marriage. It's too much," I said. Saying it all out loud gave me pause. My poor friend.

"What are we going to do?" Lisa said, slumping her shoulders. "I don't know what to do."

"Well, we're going to take it one step at a time," I said, feeling overwhelmed but happy to be talking this out with Lisa. I was so lucky to have this group of friends to support me and be able to support them. It was good to be loved and to give love. Now if only I could be completely honest with them. About a lot of things.

"And we're going over there tonight to talk to her and break down some walls. We're all finally vaccinated and can be together for Gaga Night," I said, referring to our monthly ritual. The name Gaga Night had stuck early in our relationship. Petra had asked us over to watch a Lady Gaga concert on her extra-large screen television in her beautifully decorated entertainment floor of her house, also known as the basement. It was just too elegant and five-star resort like to ever refer to it as a simple basement.

After that concert, which we barely watched because we found out we had too much to talk about, we kept meeting, the screen usually dark or a movie on in the background that was barely watched. We used these nights now to catch up and really dive in. The runs were great talking times, but there was nothing like a warm drink, a fire, and some yummy snacks to really get ladies talking about the good stuff.

"That sounds like a start," Lisa said, nodding her head. "I could use a drink."

As she said this, I must have visibly shaken because she immediately grabbed my arm.

"I'm sorry," she said, her eyes frantic and the white ball bouncing on her head. "I shouldn't have said that."

"It's okay," I said. "It's not that. I'm just jumpy," I said, trying to sound as confident as possible. On the inside though, my mind raced. *I want a drink, too,* my body screamed at me from a cellular level.

Lisa

When I got home, I had just enough time to grab a quick shower and stuff a bagel in my mouth before I had to head out the door.

"The car won't start again," I heard my daughter, Brenda, say from the garage. She made a point of starting my car for me on the mornings she was ready early. It was just a little thing, but in the world of angry teenage hormones that we lived in, it was a gesture that told me she still loved me, despite what came out of her mouth.

"No," I said, my mind already racing to the stack of unpaid bills on my desk upstairs. There was no way I would be able to pay for any type of car repairs right now. I could barely put food on the table on my small salary I made. Something had to give.

"Are you sure?" I asked, hoping that it had just been some kind of misunderstanding between Brenda and the machine.

Brenda shrugged, her tall lanky form coming into the kitchen and handing me the keys. "Don't know. You try," she said, swinging her long ponytail off her shoulder in a gesture that told me she was frustrated but trying to keep it together.

I raced to the garage and prayed for a miracle. Sure enough, the car wouldn't give, just like Brenda had said.

"Oh, no, no, no," I whimpered, knowing I was royally screwed. My options were very limited having very little support. My ex was a no-go, and I had no local family here, except for his, which couldn't be bothered after I had the audacity to divorce their son. My parents were five states away and still, sixteen years later, holding a grudge that I had gotten pregnant before I'd been legally married.

"Get over it," I yelled aloud, feeling a wave of frustration wash over me. I hated that their easy dismissal of me still got to me in these desperate times, but try as I might, it still did. I would never do that to one of my daughters.

"Get over what, Mom?" Brenda asked from the doorway.

I hadn't realized she was still there.

"Nothing," I said, laughing a little at myself. Maybe I had to get over it. My parents had ditched me a long time ago. I didn't live up to their expectations of what a proper daughter should be and they had dropped me. Perhaps I was the one who had to face that and "get over" them. Did I really want people like that in my life? I certainly didn't want fair weather grandparents in my kids' lives. That wasn't what I wanted them to see as an example.

It was just that in these desperate times, when I had no one to turn to, no siblings, no spouse, I wanted my parents to be the kind of parents that hung in there and helped out. I wished for that so badly in these moments.

"Brenda, I have to take your car," I said, referring to the car my daughters shared, which was also on its last leg. Two months ago, I bought it out of desperation from a neighbor for a second mode of transportation. It had one hundred and seventy-five thousand miles on it but was priced right at five hundred dollars. "I can't miss work."

Brenda visibly cringed, her beautiful features forming into that snotty, teenage, "Eww" look they all seemed to have.

"What about volleyball practice?" she said. "And Veronica has track. She's going to shit."

"Don't say shit," I said, trying to stick to my hard rule of no swearing in the house, an aggressive goal considering all these girls had heard in the past few years as their parents went through a divorce.

"I can't believe I'm saying this, but maybe we should call your dad to help," I said, feeling we had no other choice. I honestly didn't know if he was still in town. I'd released him to the universe and it had felt amazing. He was simply, no longer my problem. But there was no denying, I could sure as hell use his help with raising these girls every once and awhile.

"Mom, don't worry about it. Take the car. We'll either figure out carpools, or we'll get a ride from Dad. Just go. I don't want you to be late," Brenda said, shocking me into silence.

I closed the car door and walked around it, keeping eye contact with her but not saying anything. I watched her playing with her ponytail, waiting for the rest.

"What?" I finally managed.

No fights, no temper tantrums, no "my life is over" comments? She was simply going to solve her problem. Who was this calm, sensible child?

It hit me then. Perhaps she had already been talking to her father. In my mind, because they hadn't updated me, I assumed that all was status quo. It was us against the world and Rick had abandoned all of us. Was I wrong?

"We'll get rides," Brenda repeated.

"From your dad?" I asked, still unsure what was happening.

"Do you think he would do that?" she asked, her eyes shining with hope. She looked so young and naïve in that moment, staring back at me in her light pink pajamas, her brows elevated up on her forehead, not a hint of a wrinkle on her sweet, delicate skin.

These poor, poor girls. They still believed.

"Maybe," I said, unable to dash what glistening bit of youth she had left. *And maybe Santa Claus really will come down the chimney this year with the Barbie Dreamhouse*, I thought.

I reached over and pulled her into an embrace, smelling a combination of her minty toothpaste and strawberry shampoo. I should have left him earlier. I'd hung on for too long thinking Rick would improve, that we would improve. That it was important to keep family together. What had it really done for these girls? Look where they were now. I should have showed them earlier it wasn't okay to be treated poorly, and it wasn't okay to hang onto false promises.

"Thank you for being so understanding about the car," I whispered into her hair, holding onto her much longer than I'm sure she wanted. It just felt so good.

"It's fine, Mom," Brenda laughed back.

"Will you text me when you know your plan?" I asked, still keeping a tight squeeze.

"Of course," she giggled in that "I'm a teenager and I'm totally uncomfortable but also loving this" kind of way.

"Okay, I'm off then. Tell your sister I said goodbye and I'll check in later," I said, running inside to grab my bag and head to the hospital.

I drove to the hospital on a high. Even though I was broke, I no longer owned a home, and I was on sketchy transportation, there was no denying I was happy. Or happier than I'd been in a long time. And talking to Janie this morning about my crush, finally confiding in someone, felt good. Made it more real. Also, a little more ridiculous, but more real. He was probably not "the one" with the age difference, but I was abundant in "interest in life." I was interested in my schooling, I was interested in my job, I was now interested in a guy. I think I had been in a depression for so long, I didn't even know what happiness felt like anymore. This had to be it. Feeling joyful even when my car wouldn't start and I didn't have money to pay for it. This HAD to be happiness.

A few hours later, that feeling of happiness came to a screeching halt when Brenda sent me a text. I stared at in in disbelief, feeling my feet start to vibrate with anger, resentment and just plain shock. It read:

> **Hi Mom! Dad said he will drive me and Julie will drive me home. He said your friend Janie is helping him buy a brand-new house in our old neighborhood and that there is even space for Veronica and me. I'll see you tonight!**

Petra

"Gaga Night!" the humongous sign, beautifully arched over the fireplace, read. On one side, a pink balloon garland I'd found through an entertainment company completed the over-the-top look I was going for. They'd been here for over an hour perfecting the look, and I tipped them generously for dealing with my perfectionism. My kids were running around squealing, driving me nuts but also making me laugh. I couldn't blame them for being excited. It had been so long since we'd had guests. And probably a long time since they saw their mom this happy and excited.

Entertaining my friends and family, as well as throwing parties and events for my staff at the hospital, were the way I found joy and also stress relief. I was a Pinterest and Instagram junkie, pulling off all kinds of entertaining ideas and recipes to bring smiles from my guests. If I ever tired of being a doctor, my next career would be being an event planner. This was my happy.

The fact that I wasn't able to do this for so long had been hard on me. Covid shut that all down. It was inappropriate to entertain or even be happy for that matter. Life had to stop. And for me, as a doctor in the ER, it was tough to find any joy. Celebrating felt wrong. It even felt inappropriate to laugh.

"Wow," Paul said, coming up behind me and putting a hand on my shoulder. "You've really outdone yourself this time," he said, admiring my work. Or, really, the entertainment company's work.

"Do you like it?" I asked, turning to him and looking into his dark brown eyes. I smiled at him, feeling bad for the way I treated him yesterday when I came home from the hospital. This was how it was with us right now. Outbursts followed by guilt followed by remorse and then us struggling to reconnect. This wasn't healthy. I knew that, but I just couldn't seem to get a grip on the cycle of grief. It was like a hamster wheel that never stopped. I hated the theory that there were stages of grief. That made you think you could actually make progress. Like a ladder you could climb. I didn't feel like I was making progress, though. This was no ladder. It was a wheel that could turn any which way at any time. It was maddening.

But today was a good day. My friends were coming over, my shifts at the hospital were over for the week, and for the first time in a long time, Gaga Night had given me a sense of celebration that I needed so badly.

"I love it," Paul said, moving closer to me and pulling my body close to his.

After I'd returned from my rage drive yesterday, he met me at the door with another apology. Our housekeeper had separated the kids from the garage entrance, as I'd always demanded, so I could go shower and remove any last bit of germs that clung to me before I saw them.

Normally I asked Paul to give me extra space as well to take a shower. He was so distraught though from our fight, I allowed him to follow me up to the shower and eventually join me inside. We showered together in silence at first until our hands found each other and we connected in the way we needed to. At that moment, I didn't even care if he was seeing my scars. He certainly didn't seem to mind. It had been months since I allowed him to touch me like that. I just needed time.

That moment in the shower together had been a small reprieve from our arguments and disconnection. Today felt so much better. Sex wasn't going to solve all of our problems, that was for sure. But it certainly helped.

"I love you," he said, nuzzling my ear. "Got time for a quick shower before your friends come?" he asked in a deep, sexy voice quiet enough for the kids not to hear. His minty breath, combined with his signature sandalwood and lavender scent made my pulse kick up a bit. My body had missed intimacy with him so much it was certainly ready for a round two.

"Daddy!" my youngest, Devin, yelled. He hit Paul's knee with a stray balloon that had detached from the arch.

"No, I don't have time," I laughed, playfully rejecting his offer. "They'll be here in fifteen minutes. I have to go get dressed."

"Daddy, leave Mommy alone," Devin yelled in his little man voice.

When Paul looked down at him, Devin flashed his killer smile, so similar to his father's and raised his hands up in a gesture saying, "pick me up."

Devin was extremely territorial when it came to Daddy time. He had gotten so much of it that he wanted Paul to himself all the time.

"Okay, my little friends, let's get out of here," Paul said, bending his big form down to pick up little Devin with one arm. The other muscular arm reached out to me and kissed me on the lips before announcing to the kids, "We need to clear out of here and let her have her time with the friends."

"We can't stay for the party?" my daughter, Ellie, protested for the tenth time. "But I want to have cupcakes," she whined. There was no making her happy.

"I'm taking you out for dinner and treats, remember?" Paul said.

"We can get our own cupcakes?" Ellie questioned. "And Mommy will save some of hers?" She spun around in a circle, making her black curls and her rainbow-colored skirt fan out in a circle around her.

Always the negotiator, this one was our future attorney, for sure.

"For the one hundredth time, yes. Now let's go. Have a great time, honey. You deserve it," Paul said, smiling at me before turning to go. "We'll catch up with you later," he said, turning and bouncing his eyebrows up and down in my direction. "You look beautiful by the way."

"Thank you," I said, feeling hopeful about us for the first time in a long time. I knew my brother would want me to forgive and move on. I could see him in my mind, nodding his head yes. He was always the peacemaker in the family. The gentle soul. But also, the fragile soul. After his death, I'd had the opportunity to speak to our pastor a few times. I was so numb at the time, but there was something he said that flashed through my mind. I'd forgotten about it until now. Though technically not deemed a suicide, I'd had my doubts and my questions about what Danny had intended that afternoon.

"This world is unkind. It's hardest on those like Danny. God knows that," my pastor had said. I'd been expecting some kind of warning or even some kind of plan to pray Danny out of Hell since he'd been a suicide. I should have known that Pastor Frank wouldn't approach it that way. The way some of the priests I had growing up viewed it.

Turning back to my balloon arch, I smiled, wiping away a tear. I couldn't help thinking how much Danny, having run his own event planning business for years, would love my Gaga Night display.

"How did I do, Danny?" I asked to his ever-present ghost.

I nodded my head, hearing him say, "You did just fine."

Janie

At exactly seven o'clock, I rang Petra's doorbell with the bottle of Veuve Clicquot I bought specifically for this occasion, as well as my special bottle of sparkling water. The girls knew I didn't drink, and though I knew Petra would have the non-alcoholic drinks stocked just for me, I always felt empty handed unless I brought a few bottles.

I was riding the struggle bus today. Standing here in the freezing cold with my fur-lined coat wrapped around me, I questioned if this was the right decision to come. Not ten minutes ago, I got the contract for Rick the Dick's new house signed. That weighed so heavy on me right now that I could barely stand up. All I could think about was getting in front of Petra's humongous blazing fire on her plush, oversized couches and chilling out. I was wound so tight; I didn't see how I was going to be able to relax. What I should have done was stay home and call my sponsor to tell her where I was mentally.

Things were not good in my head right now. I hadn't spoken to Lisa yet about what was going on, my anxiety wasn't getting settled like it normally did by my morning runs, and on top of that, my kids were crying tonight when I left. My daughter, Nola, actually said to me, "I never see you, Mama."

Ugh. Like a knife to my heart. She wasn't wrong. I was working so much more than normal right now because of the burst in housing sales. I had to strike while the iron was hot. And normally a night like tonight was what recharged me. My girl time was more beneficial to my soul than therapy or time with my sponsor. These ladies knew my struggles and could talk me off of any ledge.

It's just that tonight was different. I had a big secret and it was going to break Lisa's heart. How could I tell her? Why did I do this?

My only hope was that before he could move in, Rick's clueless girlfriend would see the light and break up with him. I noticed she didn't include him on the paperwork. Maybe there was hope.

The door whipped open, revealing an ecstatic-looking Petra in head-to-toe ballet pink lounge wear. It was reminiscent of the Juicy Couture track outfits that were so big in the late nineties. Hers
sparkled in the upper right-hand side.

"Is that your name in sequins?" I asked, immediately taken in by her bling.

"I've got matching ones for you guys!" Petra called out, welcoming me into a hug.

Seeing her like this rocked me a little. She was much different than the Petra Lisa described this morning to me on the run. Lisa said she was a bit obsessive, quiet, and worried. That description didn't resemble the woman standing in front of me at all. Though, in my opinion, mood swings were completely permissible right now. Weren't we all constantly going through the ups and downs? It was more the exception than the norm to remain steady and unaffected by these uncertain times.

"Come on in. No Lisa yet, huh?" Petra asked, looking past me.

"No, I haven't seen her," I said, walking in and spotting my matching pink track suit hanging up in the kitchen. "Wow, look at that," I said, reaching out and running my hand along the soft velour, my name glistening in sequins.

"Do you like it? We all know that loungewear is here to stay for a while, but Juicy Couture coming back?" Petra laughed. "I couldn't be happier. I used to live in those when I was in medical school. Probably much longer than the initial trend allowed. I just couldn't give them up."

"Did you save any of your old ones?" I asked, laughing at the image of Petra cruising around The University of Chicago in her little Juicy pants. She was probably a hot little number back then. She still was.

"Unfortunately, no. I should have," Petra said, motioning for me to grab mine. "Put it on if you like. But don't feel pressured," she said, looking doubtful all of a sudden.

"I will definitely put it on. It looks tons more comfortable than what I have on. I'll change in there," I said, motioning to one of her many bathrooms.

"Okay, what can I fix you to drink while you're changing? Do you want that virgin blueberry mojito you loved so much last time?" she asked, smiling at me.

I took just a second too long to reply, taking in Petra's appearance. Her long, black hair looked freshly washed and cascaded down around her shoulders. Her make-up, perfectly applied, accented her deep brown eyes and her high cheekbones. I had a flashback to attending Petra's talk about civil liberties for immigrants at the Chicago Union League Club two years ago. I'd attended as her guest, but spent most of the night with my jaw on the floor, admiring my friend's courage and strength. I felt like that again right now. Something about this moment reminded me of the Union League Club. She was fighting for something. Working hard. I could tell. Behind that happy, confident exterior, I could see it, only because I knew her so well. Lisa had been right. Something was up.

"What?" Petra asked, after I didn't respond to her offer of a drink.

"Nothing," I said, struggling to remember what she had asked me.

The doorbell rang suddenly and Petra turned her head, looking in the direction of the front door with eyebrows down in concentration, almost as though questioning who was on the other side of the door. That was odd. She knew it was going to be Lisa, right?

"I'll change quick," I said, trying to buy myself more time to figure out how to talk to Lisa about Rick's new house. "And yes, I'll take that blueberry mojito!" I said enthusiastically, remembering what she had asked. I left the word virgin out accidentally, but part of me wondered if I had done it on purpose. It was going to be a miracle if I made it out of Covid with my sobriety intact.

Lisa

Before ringing the bell, I took a deep breath in and then released it. I was so angry right now. How was I going to hold it together?

There had to be a good explanation. I knew my friend. I was secure enough in our relationship to know at my core that there were no ill intentions. Surely, once I talked to her, I was going to feel better.

I didn't even care that Rick was moving back into our old neighborhood without me. He and his young lady could have the biggest, newest, grandest house in the subdivision. Who really cared about that? Besides, my gut knew in the end it would all blow up for them anyway. Everything always did for Rick. He simply couldn't maintain anything steady whether it came to his investments, his relationships, and his commitments. Sooner or later, hot lady was going to figure it out and leave him. It didn't take a genius to figure that out. The only thing that affected me was the thought of my girls once again getting something ripped away from them.

Were they going to move back into glossy bedrooms in our old neighborhood and for a second time have to leave? The thought of that made me sick. And angry.

"Hey," Petra said, conspiratorially, taking a step out onto the porch. "Can I show you what I was talking about?"

"What are you wearing?" I asked, stepping back to take in her pink sweatsuit with her name flashing at me proudly from the upper right-hand side of her top. Over her left arm, I noticed she held her winter coat.

"I'll tell you later," she said, pulling me down the porch and in the direction of her driveway. I allowed her to drag me, a little freaked out by her determination. What the hell was going on? My curiosity almost wiped out my anger. Almost.

Petra stopped abruptly when we got to the far side of the driveway and pointed.

"Look!" she said. "I can't believe it. I told you! Look there," she said, frantically pointing her finger out toward Carrie's darkened house.

"Look at what? What am I looking at?" I asked, feeling a bit concerned that maybe Petra was seeing things now. Was that part of PTSD? I wished Janie was here with us. A few seconds earlier, I was dreading seeing her and now all I wanted was for her to be here witnessing this as well. I wanted her help.

"The light is out now. It was on last night," Petra said, grabbing my arm. "See. Someone is home."

I nodded my head, turning to look for Janie.

"Is Janie here yet?" I asked.

"She's inside putting her Gaga Night outfit on," Petra said dismissively. Clearly that information was not as important right now as what we were seeing at Carrie's house.

"Gaga outfit?" I asked.

"Never mind, I'll tell you later. Lisa, someone is in that house, and I think they were screaming yesterday," Petra said, tugging at my arm to follow her to the house.

"Wait, what are we doing?" I asked, starting to panic as Petra pulled me in the direction of Carrie's property.

"I just want to check something out quick," Petra said, stopping and turning to look at me. "Please, just please come see this with me, Lisa," she begged, tugging at my heart strings. "Paul thinks I'm crazy and doesn't believe me. You're the only one I can talk to about this," she said, her shoulders slumping.

That got me. I thought about all the times I was alone in my own head during my marriage. Scared and alone. I wouldn't allow that to happen to Petra.

"Lisa, I'm not crazy. I know how I've been acting after Danny died. I lost it a little bit, yes. And, I'm going through a hard time with my husband on top of recovering from all I saw at the hospital. I own all of that. But you see me at work every day. You see how I have it together now. I'm getting better. Everything is better," she said, waving over her body as if to indicate the physical scars left over from the fire. "Here, too," she said waving over her head and her long, black hair.

She said she doesn't want to be here anymore, Paul had whispered into the phone, begging me to come over that night. He'd found Petra crying in the bathroom in the middle of the night, alone and at her bottom. He'd begged me to come over because he was overwhelmed and didn't know what to do. Janie and I were there within minutes.

As though reading my thoughts, Petra said exactly what I needed to hear.

"Lisa, please don't judge me by my darkest days," she said solemnly. "I'm not there anymore."

But that was only six months ago.

Standing here in the freezing cold, my mind told me to get Petra inside and talk her out of whatever she had planned. This wasn't normal. But my heart said differently. This was my best friend, standing in front of me, asking me for help. And she did have a point. Out of everyone around her, I probably saw her the most because I worked with her. She excelled there. Based on what I saw at the hospital, she certainly seemed like she'd moved past some of the demons that haunted her. She was never glazed over, or late, or checked out. From what I saw, she was engaging with patients, accountable with her staff and fellow physicians and approachable.

"Okay, but should we get Janie?" I asked, hoping for another compadre in this. I didn't completely trust my own judgement when it came to Petra. I was devoted to her and might be a bit blind here.

"This will only take a second," she said, pulling me closer to the darkened monstrosity that was Carrie's house.

Petra

Lisa's hesitation felt like pulling a heavy weight. Maybe this was a mistake. She looked terrified. Like I was dragging her into a party she didn't want to attend. I stopped for a second in my urgency and got cold feet.

"Maybe you're right," I said, just as we got to the stairs leading up to the side door into the garage. "This is nuts."

"What if we went back and got Janie?" Lisa suggested again, putting her arm around me. "Maybe it would help to have another set of eyes."

I stood silently for a second, trying to reason with my own paranoia. I couldn't tell my friends about Carrie coming to the E.R. with the suspicious bruises. It would violate my code as her doctor. I just wish that Lisa had been there when she had come in. She hadn't started at the hospital yet when it had happened, but she'd seen her fair share of injuries from domestic violence since her start there. We had definitely seen an uptick of it as couples were isolated in their homes, stressed out and freaked out.

I nodded my head, ready to call the whole thing off. Standing out here in the pitch dark, my plan didn't seem very reasonable or thought out. What were we really going to be able to see?

As though the heavens were listening, Lisa and I were suddenly flooded in light. We grabbed onto each other; our eyes glued now to the top of the stairs.

"Oh my God, you were right," Lisa whispered. "There is someone here."

Her shaky voice and tight embrace sent my brain into overdrive. Why had I brought her here? Had I put her in some kind of danger? She was a single mom now. I couldn't risk anything happening to her.

"We have to get out of here," I said, pulling her back in the direction of the house.

Before we could make a run for it, the door at the top of the stairs, leading into the garage was flung open, and a woman bearing a large shotgun stepped out.

"Get off my property," the woman shouted down at us.

Lisa and I screamed in unison and scrambled to do exactly what she had said. Bolting through the deep snow, Lisa and I held hands, screaming as we ran. Just as we were about to hit my driveway, Lisa stopped abruptly.

"Wait," Lisa said, stopping us in our tracks.

"Heather Platt?" Lisa called out to the woman standing on the porch.

"Lisa?" the woman said, lowering the shotgun.

"What?" I asked, bowled over by this change of course. No way this was Heather Platt. What in the world was the neighborhood busybody doing here?

"Hold on a minute," Lisa said, letting go of my hand to walk back in Heather's direction. Before she could close the gap, I grabbed the back of her coat.

"What are you doing? She has a gun," I said, feeling the strong urge to get back in the house and away from whoever this crazy woman was.

"It's our neighbor. Well, your neighbor now. Heather Platt," Lisa said, turning back to her. "Just give me a second."

Heather kept her gun lowered and allowed us to approach her. She turned back into the garage and suddenly the yard filled with more light.

"Yes, Heather, it's me, Lisa. And Petra from next door," Lisa said, pulling me along with her to talk to Heather.

"I'm sorry about the gun. Never can be too careful these days though. What are you ladies doing out here?" Heather asked, setting the gun back into the garage. This act finally settled my mind a little bit.

"We were just looking around. We thought we heard something," I said, feeling like I had to defend my actions, considering I was the one that had drawn us into this mess.

"What are you doing here?" Lisa said, volleying back at her.

"Oh, I'm just here checking on the house. Carrie and Tom asked me to watch it for them while they were out," Heather said, smoothing her waxy, brunette hair. "You guys gave me a good scare. There are cameras on in the house, and I saw two people walking around where they shouldn't be. I thought you were going to try and get in."

We were, I thought.

"And you know, you can't be too careful in this silly 'Black Lives Matter' time. They'll come and loot your house just because they think they're entitled to even though we worked hard for everything we have."

I rolled my eyes, not caring if she saw or not. She must have forgotten or simply didn't care that my husband was black.

"I thought I heard a scream earlier this week coming from inside the house. Are you staying here, Heather?" I asked, knowing our time was limited. From the few encounters I'd had with her at school functions, I knew she loved to talk about herself and had the tendency to trap her audience once she got going.

"Oh no. I'm just on an on-call basis. Tom called me and asked if I would take a look around," Heather said. "What do you mean scream? You heard it from inside the house?"

The cameras must have alerted Tom earlier when I was approaching the house and he had called in his dogs. Or in this case, Heather.

"I must have been wrong," I said quickly. "When will they be back?"

"Oh, I don't think they are coming back. Haven't you heard?" she said.

This whole time, we were standing out in the cold. She hadn't come down the stairs nor had she asked us in. She just stood up there, talking down to us, which was how I imagined Heather preferred things. She was the ultimate one-upper, with a superiority complex. Her kids were known in the neighborhood as being the class bullies, no big surprise. She was probably too distracted running all the school activities and religious programs at one of the local churches to discipline her own obnoxious kids. Whatever your kids were doing, hers had already done and had done it better. She was going to let you know that.

"What do you mean?" Lisa asked in response to Heather's statement.

"They're buying a place in Florida. They've asked me to sell this home. Tom runs his business from home, so he can really live anywhere. They decided that it would be better to live in a better climate. Illinois is going downhill anyway," she said, her lip sneered up in disgust. "I'm going to list the house next week."

"Oh," I said, shocked to hear this. "I didn't realize you sold real estate."

"Well, I have not for years. I've never needed to work, but since the market is so hot, I decided to reactivate my license and get in on the fun. The kids are older now and don't need me as much. They're straight-A students without my help. Also, just heard that Frankie, Jr. is getting a scholarship to Yale," she squealed.

Lisa groaned loudly next to me and I nudged her. While Heather babbled on, the skies opened up and flakes of snow pelted us from above as we looked straight up at Heather. It was getting awkward and uncomfortable to look up at her. Like a motor, she kept running her mouth at us. It didn't even register with her that we were getting dumped on. She was happy going on about her children and their success without really checking in on our status.

My guess was we could walk away and she would still be standing there, going on and on. It made me nuts. She bounced from her daughter's tennis, to her husband's business, to her twin sons graduating Princeton and now her next son going to Yale. All of this while we stood in the freezing cold and she had the benefit of coverage from the roof over the stairs.

"I didn't know you were even friends with Carrie and Tom," Lisa said, cutting her off rudely.

I noticed since Lisa moved out of the neighborhood and outside of this social circle, she had very little tolerance for bullshit. She didn't even try or care anymore. I was sure in her mind, she'd moved on and simply didn't care for playing the game anymore.

"Well, I'm friends with everyone. That's how I'm so successful in real estate," she said, buying into her own bullshit as usual.

"But I thought you said you're just getting back into it?" Lisa said, calling her out.

"Okay, well, it was nice talking with you. Glad everything is okay. We have a pizza coming any minute," I said, holding up my phone as though I'd just received a message. "I gotta run in and get tip money and he's almost here. Talk soon, Heather!" I called out, linking my arm around Lisa's and pulling her with me.

I'd had enough. She'd have us out here all night. This was a dead end.

"Okay, well, let me know if you know anyone looking to buy a home," she called out to our backs enthusiastically. She kept talking, but we blatantly ignored her now. When we finally got to my front porch, I turned to look back one last time and saw her still up on the stairs, watching us. And it looked as though she was still talking. I turned and walked with Lisa up my front stairs and into the house.

Janie

I stood by the front door, watching my friends walk slowly down the stairs. When I saw them bolt to the side of the house, I opened the door and stepped out, wondering what the hell was going on. I almost called out to them, but when I saw where they were going, I stayed quiet. I was this close to pulling my coat on to join them, but stopped and turned back inside. As juvenile as it sounded, I felt left out. If they had wanted me to come with, they would have asked me. Maybe they didn't want me there for some reason.

Or, worse. Maybe Lisa knew about the sale and wanted Petra alone to talk about me. Maybe Petra was trying to calm her down and pulled her to the side yard for some time alone. No. That didn't make sense, either. They would have just gone out on the porch. They were walking at a pretty fast speed in the direction of Carrie's house. They appeared to be on a mission.

Feeling frazzled and not knowing what to do with myself, I went downstairs to the basement where we normally hung out. I paced back and forth, taking in all the decorations Petra had set up for our event tonight. How beautiful. If only I were in a better place to be able to appreciate it all.

Seeing the decorations made me feel silly. Everything was fine. We had been friends for over seven years now. Our kids were growing up together. In those years, we'd been through a lot and had been very open with each other. Our marriages, divorce for Lisa, death for Petra, kid issues, my addiction issues. All of these things had been openly discussed. We'd been vulnerable and loving with each other. This stupid house sale wasn't going to break us apart. Who was I kidding?

To settle myself down, I plopped down on the plush, oversized couches that ran almost the entire length of the room. I let them swallow me up while I waited for the ladies to come down. Lying back in my new loungewear and pulling out my phone, I allowed myself to believe that everything was going to be okay. Until I started flipping through social media.

Rick the Dick had posted a picture of himself and his girlfriend bundled in winter coats in front of his new house with the caption, "She said yes! Manifest it and it can be yours!" They hugged each other and jangled a set of keys in front of them. Not keys to the house yet, obviously. They hadn't closed, only just signed initial paperwork. What a bunch of thirsty people.

What a douchebag. The ink was barely dry on the house deal, let alone the divorce papers from his first wife who was struggling to make ends meet. Now he was showing off his new property while people were still suffering with their health and financial struggles as the world tried to recover from the shutdowns that were still going on. Who did he think he was?

My head started to pound and my cheeks flared red as I bolted up from the couch. Surely, Lisa had seen this. She told us stories about how she still followed him on social media to make herself feel better. We knew this was also part of her healing. Although she claimed to be happy away from him, it had to still hurt a bit to see him bragging.

This was really going to sting. And it was just a matter of time until she put two and two together about the sale of the house.

I walked over to the bar where Petra stashed her usual small fridge of non-alcoholic drinks for me and started rummaging through. Grabbing a blueberry carbonated water, I stood up and started to reach for a glass she had set out on the counter when a bottle of Cabernet Sauvignon caught my eye. It was set out on a little tray, already opened. They would never know.

I set my water down and stepped back from the bar, my heart racing. I had to get out of here. I was in big trouble. I could hear the voices in my head battling it out. This was how it was when I had one of my episodes.

Get out.

Drink just a little bit. Just a half a glass will take the edge off. Better yet, look for the vodka. They won't smell it.

"I have to get out of here," I said aloud.

I turned and ran up the basement stairs, noting that the ladies still had not returned. I could leave and just text them as soon as I got home that I had an upset stomach. A sudden bout of the flu.

Or you could check Petra's medicine cabinet upstairs and see what kind of pills she has. You know she has the good stuff. Especially since the fire.

Before I could stop myself, I was halfway up the stairs, leading up to the second floor. Just a look around wouldn't hurt anyone. I wasn't really going to take anything. Or maybe one Vicodin would calm me enough to stop this episode. One wasn't going to hurt.

Just as I got to the first landing, I heard the front door open.

"We're back," I heard Petra call out. Her eyes immediately met mine, and I could feel my stomach drop to the floor like a kid caught with a hand in the candy jar. Her eyebrows scrunched down in confusion, and my heart broke thinking about what she must be thinking.

Lisa

"Everything okay?" Petra asked, sounding confused.

It took me a second to figure out what she was looking at, but then I spotted Janie, peering over the banister, a sheepish look on her face. Her eyebrows were raised, her blond bob askew, and her mouth was curved into what looked like a forced smile. The look reminded me of how Veronica looked after I'd found her texting on her phone after midnight one night-an act strictly forbidden in our household.

"I was looking for you guys," Janie said, her voice noticeably shaky. "Where did you go?"

Janie started to walk down the stairs, then seemed to reconsider. Clothed in the matching pink sweatsuit to Petra, she turned to head back up, then once again began her descent.

"I went to go show Lisa something next door. Are you okay, Janie?" Petra asked.

Janie sat down on the stairs and put her head into her hands.

Petra and I both turned to look at each other, sharing looks of confusion, before we both bolted up the stairs to see what was happening.

"What's wrong?" Petra asked, making it up before me to Lisa's side.

Janie didn't respond, just kept her eyes hidden from us in her hands and shook her head.

"I'm so sorry, Lisa," she managed to get out in between sobs. "I shouldn't have done it. I didn't know how to stop it. I planned to give you the commission. I think that's how I justified it in my mind, but it's still not right."

When Lisa finally lifted her head up, her cheeks were so red, they reminded me of the red tulips on my kitchen table. She was having trouble catching her breath and tears poured down her face like someone had left the kitchen sink running. Seeing her like this, my heart broke into a million pieces. Though, I was still a bit hurt. I wished she would have told me. It wasn't that I judged her for taking the sale, I just thought because we were so close, she should have told me first. Instead, I had to hear it from my kids. Always the last to know, once again.

What she said next though, wiped all of that clear.

"Petra, I was going to go look for pills in your bathroom," she sobbed. "I almost drank the wine downstairs."

"Oh, honey," I said, pulling her into a hug. She sobbed uncontrollably for a few minutes while I rocked her and rubbed her back.

"I'm so stupid," Petra said. "I never should have left that open bottle out like that. I wasn't thinking," she said, reaching out and rubbing Janie's arm.

We let Janie release her tears, reciting words of encouragement and comfort, knowing that sometimes these breakdowns had to happen. It just had to come out.

Janie's sobriety was more important and critical than some stupid house that Rick the Dick was buying. I felt terrible that the stress of having to tell me may have pushed her to this edge. It made me look at the whole situation differently. Was there something about my demeanor that made Janie think she couldn't tell me? That I wouldn't understand? We would have to talk about that once there was a window to do so. Not right now.

When Janie finally caught her breath, she pulled away from me and sat back, leaning on the wall for support. She looked like a tiny, deflated balloon. I noticed she'd gotten mascara on her new sweatsuit and her lips were puffed up from crying. Her normally perfect bobbed blond hair was a mess, sticking up in all directions.

"It's not your fault, Petra. I should be past this by now. I should be able to walk by an open bottle no problem. It's been years now that I've been sober. I'm acting like it's my first week. When will this go away?"

"I think that's just it, Janie," I said, as delicately as I could. "It's not going to. You can't expect that of yourself."

"I'm under so much pressure at work," Janie said, opening up. "I know my job is not like yours. I'm not seeing what you guys have to see on a daily basis, but there's still a lot of pressure. This housing boom has been great, but there's a lot of pressure to perform while things are hot because we know things will stop. And then Rick the Dick called me, Lisa," she said, looking at me with those blood-red eyes. I noticed she was barely able to make eye contact when she said it. Her body seemed to vibrate, shaking as she spoke. "And he just kind of took off. He didn't really even let me say, no. I don't know how to explain it. I should have told you immediately."

"Trust me, I get Rick's bulldozing. He's very persuasive," I said, trying to make her feel better. "Wait, scratch that. He's not really persuasive. Who am I kidding? He's too much of a narcissist to worry about persuading someone. He just takes what he wants."

"Janie, you understand that I'm just hurt that you didn't tell me, right? I know that you had to do it. I just wish you felt like you could have told me. I wouldn't have blamed you. Rick is a dick, but you are my best friend."

Janie put her head back in her hands and started crying again. Uh oh.

"I'm just telling you the way I felt, so you know that I hold nothing against you. This is not your fault. You had that listing, he bought it. Now I want us to move on. Water under the bridge. It's really not a big deal. What is a big deal is you. We need to help you right now. Tell us why your sobriety is in question here. What about your sponsor? Have you been talking with her? Does Susanna know?"

"Yes, and what should we do now, Janie? We can take you to the inpatient unit tonight. I have an in," Petra smiled. "And you should not feel so bad. The addiction and behavioral health units are busting right now. You are not alone in your struggles. The pandemic has made everyone crazy. Look at me! Do you know where we were just now? I dragged Lisa next door to break into Carrie's house because I think she might be held captive in there by her husband!" Petra laughed.

"Wait, what? We were going to break in?" I asked, turning to Petra, my brows burrowed in worry.

Petra just shook her head and waved her hand as though she were kidding. But was she?

Janie finally started laughing and lifted her head up, allowing a bit of brevity into the situation.

"So, I'm not the only one feeling crazy right now?" Janie asked, accepting the Kleenex offered by Petra.

"I'm telling you; the world is imploding with pandemic stress. It's gone on too long. You are not alone," Petra said.

"What do you do in your program when you have a moment like this? What do they suggest?" I nudged, trying to figure out the next steps.

"The first thing I need to do is go home and tell Sam. And then I have to get on the phone to Susanna. I haven't spoken to her in a month," Janie said, cringing. "And since I'm being honest, I stopped going to meetings. They were no longer in-person and I was just too busy. I know I blew it."

"Okay, we'll take you home. It's going to be fine," I said, helping Janie to her feet. "Come on."

When Janie stood up, she steadied herself against the wall then turned again to hug me. "I'm so sorry," she said.

"Janie, you don't have to apologize. I'm so over Rick the Dick and his bullshit. I'm happy now. I don't care about the house. I just want us to be okay. You know you can talk to me, right?" I asked, squeezing her back tight.

"I just don't want to disappoint you guys. I want the world to think I'm strong. I want you guys to respect me and think I'm okay. That's so silly," she said. "But that's me."

"That's all of us," Petra said. "We're all scared of failing ourselves, each other, our families."

I stared at Petra over Janie's shoulder, thinking about how much Petra could relate to what Janie was saying. When Petra had her nervous breakdown after her brother died, it took us all a very long time to know she was suffering. She hid it well. Was she hiding it still?

As we were putting on coats, the front door opened. Paul and three crying children came stammering in, Paul looking the worst of all of them.

"What happened?" Petra asked her husband.

"They fought the entire time and kept begging to come home to you," Paul said, his signature smile nowhere to be found. He had a big red stain down the front of his shirt that looked like ketchup and he held one of the kids in his arms. "I'm sorry, honey. You just ignore us. I'll take them upstairs." Paul looked around at our group. "Wait, is everything okay? Are you guys leaving?"

Petra put her hand on his arm and picked up one of the kids. "It's fine. Janie's not feeling so hot, so we're gonna make sure she gets home."

"Mom, I'm hungry," Ellie said into Petra's neck.

"You stay, Petra," Janie said. "You have your hands full here."

Petra's kids were all over her, so I opened the door and ushered Janie out with me. I had a feeling we had to act fast. We needed to make sure Janie got safely home and on the phone with her sponsor. I didn't know much about addiction myself, having never experienced it, but I would assume it would be much easier and much more comfortable to just say, "Never mind I can handle this on my own," and not call.

"Thank you for not being upset with me, Lisa," Janie said quietly as we were walking up the street to get to her house. Cutting through the yard wasn't a good idea at this point because the drifts of snow were just too big between Janie and Petra's home. When we got to the start of Janie's driveway, I looked back at Petra's house and to Carrie's home beyond that. These lots were huge. And though these women appeared to have it all, I knew, my arm slung around my sweet, sick friend, that that lie simply wasn't true. Rich or poor, women were getting their butts kicked during this pandemic.

Petra

I stepped out on my porch, after making promises to the kids that I would be right back. I was still in denial that the entire night had blown up in my face after I'd worked so hard to make it special for the girls. That was to be expected right now, though. You just could not really plan anything in this moment. It was better to just plan that things were going to go badly than assume that things were going to go well.

I slipped on my coat to head over to Janie's. I had to see for myself that she was able to get a hold of her sponsor and make that important connection. And if need be, I would be the one with the most pull to get her into a facility tonight. I wasn't an expert on addiction, but in my medical opinion, I always thought it was best to act fast.

Poor Janie. I was so distracted by my own problems; I'd missed seeing that she was dealing with this. What else had I been missing? I allowed that one to sink in and do its damage. I swore after my brother, I would be more tuned into family and friends. But my grief had done the opposite. It had isolated me and put me deeper into a shell.

What took you so long? Danny had said.

He'd been calling for a few weeks in a row every day until the calls had stopped completely. My parents were done with him, having completely drained their savings years ago, trying rehab after rehab, and my other siblings had had enough. Even when he appeared to turn everything around and develop an insanely successful entertainment company, they all kept their distance. I was the only one left who would take his calls. But then Covid hit, and I was trying to keep the world alive. Danny had slipped through the cracks. I'd just happened to stop by that night on a whim because my sister said she'd received a haunting message from him earlier in the day. By the time I arrived, the neighbors had called the fire department. Even though I was able to drag Danny's body out, he was barely alive and was gone before we got him to the hospital. I was never going to forgive myself, I accepted that. I was never going to fully forgive Paul. I'd begged him to check on Danny while I managed shift after shift at the hospital.

He'd always been too busy and too preoccupied to be a part of the Danny Drama, as he had called it back then. He was dismissive of Danny, not trusting him because he saw him hurt too many people.

And now Paul and I were in therapy because we had not communicated well during that trauma, had not worked as a team, and I couldn't get over it. His compassion came too late, and my acceptance of his apologies was just not coming at all.

Shaking my head, I walked with determination down my driveway to Janie's house. I couldn't save Danny. But I could definitely help Janie.

Just as I was about to turn the corner at the end of my drive, I heard it again. The scream. The same distinct one I'd heard the morning of our run this past week. I stopped and turned in the darkness, my breath creating a cloud of smoke. Staring at Carrie's house, I waited for a second, trying to decide if the girls could have been right the other morning. Could it have been a call from a lone coyote calling to its pack? It had to be. We knew now that the house was empty. Carrie wasn't there. In fact, Carrie had most likely moved to Florida permanently, fleeing the Midwest like we'd seen so many people do during the pandemic.

My mind raced back to the night I'd run into Carrie in the ER. The look of desperation on her face under the coating of shame and defiance she wore.

Are you afraid of anyone in your home? I'd asked, not looking right at her as I read the question so that she wouldn't be intimidated to answer honestly. We'd been trained to make them feel comfortable, make them feel like you weren't drilling them with questions. I was doubly challenged because of the fact that we had somewhat of a personal relationship. She was my neighbor and a parent at my children's school. Looking back, I should have called someone else in. Maybe she would have been more open.

But wait.

A chill ran down my spine as a memory from that night sprang to life in my head. She'd requested me. That's right. There were two doctors on-site that night and she'd specifically requested me. I remember Maggie walking into my office and saying, "Special request for Doctor Petra in Room 12."

I'd completely erased that from my memory of that night until just now. She wanted me to know.

At the end of my driveway, against my better judgment, I made a decision. I just had to. I turned on my heel and began to run in the direction of Carrie's house.

Lisa

"Thank you so much for bringing her home," Sam said, sitting with me at the long, wooden kitchen table. He kept nervously looking over my shoulder, presumably to see Janie through her office door. As soon as we walked in, we'd filled Sam in on what was going on, then quickly got her connected to her sponsor who'd picked up her call right away.

Sam looked like he wanted to burst into tears as he stood up and started the routine of making me coffee and being a gracious host. He was such a classy man, still dressed in his button down and dress slacks this late into the evening. He was clearly someone who cared about his appearance and how he projected himself to the world. But not enough that he would hide his emotions for his wife. There was no mistaking that he was crazy about her and the children she'd given him. The way his hands shook while he poured the coffee told me everything.

"Still like cream, right, Lisa?" he asked, plastering what looked like a forced smile on his face.

I reached my hand out and took his in mine.

"We've been here before, Sam," I said quietly. "She'll be okay."

Sam squeezed my hand back and set my mug down with the other, stealing a glance in the direction of Janie's office.

"I missed it. Again," he said, meeting my eyes. The panic behind his glass blue eyes was palpable.

"So did I," I said quickly, trying to make him feel better. "I'm supposed to be her best friend and I missed it."

"I'm her husband. I sleep next to her every night and I missed it," he said. "What kind of a husband am I?"

I shook my head and stayed quiet.

"I feel like I did see some things now that I look back. She's obsessed with her job. But I thought she was loving it. I didn't realize it was pushing her over the edge," he said, shaking his head and lifting his cup to his mouth. Before he took a sip, he set it back down and looked past me to the office, an intense gaze on his lined face.

"Do you think she's already using? Has she crossed the line?" Sam asked, turning his gaze back to me.

"I don't think so," I said, shaking my head and angling my body to take a look into the office. "Based on what I saw at Petra's house. She looked like a woman on the edge who decided not to jump."

"Good," Sam said with a sad smile. "I will do whatever it takes. Get her whatever helps she needs. Money is no object."

"She knows that, Sam," I said.

I could tell he was feeling very insecure about his role in all of this. That he hadn't done enough. Perhaps he felt like he had enabled her somehow. I was going through that in my own head. What had been my part in all of this? Had I missed red flags because I was so distracted by my own troubles? Maybe I'd talked too much on the runs when she had needed more air time.

"She has to be willing to take the help though, Sam," I said.

This silenced Sam as I think it does most of us that don't deal with addiction themselves. In the end, as the support team, we really don't have control. We think we do, but we don't. It's the addict who has to take control of the situation.

Sam's shoulders sunk as he sipped his coffee. Seeing him like this made me understand a little more why Janie may have hidden her pain from this dear man. She'd finally married a man who loved her, took care of her and cherished the kids. She didn't want to put him at risk. Normally such a youthful man, he looked his age tonight.

"I'm going to check on the girls," he said quietly. "I'll be right back." The chair squeaked on the wood floor as he pushed it back and stood up.

I nodded, not knowing what else to say.

"I'm going to stay a little longer, Sam, if that's okay? I just want to see where this call goes and if you need help. If you need a next step, I mean," I said.

Sam had already started walking over to the stairs. When I said this, he turned around and nodded his head, his eyes meeting mine after a minute.

"Lisa, I'm not a man that is too proud to ask for help. I think I need help with this one. You and Petra are her best friends. I would love it if you would stay," he said, smiling a sad smile with only one half of his face. I could see the internal battle going on inside him. Addiction is a private, family matter, but sometimes it's not. Not when you finally look at it and say, "It's too big."

He turned to head upstairs, and I got up to look out the front door. I thought for sure that Petra would have been here by now. Even though I had told her to stay home with the kids, I had a feeling she would still come by eventually. Maybe the addiction stuff was just hitting too close to home with the recent death of her brother. I didn't know what to think with Petra right now. She was going through something, that was for sure. What was that earlier today, dragging me over to Carrie's house and her theories that she was in there? That was weird.

But these were weird times. No one could deny that.

Still, what I did know for sure about Petra was that she was an excellent friend. And I was pretty sure she would come over here to check on Janie sooner or later. So where was she right now?

And how did I become the most stable person in the group suddenly? I was the hot mess dealing with divorce and destitution. I chuckled quietly to myself thinking of that. Just more proof that happiness was an inside job. On the outside, I'm sure my story didn't really look good right now, but on the inside, I really was happy.

I sighed, back to worrying about Petra. She absolutely would not hear no this evening about going to check out Carrie's house no matter how much I tried to push back.

I scanned the street, looking for her tall form walking up the driveway but was disappointed when all I saw was snow. Oh well, maybe she'd be here soon.

Janie

"Amen," I said, into the telephone after Susanna ended the prayer she was leading us in. I'd met Susanna over five years ago now when I entered the AA program. By that time, she'd had over twenty years of sobriety under her belt. Her story was much different than mine, yet somehow, the stories all felt the same. In her case, though, she had hit rock bottom when she lost custody of her children, lost her home, and had to be paddled not once but twice to bring her back to life. She was very open to share those experiences and didn't hold back from crying or allowing me to see how much her addictions had destroyed her. Still, to this day, two of her children had cut ties with her and never let her back in. I lived in fear of that. So much so that just speaking to her once a week had kept me solid for a few years. So, why had I slipped?

"So, tell me more," she said softly. "I'm here to listen."

I glanced out my glass double doors into the kitchen where I could see Sam and Lisa talking. It made me put my head in my hand and mutter, "ugh." I was so embarrassed that it came out this way. Lisa was the one I had turned to last time when I finally admitted I had a problem. My kids were so young then. I remember how desperate I was back then. I thought someone was going to take my kids away from me. I couldn't get a hold of myself. Sam and I had just moved into this glamorous new house, we'd had two beautiful children, we were entertaining all the time, and I'd just started trying to go back to work. Then I fell on the driveway. It had been a simple back surgery to help the slipped disk, but that had started the pills. And then the drinking. I'd been ashamed that I couldn't handle it all. I hid it until Lisa finally figured it out and confronted me, making me look at myself.

She was firm but also phenomenal. I never felt judged or criticized. Somehow, I still don't really understand how she did it, but she managed to make me feel empowered by challenging me to take on my sobriety. And now here we were again, years later, and I was back at ground zero.

"I just can't believe I'm here, Susanna," I said, wiping a tear away from my cheek. "I thought…I mean, I really…" I stopped, turning my body to look out the big floor to ceiling windows on the back wall of my office, facing the small pond that lined the back of our property. During the day, I loved watching the geese and the ducks fly in and out. Often, I fantasized about what kind of "real estate" they had. Did they also have to "buy" land? Did they have land agreements like humans did? Constant negotiations going on like we had?

"Don't be afraid, child. The Lord is here," Susanna said.

Susanna was from the south side of the city of Chicago. She sang in a gospel choir, fed the poor, took in people who needed shelter, and counseled addicts like me. She had truly found God and was courageous in her beliefs. She felt no shame in speaking constantly about her love of Christ and her need of Him. Normally, I could be turned off by people who were too much into proclaiming their spirituality. Susanna wore it right, though.

"I thought I would be more like you right now. Honestly, I thought I would be someone's sponsor by now," I said, shaking my head. "I thought I had overcome so much of this."

"What set you off?" Susanna asked. "And by the way, I just want you to know that you are not alone. I've taken five calls tonight alone from other addicts."

"Really?" I asked, floored by this news.

"This pandemic is killing us. And not just in the way you think. We have got to get back to our in-person meetings. This Zoom nonsense is not doing anything for our groups," she said. "Oh, speaking of, I meant to ask you, would you rather FaceTime?"

I looked up in the mirror across from my desk and took in my reflection. My blond bob was stringy and askew and my mascara was all over my face. I pulled a Kleenex out of the box sitting on my desk and wiped frantically at my eyes.

"Oh, hell no," I said bluntly.

Susanna laughed her deep, belly laugh, which made me laugh in return.

"Good. Cause you don't want to see what I look like right now. I'm in my pajamas watching Food Network. But you know if you need to see me, I can come to you," she said.

"I know," I said, nodding my head and thinking back to Susanna coming to my inpatient facility day after day years ago even though I knew the commute was killing her.

"And honey, as much as I love talking with you and don't plan on going anywhere, you know I gotta ask. Have you found something closer to home yet? You know, something that would be more convenient for you? You're probably not going to meetings because it's too hard to get here. You've got that big job now," she said, bringing up a topic I'd been avoiding for over a year now.

I stood up and walked to the windows to look out. She was right. I knew it. I knew it a year ago even before things changed in the pandemic but hadn't done anything about it. I was too scared to find a local chapter of AA because I was scared to run into someone I knew. I was too well known in the community and didn't want people making judgments about me. Going into the city, I felt safe. I felt protected. And I loved Susanna and the group I had met there.

While trying to decide how to respond, I stared out the window at the dark pond. It was silent and peaceful tonight. Snow fell in quiet determination down from the dark sky onto the frozen pond, creating a scene of winter serenity. My eyes scanned the long grass at the edge of the pond, looking for coyotes or other creatures that might be exploring the evening snowfall. My gaze fell on a darkened shape hunched next to the grass near Petra's property. At first, I assumed it was a coyote. But then when it moved slightly, I realized it was rather large to be one. Possibly a deer then.

I gasped when I realized what it really was. What the hell was she doing out there?

Petra

Just a peek. That's all I needed, just a quick peek into the back windows, and then I would be out. It would only take a few minutes and then I'd bolt over to Janie's. I wouldn't sleep tonight if I didn't at least go check this out. Janie would be on the phone with her sponsor for at least a little while and there would be a waiting period anyway for Lisa and I. I wouldn't be missing anything.

But what if you're wasting precious time and you could be on the phone using your influence to get her in somewhere? In my mind, my brother's beautiful hazel eyes I saw close for the last time as I held his dying body reopened one last time to say these words to me.

I halted in my tracks and rubbed at my eyes. Fine, Danny. I personally didn't think Janie was at that point, but he was right. Why go chase trouble when I already had it? My friend needed me, and I was out here in the cold like a lunatic, on a wild goose chase. I turned and headed back in the direction of Janie's house, praying that Paul wasn't watching me from the house. He'd be furious. Or maybe that wasn't the right word. He'd be upset, that's for sure, but maybe furious. And curious. Curious about my mental stability. And I didn't need that right now.

I kicked into a light jog up the incline of the street that led to Janie's house. She was at the top of the hill before the subdivision started the slight decline. I knew this road well because we ran it so many times on our morning runs. Janie's house was sometimes the finish if we were feeling the need to end with a challenge by getting to the top of the hill. But we never went past it down the other side since that led to Danny's house.

Shaking my head again, I turned my body to look back at my house, trying to stabilize my emotions. Would I ever be able to? Did I have to move? I didn't want to move. I loved my neighborhood. I loved the schools, my friends, my job. But how long could I go on not being able to drive down my street without being haunted?

"*The biggest lot in the division*," he'd bragged when he was building. It was how Paul and I had found our own lot. We'd fallen in love with the area when we came to visit his build. He'd been in full recovery for almost ten years by that point and turned his life completely around. I thought he was over the hump and was so proud of him. He ran a successful business, traveled all the time, and had relationships. He traveled so much, in fact, that I didn't second guess moving so close to him. Sure, we'd be able to see each other, but he was gone almost nine months of the year with travel, so it felt great that home base would be so close to each other.

"If you're traveling so much, why do you need this big monstrosity of a house?" Paul had asked him.

"Because I need a physical reminder that I'm successful," Danny had half joked back to Paul.

I remember shaking my head and laughing, but knowing it was a solid plan. Home base and a strong base was going to keep him grounded.

A tear escaped, rolling down my cheek, as the guilt overtook me. I'd been so blind.

Just as I turned in the direction of Janie's driveway, determined not to let my friend down like I'd done my brother, a beam of light coming from Carrie's house stopped me dead in my tracks. I wasn't able to see the light from my house, not being high enough up. But here, at the top of the hill, I could see it. A skylight at the very top of Carrie's second story was on. Why?

Wiping the tear away, I put together a plan. If the layout of their home was similar to mine, the best view of that second story would be from the back of the house, near the pond.

Lisa

The sound of screaming felt so out of place in this quiet house that I wondered if I had fallen asleep leaning against the front door waiting for Janie to get off the phone. It wasn't out of the realm of possibility, considering how tired I was from burning the candle at both ends trying to manage school, work, and the kids.

But the pounding of Sam's feet down the hardwood stairs confirmed what I was afraid of. Janie really was screaming from the office.

I pushed myself away from the door and rushed over to join Sam at the bottom of the stairs.

"What happened?" he asked me, his eyes wide with panic and his normally calm demeanor gone.

"I don't know," I said, grabbing his arm as we both rushed to the office.

As we were rushing to the doors, Janie ripped them open and started talking a million miles an hour.

"She's out there," Janie yelled frantically, reaching out and pulling both of us forcefully over to the windows.

"Who?" Sam demanded, running over to the gigantic floor to ceiling windows. "What are you talking about?"

My stomach sank thinking about my adventure with Petra earlier in the evening. Janie had that same level of panic in her voice that Petra had earlier. And sure enough, she ran to the window and pointed in the same direction Petra and I had done our search earlier in the evening.

"Turn the lights off, Lisa," Janie demanded. We will be able to see better. Why are you looking at me like that? Hurry up. Turn the lights off and get over here. There's a woman by the pond, almost in the pond. I think it might be…"

"Mommy?" Janie's daughter called out in a frightened voice from the door of the office.

Janie's two daughters, Zoe and Nola, were there, wearing matching pajamas and looking like they'd just been pulled out of a dead sleep. The girls, six and seven, both had short blond bobs, much like their mother and clear, crystal blue eyes like their father.

"There's a ghost out there? The Lady in the Lake?" her eldest, Zoe said. She reached out and grabbed the hand of her sister, Nola, who had started to cry.

"I don't like ghosts," Nola said, her lower lip trembling.

All of the adults in the room froze as though unsure of what to say. Finally, Janie made a beeline for her kids.

"No, honey, I saw a big coyote out there. I wanted daddy to see because I thought it was a mommy coyote looking for her cubs. I thought he might want to go help her."

"Help her? No," Zoe said. "We're not supposed to go close to those coyotes. They eat puppies! They ate my friend's puppy. Remember Joey's puppy?" she said, reaching out to grab for her mother.

I noticed Sam had moved closer to the window when Janie started for the girls. I did, too.

"I have an idea. Remember our midnight snacks? Why don't you guys go pick out a midnight snack from the cabinet and I'll meet you in there in a second," Janie said, using the most successful method of mothering on the planet. Diversion.

Sneaking a peek back at the girls, I could tell immediately it was going to work.

The girls looked at each other first and then turned back to their mother.

"You mean the cabinet for the school snacks?" Nola asked, already making deals.

"Well," Janie said, hesitating and putting her pointer finger up to her mouth. I could tell it was just an act to make the girls feel like they were going to get something they really wanted by using their negotiating tactics well.

"Maybe. But only if you let us have a few more minutes of quiet in here. Do you think you can do that?" Janie asked the girls. 'I'm not sure if you can reach those snacks by yourself, and we need a few more minutes to talk."

"We can. We got them yesterday by ourselves," Zoe insisted, revealing herself. Nola nudged her and shot us a smile as cover.

"Oh really?" Janie laughed.

"But we were just getting them to put in our lunches," Nola added quickly.

"Okay, go ahead and pick out one bag right now and I'll be in there in a few minutes. Eat at the counter," Janie added.

"Okay. Have fun looking for the Lady in the Lake," Zoe said before turning and making a beeline for the kitchen.

"Have you seen her before?" Janie asked, but it was too late. They were already halfway across the house. Janie sighed and flipped the light switch off and closed the door slightly before rushing back over to the windows next to Sam and me.

"Over there. Did you see her?" Janie said, pointing her finger in the direction of Petra's house. "Further, by Carrie's house."

We were all leaning over each other and squinting our eyes. It was so dark and the pond was very poorly lit at this hour. There had been talk of the subdivision putting in lights around the pond, but nothing had been done thus far.

"I'm sorry, honey, I don't see anything," Sam said, looking back at her. "What do you think you saw?"

"I didn't think I saw anything," Janie said, sounding aggravated. "I know I saw a woman," she said.

I couldn't help but note that the tempo and pitch of her voice sounded almost identical to Petra's earlier. It was the sound of a woman being told what she saw or thought wasn't true. And we all knew how aggravating that could be.

Janie

Ten minutes later, there was a quiet knock on the front door that sent chills up my spine.

"I know who that is," Lisa said in a calm voice, standing up to go answer it. Lisa's long brown hair was up in a top knot now, and her eyeliner looked a bit smudged under her eyes. This was turning out to be quite a long night.

"Who?" I demanded, standing up, still holding the phone to my ear.

"Just Petra," Lisa said, turning her hands up at her sides and walking out of the office. "Who else?"

"Oh," I said. "Sorry. I'm just a little freaked out. I'll be out after my call," I said, holding my hand over the phone.

My sponsor, Susanna, had called back a few times and on the third time I'd finally picked it up. I'd hung up on her when I spotted the person by the pond, or as my kids had labeled her, The Lady in the Lake. When I'd pressed them on this, Zoe said she'd seen a woman walking by the pond a few times but was hazy about the details. She also told me that she thought she was a ghost not a real person. Nola just nodded her head and said she wore a big coat. Not wanting to stress the kids out, I'd sent them back to bed and told them we would talk in the morning.

Between the kids' stories and my fatigue, I was so confused on what I actually saw that I was getting paranoid. My initial thought was that it had been a woman, just based on the way the person had moved. Something about the walk. But now I had myself so worked up that I wondered if I had even seen anything at all. No one else had.

Susanna, as much as I loved her, was on me now about getting to a meeting as soon as possible. I agreed with her, but was still set on not going to a local meeting. The Zoom meeting set for the group I normally went to was scheduled at the same time I had one of my showings tomorrow. My sobriety was getting in the way of my success and my family. I didn't have time for this.

"Okay, then I'm coming to you," Susanna insisted.

"But I have to work tomorrow," I said, glancing out through the glass office doors and into my living room. Petra sat on one of the oversized couches with Sam, and Lisa was nowhere in sight now. Neither were the girls. Maybe she had taken them back upstairs to bed. Hopefully that was the case. I didn't have the bandwidth for the girls at this moment, as terrible as that sounded.

I noticed Petra had changed out of her Gaga Night pink sweatsuit into jeans and a sweater. Uh oh. Did that mean she wanted to take me somewhere?

"Then I'll come after work," Susanna said.

"That's so late for you and so far, Susanna," I said, feeling bad.

"Are you calling me old?" she laughed.

I couldn't help but laugh, too. She was getting up there. That was true. But there was no way I would say that to her. She had more energy than me at seventy-five. I wish I could have half of her gumption and vitality.

"How about this? I need to head that way to see my sister, anyway. I'll pack a bag and come after your open houses. You know you don't have to put on a show for me. I'd love to come see the girls. If you need me to stay a night, I will. Or I can leave straight from your place and head to Beatrice's. I've been looking for an excuse to get out there to see her," she said warmly. "And I'm vaccinated now. Got moved to the front of the line with my age and health status. I need to show off my new antibodies."

I smiled, thinking of Susanna in my house. My family adored her. And she was right. There was no pressure to put on a show for her. She had seen me at rock bottom, driven me to inpatient care when I was so drunk I couldn't keep my eyes open. We made a point to see each other as much as we could, but it wasn't nearly as much as we would have liked to. This would give us an excuse to spend some time together and figure out a plan for me.

"I would love that. And it would be great if you would stay here. Sometimes I really don't get to have adult time until late into the night when the girls are down. If you stay over, we'll really get a chance to talk," I said, hoping she would say yes.

"You bet I will," Susanna said.

"Susanna, would it be okay if I let you go and called you back in the morning?" I asked, feeling the need to go out and talk with Petra. I had already looked her over a couple of times but it was hard to tell. I would just have to come out and ask her. Whoever I'd seen by the pond would look, well, wet. I could have sworn I saw the person take a stumble near the pond. But as far as I could tell, she looked completely dried off and relaxed, sitting with Sam on the couch. Not like someone who was just acting as "The Lady of the Lake." But she had changed her clothes. There was that.

Could I have seen Carrie? Maybe Petra had been right and there was something going on next door or that scream we had heard was really not a coyote, maybe Carrie?

I didn't really know her that well having met her just a couple of times through school events. We both had girls in the same classroom at school, and we'd both volunteered together for a Fun Fair event. From what I could remember, Carrie had been extremely quiet and almost painfully shy. Her brown hair was cut into a stylish bob and her figure was extremely petite, almost to the point of looking malnourished, but I knew she was into working out.

Wait, yes, I did remember something now. I had spoken to her about running and she noted that she saw us running most mornings. I took that as a hint that she might want to be invited, and she had very bluntly said, no, that her husband wouldn't like it. I remember thinking at the time that it seemed odd that her husband would care one way or another. She had made a point to extend the story and tell me that she was the one that got the kids out the door in the morning. If she was running, her husband would have to do it and wouldn't do it as well. That I could relate to. Most mothers probably felt that way when it came to the morning routines of the kids. But I told her specifically that we went very early so that we could all be home to be there when the kids woke up. Carrie balked at this and mumbled another excuse. I just remember thinking that it was best not to push the topic. She didn't seem to want to join us, so I backed off.

Hanging up the phone, I made my way over and sat down on the couch next to Petra, who immediately reached out to take my hand in hers.

"How are you doing?" she asked, placing her mug down on the table and moving closer to me to give me her full attention.

"I'm okay. I'm better," I said, noting how cold her hands were. Could that mean? No. Petra's hands were always cold. It was a running joke we had with her. She always said, "Cold hands, warm heart."

Sam stood up and said, "I'm going to go check on the girls. I'll give you a minute to talk. Is there anything I can get you ladies when I come back?" he offered.

I took a minute to examine him. He looked exhausted. Normally Sam chose to go to bed very early and then get up before the sun rose. I was similar except for the times when we had negotiations go late into the night on house sales, which was happening more and more lately.

"Honey, why don't you head to bed," I suggested to Sam. It scared me too much to think of him not sleeping or not resting. I just wanted to lock him away and keep him safe from the world. Safe from me tonight.

"I'm fine," he laughed, leaning down and kissing me quick. "Don't worry about me. Talk to Petra for a bit. You're so lucky to have a doctor as a best friend. Let her help you," Sam said, pulling away and heading upstairs.

I turned to look at Petra, grateful that she was here. I felt so much better than I did a few hours ago.

"What do you want to do?" Petra asked me.

It made me feel so good that she asked me that way. It gave me some power back. I knew what she was asking me. She wanted to know if she should take me somewhere tonight. She had the ability to do that. But in truth, I didn't want that. I had work, I had the kids to keep up with, I had too much that needed to be done.

"For now, I just want to have Susanna come tomorrow and regroup. Then decide from there," I said, trying to sound confident.

Petra nodded her head, and squeezed my hand in hers. If she believed in me, I believed in me.

"Petra, can I ask you something?" I said, feeling now that I could. The distraction felt good.

"Anything," Petra whispered, smiling at me.

She probably thought I was going to ask about her recent breakdown. How she did it, how she came back, what steps she took. If there was anything I learned in this pandemic, it was that the women took care of each other. The men were here, too, of course, but the women were the ones that picked up each other by carrying the loads, making sure the spirits were up, delivering the food to the sick, helping with the kids, making sure everyone kept going, getting beyond the grief, staying on target. I could ask her a million different questions about how she did it after her brother died. How she put her stress and grief aside and dove back into working in the E.R.

But instead, I asked her something else.

"Petra, where you just outside? By the pond?"

Petra

At the hospital the next day, I checked our latest stats and smiled to myself. Finally, some bit of progress. We were already doing the math on when we might reach herd immunity and based on the aggressive way the United States was moving the vaccine, I was full of hope. How nice. How nice to feel something besides fear. I was so tired of the fear.

That was part of the problem though. We had been so pumped with fear that it was nearly impossible to get everyone to turn the corner. No one believed anyone or anything anymore. How were we going to get people to accept this vaccine and believe in it? Even my own staff was doubtful. The nurses I thought would be the first ones in line had asked me, "But how can you be sure?" and "I want to wait for more data."

I'd been trained on how to speak calmly and logically to doubters and not push too hard. I didn't blame people for feeling unsure or afraid. It was to be expected after what we'd been through. Time would tell. Once the right amount was vaccinated without adverse effect, the public would have what it needed.

"Did you talk to her yet today?" Lisa asked, popping her head into my office. Even though I was supposed to be off today, I ended up getting called in because we were short staffed. In a way it felt good to be at work since last night had gone off the rails. We were both on the early shift this morning and things weren't as hectic as normal, so I waved her in.

We'd skipped the run because we would have had to get up at four thirty to get it done in time, and I think we all knew that wasn't the right thing to do. Especially with the current circumstances.

"No, not yet," I said, glancing down at my watch. "Think she's up?"

"Oh, yeah," Lisa said, sitting down in one of the comfortable seats in my office. "She's probably been up since five. She's got a bunch of showings today and said the heat is on with all of them. I have an idea."

"What?" I asked, intrigued. There was a part of me that hoped her idea had something to do with mine: another reconnaissance mission tonight at

Carrie's house. I'd found a hole in their security setup, and I planned to use it.

"Let's just kill off Frederick," she said with a straight face. "Can you imagine the amount of stress that would be lifted from her shoulders? She said he's the only one that's anywhere near her in the competition they're holding."

"You know what we don't need more of right now?" I said, raising my eyebrow. "Dead bodies. We're working our butts off trying to not have any more of those. And now you want to add to the stats?"

Lisa laughed and looked at her watch.

"Okay, I gotta get back to work. Mrs. Ubel wants to know when her daughter can come. She's getting very anxious. I have to go talk her down before she starts flipping tables," Lisa said, standing up. "Wait, seriously, she was cleared by psych? I still think there is something a little off there. Maybe we can check in on her again? Her mood has drastically taken a fall over the last two days."

"I'll get on it. You think something is off?" I asked, making a note for myself.

"I think the longer these patients stay in this isolation, the further they go down the rabbit hole. You think she's going to be okay?" Lisa asked.

I turned to my computer and pulled up her details.

"I do. She looked really good this morning. She's showing improvement, and she came in already in pretty stable health. She just needs to wait out the quarantine period, and we'll move her along," I said, nodding my head.

"Well, between you and me, my radar is up on that one. Something in her eyes seems off," Lisa said.

"Do me a favor and talk her up a bit when you go in. Tell her the plan is to get her out of here as soon as possible. I swear that helps the psyche. And give her a sense of control in the plan," I said. I took Lisa's words seriously. I'd seen it happen too many times where the patient was doing well and just when you thought they were about to go home, they fell off a cliff. I didn't want that.

"We're going over to Janie's again tonight, right?" Lisa confirmed before leaving the room.

"I think Susanna is still there, but yes, I think we should. The more she sees our faces, the better. You know how this is," I said, running through in my mind what was left in the fridge. I'd volunteered to make dinner tonight and bring it over to Janie, but I just realized I had nothing in my fridge to make that happen. I would have to stop at the store and that would cut down on my time to perform my mission.

"One last thing. You're not still…" Lisa paused and began rolling her finger.

I had an idea what she was referencing but played dumb.

"What?" I asked.

Lisa stopped her rolling and just pointed her finger straight at me.

"Carrie," she said simply.

"No. Definitely not. I see now how crazy that was and I'm over it. She's fine. She's in Florida with her husband. Done," I said, shaking my head no.

"Good," Lisa said, backing out of the doorway but never breaking eye contact.

I'd made the decision the night Janie's sobriety broke that I was going to do this alone. No one needed anything else on their plate. Especially my ladies. They all had enough going on. Janie was so much more fragile than I thought. And Lisa looked strong, but she had to be hurting inside with the news of her ex moving back into the neighborhood they'd raised their kids in.

When Janie had asked if I'd been by the pond, I'd lied. Thank God for the extra clothes I'd kept in the garage for when I wanted to change after hospital shifts before seeing my family. My wet clothes were still hidden in the garage. I had to get them out of there as soon as possible. If I was watching them for signs of trouble, they were definitely watching me.

Lisa

At class that night, all dressed up in my scrubs for clinical, I lifted my wrist to my nose to see if I could still smell the grapefruit mango perfume I'd applied before leaving the house. Was it bordering on obnoxious to wear perfume to class? Possibly. I was turning into a desperate housewife. Wait, scratch that, I was no longer a wife, so I wouldn't fall into that category anymore.

I was just straight up horny. There. I admitted it to myself. It had been years since things were decent in the bedroom with Rick the Dick. He certainly didn't live up to his nickname, let's just say that. Probably over ten long years if I was being honest. Somewhere when the kids were very young, we just gave up. Well, I shouldn't say that. I kept trying to keep things going but there had been many years of suspicion surrounding Rick's behavior. And it was hard to find someone you didn't trust sexy. I felt like I always had one eye open, even during sex. Not until I'd fully checked out and we started the divorce proceedings did I accept how bad it had been. How gross it was to sleep next to someone you thought was cheating on you financially, romantically, etc. He was just untrustworthy. And my dead libido was the first to try and tell me.

But now, sitting in the car, about to go into class, my sexuality was so alive, so awakened, so powerful, it could have started the engine on its own. That was how hot my motor was running. How ridiculous. I'd only seen Erik on a computer screen, and I wanted to run in and jump his bones. Pathetic.

Taking a deep breath, I opened the car door and stepped into the parking lot. I could feel my phone buzzing in my pocket, so I stopped and pulled it out. Ugh. Speak of the Devil. Rick the Dick was calling. Everything in me wanted to throw the call to voicemail, but the mom in me felt it best to take it. It could be about the kids. I would never be fully released from Rick because of the kids and that killed me. All those wasted years with him and now it was like having an ankle chained to him for the rest of my life.

"Hello?" I said, continuing to walk toward the building.

As though the universe wanted a laugh, a black truck pulled up in front of me and Erik jumped out, taller, hotter and much more put together in person than what I had imagined. His clothes looked tasteful and expensive. That gave me hope. Maybe he was older than I thought? But then he turned and his unlined, glowing skin knocked me over. Nope, this man was young.

"Hi," he called toward me. "It's Lisa, right?"

Practically swooning, I closed my gaping mouth and immediately disconnected my call with Rick. The girls would have called me if something were really wrong.

I nodded my head, willing myself to say something, anything. Erik was even better than I imagined, dressed in boots and a winter jacket. He was standing there holding his man bag and a Yeti cup like a mountain God who decided to grace us mortals and take some clinical classes. His dark, wild curls fell lazily around his face, making him look carefree and sexy. That spark I thought I had imagined over the Zoom classes was real. Maybe.

"Yes, Lisa," I said, pulling myself up to my full height of 5'1." He was definitely over 6 feet and from the way he had to gaze down at me as he walked closer, my guess was he was well north of that. "I'm Erik," he said, extending his hand. He smiled, his teeth giving off their full megawatt glow. No coffee stains, healthy looking gums. My age estimate jumped down another rung. Could he even be twenty-five? My God, what if he wasn't even twenty-five? Get a hold of yourself, Cougar. But wait. Maybe Covid lifted any age restrictions? Maybe the world would be less judgy?

My phone buzzed again in my pocket, alerting me to the fact that Rick was most likely calling back. Let him leave a message.

After our handshake, I pulled back, trying not to freak out. We weren't supposed to shake. This was still Covid. But either it was my imagination or my desperation, something made it impossible for us not to connect.

"It's so nice to be here. Like, live. Rather than just over the Zoom calls. I feel like I've been waiting for this moment forever," I said.

I tripped over my words a bit and my statement was over the top, but I was happy to have at least come across as coherent. I had to remind myself that I was a mature mother of two, who'd owned homes, graduated college, been married, and once managed a large bank account. Sure, some of that was gone now, but I knew how to handle myself. This crazy crush was not going to get out of control.

"I've been watching you," Erik said, smiling. "Should we head in?" he asked, turning casually. "We don't want to be late for our first round of clinicals."

"You've been watching me?" I laughed, trying to keep it casual. I couldn't help but wonder what his feeling was right now. Was he disappointed? Was I much older than he thought? Too old? Was I shorter than he thought? Did that bother him? Did he see my hair live and notice how unkempt it looked?

"Yeah, in Zoom. I noticed that you and I seem to laugh at the same things," he said, warming my heart.

A sense of humor was my number one. The first thing that I was attracted to in a person and probably the one thing that kept me with my ex for so long. Unfortunately, he'd had a great sense of humor. I see now that he used that to keep me on the line for a long time. It took me a while to figure out that ultimately, I was the butt of his jokes.

"Oh," I said, smiling, not sure what else to say.

"Mrs. Francis is a hoot. I think she'll be even better live," he said, pulling open the glass door for me. A gentleman, too. This just kept getting better and better.

"I think so as well," I said, pulling up my mask.

"I'm happy so far. I really need this to be worth it. I gave up a well-paying career for this. I'm taking quite a risk to get this degree. But I think I'm doing the right thing," he said, smiling down with his eyes, his beautiful face now covered with a mask.

He'd just said the magic word, career. His age jumped back up a notch in my mind. Surely if he said the word career, that meant he was older than twenty-five?

"I hope I'm doing the right thing as well," I said, pulling open the classroom door and smiling at Erik, my heart jumping at the smell of him when he reached over me to hold the door so I could enter. His deodorant or after-shave, or something he'd lathered on his body, smelled of sandalwood and vanilla. The two scents I adored. Saliva built up a bit in my mouth and I had to stop myself from leaning in to get a better whiff. I was in trouble.

Janie

I sat in my home office tweaking some of the descriptions for my most recent postings. It was amazing how little I had to do to sell a home these days compared to just a few short years ago when real estate was in a very different place. That was part of my stress. I had to strike while the iron was hot. God only knew when things would turn. I had five closings tomorrow alone. This market was not going to last.

Susannah had just left for the night. We'd spent the last two days digging and analyzing and trying to figure out what had happened to push me close to the edge. Close. But not over. I felt so much better today. I knew the deal with Rick the Dick was the final push. But it had been building. It was what it always was. Stress.

Years ago, I drank to calm my anxiety and stress. Then I drank too much, so I quit and got into exercising and talking through my problems. Talking with friends, talking with group therapy, talking with fellow addicts. The pandemic had shut all that down. I'd turned away from my groups and focused on work, and that wasn't working for me. Susannah was right. I could handle the stress as long as I had my outlets. My runs with my friends were great, but when I was doing that plus getting therapy, plus staying active in my AA meetings, I was solid. That combination was the perfect tonic for me.

She'd made some calls and pulled some strings and found an in-person meeting for me thirty minutes away.

But no more than twenty minutes after she set this up, I got a new listing for a house in that same suburb where the meeting was to be held. I couldn't risk having someone from the community find out that I was attending a meeting there. As much as we were supposed to be anonymous, I was constantly noticing that people shared names and stories too much. I trusted my group on the south side, but they were still not meeting in person.

I didn't have the heart to tell Susannah that the new group would not work, so I let it slide, telling myself I would just think about it more.

After she left, I sat alone at my desk, enjoying the quiet. Sam had left for a work meeting and the girls were still at school for the day. That gave me thirty more minutes alone in the house.

I clicked off the screen of my listings and went back to Facebook. This morning while Susannah was on the phone, I'd done a dive into my mysterious neighbor's account. I couldn't stop thinking about what I'd seen the other night outside my window. The Lady of the Lake. And now that I was in a better, clearer place, I knew it to be true. I'd seen something. I'd seen her.

Petra had been asking about Carrie. The other day she said she thought she'd heard a scream. Could she have been right? Was she the "Lady of the Lake" that my girls had reported seeing? But how was she in her home screaming when her Facebook page had recent pictures of her and her family dancing around Florida?

I should have gotten to know Carrie better. She lived two doors down from me. How hard would it have been to walk down and knock on her door? Ask her over for coffee? I had not been a good neighbor. I allowed myself to be buried in my work, my own family, my own drama. Wasn't that what we were warned against as addicts? Don't isolate. Don't cut yourself off too much from the world. That was never good.

Logging onto my Facebook account, I pulled up Carrie's account. A new picture was up today. Oh good. See, I was being crazy. She was smiling into the camera, her kids and husband behind her on some kind of ride. They looked happy and carefree, so opposite of where I was right now.

I logged off and shook my head, leaning back in my chair. Enough. I was just trying to let one obsession take over another. I had to center myself and use this time to reflect. I had to review what I had learned in therapy and addiction counseling. Try to get to the core of what was bothering me. Check in on it, accept it and try, as hard as it was, to move on. I closed my eyes and breathed in slowly, picturing myself on a beach, alone. A safe, quiet place. My kids and husband were not there, but I knew they were somewhere safe. This is the method I learned that worked for me. Go there in my mind, be with myself, no other responsibilities, and talk to that woman within. Be kind. Get her talking.

"What's wrong?" I asked the lady on the beach, who was really me.

"I'm alone," she said.

"So what? It's nice to be alone," my mind answered.

"Yes, it's nice when you know they're coming back," she said, hitting a tender spot in me.

"What do you mean?" I pushed, lightly. A tingling feeling started in my stomach that I didn't like. My body was reacting.

"I mean, sometimes they leave and don't come back," she said coldly.

My eyes popped open and I grabbed the desk. There it was. My abandonment issues. My first husband had left me, my father had left our family and now I was worrying. Would Sam, being in the older age bracket that he was, abandon me? Maybe succumb to illness? I grabbed harder at the desk, feeling a sob overtake me. Instead of fighting it, I allowed it. My body heaved as I released my anxiety, my pain, and my fear. I'd been holding it. I was being strong and selling real estate and taking care of the kids while keeping everyone's emotions in check during Covid. Enough. I couldn't take it anymore.

With the house empty, I decided to completely release and screamed at the top of my lungs. I'd done a therapy class once that used this in practice as part of the healing. At the time I thought it a very strange practice, but I couldn't take it anymore. No more fear. No more anxiety. It had to stop. I had to pull this elephant of worry off my chest. I couldn't do it anymore.

After five gut-wrenching, wall-cracking screams. I stopped and stood up, walking to my big windows that overlooked the pond. Grabbing onto the window pane, I sucked in air and actually started laughing. Man, that felt good. What an incredible release. Why weren't we doing that at all of our AA meetings? I could suggest that next time. I felt like I could handle everything again.

The act of admitting, just saying to myself, this is beyond me, I can't carry anymore. My God, that felt good.

I allowed the silence of the house to nurture me and sing to me while I gazed out the window, my body peacefully resetting and swaying to the harmony of quiet. In just a few minutes, my house would be full again and the madness would set back in. I needed these few minutes.

Suddenly, I stopped swaying. Something clicked in my head. I jolted back to full awareness of where I was and what was happening and dashed back to the computer.

Tapping wildly on my keys, I went back to the Facebook account and pulled up Carrie's name. The picture. They had been on some kind of ride and they weren't wearing masks? How was that possible? Wasn't Disney World under restrictions?

When I pulled up her name, I was shocked to see that I was unable to find the picture again. I clicked madly, trying many different ways to see it but to no avail. This couldn't be right.

Someone had removed the picture? Why?

Petra

As soon as I could, I dashed out of work, intending to go to the store to pick up what I needed to make Lisa dinner. By the time I got to my car, my phone had dinged, letting me know that my Instacart order had been delivered. I'd completely forgotten that I'd placed this order last week, planning ahead to replenish. Apparently, I was more organized than I realized. If only I could make myself remember how organized I actually was. That would be better.

I checked the cart and noticed that everything I needed to make Lisa my famous enchilada dish was waiting for me in plastic bags on the porch, so I headed home instead of going to the store. Padded with some extra time now, I rolled over in my head exactly what I should do with that time. I knew what I wanted to do, but argued with myself whether or not that was actually a good idea or not. Pulling up to my street, I made the decision to park the car a few houses down at the bottom of the hill so that Paul wouldn't be alerted to the fact that I was home. He didn't have to be involved. Not yet at least.

Walking up this hill, I was reminded of the night I sped like a lunatic over 80 miles an hour up and over the hill to the sight of Danny's house engulfed in flames. The strange circumstances surrounding the fire were never really solved, the cause of the fire linked to candles. I'd insisted the police keep digging. Danny hated candles.

He'd been hanging around some shady people. His new girlfriend, or girlfriends, never really sat well with me. They were all openly troubled and lost-looking people. And clearly substance abusers. Their eyes always seemed beet red and darting around with a paranoia that was so intense, I couldn't even handle being in the same room as them. It was especially disappointing and sad to me because for years, Danny had been doing so well. My gut knew, and turned out to be correct, that these people would bring him down.

The police ruled it an accident, but I still never felt great about it. My assumption was, and is to this day, that whoever helped Danny along with the drug use and the fire took what they wanted and moved along, leaving my brother to die. Or, had he overdosed on purpose? That would haunt me forever.

"*What took you so long?*" he'd asked me.

"I didn't know you were home," I said aloud as I marched up the hill to Carrie's house.

That was the truth. He lived a few blocks away, and I didn't even know if he was there or halfway around the world. It was my job that pulled me away. People were dying and I was trying to stop it. I hadn't realized that death was visiting my own family just a few doors down.

I broke into a slow jog toward Carrie's house. I had to be fast and furious because Paul would be looking for me very soon.

Sneaking around to the back of the house, I used my knowledge of our own security system to slip past a blind spot by the front door and knock the camera on the back door to a different angle. Easy as that. I looked around for where our security guy told us to hide our spare key, and sure enough, Carrie's was there. I slipped it out from its hiding space.

One of the founding members of a local security company lived in this neighborhood and set up the majority of these homes. He had a great reputation, so we all used him, probably assuming we wouldn't use the information against each other.

But I was doing this to help Carrie. If I got caught, I would tell them what I heard. And I was sure I had heard screams. And the night Janie had her meltdown, I know I saw a light go on and off upstairs. And this was after Heather, the nosy neighbor, had left. I'd checked for her car. I was sure that something was wrong in the house. Someone was inside the house that wasn't supposed to be. What if Carrie was in there and she needed my help? My brother had been home and needed help.

Slipping the key in the lock, I tried blocking my mind from racing too fast. The plan was to get in, look around and then get back out and angle the camera back to where it needed to be. And to remain calm through it all. With my brother, I knew something was off but chose to just push on, hoping things would turn out. I wasn't going to do that again.

Closing the door lightly behind me, I contemplated calling Carrie's name out but stopped. What if there were other people here? I didn't know what to expect. Walking over to the security system, it hit me that there was no beeping, alerting me that I had to disarm the system. Huh? Strange. It didn't appear that any of it was enabled. Good. One less thing for me to be worried about, but still, odd. Maybe Heather had deactivated it the other night and never turned it back on?

I took a deep breath in, trying to pick up the scent of decay. Having had experience with bodies in various stages of death through my career, as well as my time in medical school, I knew what to look for. The potency was always related to the timeframe.

I made my way through the large kitchen, similar but not identical to mine. From what I could tell, it looked completely shut up-no cabinets open or dishes out. It was a dark, gloomy afternoon, the hour of sunset quickly approaching. It wasn't easy to see clearly, but I didn't want to turn on any lights.

My first impression though was that the place was in pristine condition. How you would want to leave your house if you were thinking of traveling or even putting it on the market. I turned the flashlight of my phone on and made quick work of inspecting the kitchen and main hall leading to the foyer.

The layout of the house was set up almost identical to mine and Janie's. Huge floor to ceiling windows lined the entire back of the house, overlooking the small pond. A grand staircase at the front of the house led to the second floor, which, if identical to mine, held six bedrooms. Instead of taking the large staircase, I chose to climb the simpler one at the back of the house, off the kitchen. The lights flicking on and off the other day had come from the second floor, so something told me that whatever I was looking for, I would find upstairs.

Something made me stall before going up there. Could this all just be my PTSD rearing its ugly head? Maybe Carrie had simply come back from Florida early to have some peace and quiet from the kids and husband before the house sold. What if she was here? Why did I care? Perhaps she was holed up in a dark room staring at a wall upstairs. I wouldn't blame her if she was. There were days that were so hectic in my life, the thought of staring at a wall sounded like heaven.

But then, why the scream? I was sure I had heard a scream. I pushed on and made my way up the stairs.

Just as I got to the top step, I heard the distinct sound of the back door closing shut. The same one I had just come in. I crouched down and backed into one of the bedrooms before whoever had just entered could spot me.

The sound of footsteps crossing the hardwood floor below me made me shrink back further. I had to get out of here. This was a huge mistake.

Lisa

Driving home from work, I mentally prepared myself for the onslaught of questions my kids were going to dump on me when I walked in the door. Trying to find time to study was ridiculously hard with the kids home so early from school and me working full-time. My only peace was when they went to volleyball or tennis practice, but often times, I was still at work at that hour.

We needed to set down some stronger ground rules. I didn't want to have to study away from home. I was already gone so much. But it was looking as if that might be my only option at this point. They were not respecting the closed-door policy I was trying to keep when I was studying in my bedroom. I told them to knock only for emergencies, but in their young, teenage minds, everything was an emergency. They were driving me nuts.

I smiled to myself, allowing some naughty thoughts to run through my head. If I got off work early enough, or maybe even took a day off in some unforeseen day in the future when the kids were in school, perhaps I could have guests over. Or in my case, one particular special guest. Erik. I sighed, thinking of the fun we could have getting to know each other better. In my bedroom.

The car behind me honked, alerting me to the fact that I'd been sitting at a red light for too long.

"Oh, relax," I mumbled aloud.

Everyone was so wound up. From the political atmosphere, the unsteady economy, the scary health statistics that kept pounding down on us, I was not surprised by the horn. People were ready to blow and road rage ran rampant.

My cellphone rang, alerting me that Janie's husband, Sam was calling.

"Hi, Sam. Is everything okay?" I asked, my body clenching up with worry. It was uncommon for him to call.

"Hi, Lisa. Yes, everything is fine. All seems well here," he said, but his words didn't match his shaky tone.

On the night Janie had her little meltdown, I'd spent most of my time with Sam. I could see why she wanted to keep her secret from him. He was clearly physically and mentally affected by her struggle. He'd wrung his hands constantly, walked around nonstop, and in general, seemed to age right before my eyes. He knew Janie struggled, but I think he'd gotten confident in Janie's sobriety, her strength and her achievements. She'd sold it well. We all thought she was okay, great in fact.

"Thank you for taking my call. I just want to talk to you about something," he said.

"Anything, Sam. I'm here to help," I said, kindly.

When I'd filed for divorce from Rick, Sam had been the one to help me find a lawyer and got the case moving. Sam wasn't a divorce attorney himself, but his firm had connections, and he'd helped me when I needed it.

"I don't think Janie told you. I was pushing her last week to tell you ladies, but she didn't think it was a good time," he said.

Janie was pregnant. That had to be it. And Sam was terrified that she had somehow hurt the baby with drinking or something else.

I didn't really know where she stood on this topic. It seemed like she had her hands full with her work and her two girls, but I knew she loved her children. And children in general. I knew she was really happy in her marriage. That was a given. There was no hiding her true feelings on that. Not with us.

"She won a trip to a spa and wanted to invite you and Petra to go with her for the weekend, all expenses paid," he said.

"What? Where?" I asked, feeling a bit flabbergasted. This wasn't what I was expecting. Not that it wasn't good news. It just wasn't as big as what I thought he was going to say.

"She won it through work for top sales last quarter. It was the big Christmas giveaway at her work and she won it," he said.

I could hear the thrill and genuine pride he had for his wife in his voice. For a split second, I allowed myself to be jealous of her. She was married to such a great man. I wished mine had turned out the way hers was. But I had to remember, this was her second marriage. Janie had paid the piper with her first marriage. She deserved this.

"That is amazing," I said, genuinely thrilled for my rock star friend. "She didn't tell us."

"She didn't tell you because she feels guilty about asking you guys to go with her. She knows how hectic things are with kids, job, school," Sam said. "Lisa, I know this is a lot to ask, but would you go with her? I think that it would really help her. You saw her the other night. She's spinning with stress. I feel like a change of scenery will reset her."

I nodded my head, agreeing, but also wondering how I would pull it off. What about my kids? How could I leave them?

As though he were reading my mind, Sam tossed in.

"I would be happy to pay for your girls to go if that would help. I know you are balancing a lot right now and probably don't want to leave them," he said.

As soon as he said it, my body jumped back, recoiling from that idea. The thought of bringing those two into a relaxing, serene setting like a spa didn't sit well with me. I imagined myself laying there with cucumbers over my eyes and wearing a white robe. Then I pictured them lifting those cucumbers in order to get my attention before launching into their demands: keys, money, car, when are we leaving, what are we eating? On and on and on. There had to be a better way.

"No, Sam. That's not necessary. I'm sure I could come up with something for them," I said, trying to make a list of non-existent people in my life. Who was I kidding? I had nobody.

"Will you go with her?" he asked again. "Please? You girls can give her something that I can't. She needs you."

I nodded my head, and without really thinking it through, gave him the only answer that felt right.

"Yes. Damn straight I will."

Janie

Closing the door behind me, I finally expelled the air I'd been holding all the way up the back stairs. I was inside Carrie's house. I must have lost my damn mind. But I couldn't not do it. My gut told me that someone was in trouble and how could I ignore that?

Besides, the door was open. The damn door was slightly ajar. Who left their back door unlocked when they went out of town? That alone told me I had done the right thing. Someone was in this house and whoever it was, that person needed my help. I was sure of it.

Petra had been right. She thought someone was in this house and we didn't believe her. Shame on us. But now how could I tell her? She was dealing with PTSD from the loss of her brother, from the loss of so many patients, and all of the stress that those things had put on her marriage. I couldn't tell her. I had to do this by myself.

And I wasn't sure about telling Lisa either. She was balancing enough right now with school and the kids and not to mention trying to figure out how to put a band aid on her finances. Yes, my husband's friend had stepped up and did the best he could to help represent her as her lawyer but when it came down to getting money out of Rick. Ha! That was a joke. You couldn't pump water out of a dry well. And that was sure how he looked in court. Didn't matter that he was living in the life of luxury now. That was all his new girlfriend's money. Lisa had no claim on that.

No, that was why I needed to take this on myself. Help Carrie and move on. I'd had it the easiest out of us during the pandemic. My business took off, my kids were homeschooled for a bit, but then slid right back into onsite learning without any issue, and I had Sam, who was wonderful to me.

So why then are you still wanting to drink your face off? my judgmental internal voice nagged.

"Shut up," I told that voice in my head.

And by the way, isn't this just really a distraction so that you don't have to deal with your own issues? Like making an appointment with your therapist like you promised Susanna and Sam you would?

Good Lord, that bitch was judgy today.

I shook my head to rid it of my annoying internal voice and marched forward. I only had a little time before the kids came home. It was about to be late afternoon mid-winter in Chicago, which meant darkness was coming fast.

Should I call out? Was that wise? I had no idea what I was looking for. I walked slowly into the kitchen, noting that the place was immaculate. It sure didn't look like there was anyone else here. Running my hand over the expensive granite counters, I noted what a good job the builder did with this kitchen. Everything was state of the art, and the colors really knocked it out of the park. Carrie must have worked with a professional decorator. We all seemed to in this neighborhood. It was very much a keeping up with the Joneses neighborhood.

There was something about Carrie's style that set this house apart-even beyond what Petra and I had accomplished in our homes, which were pretty spectacular. Perhaps it was in the light fixtures? Something was a step above, there was no denying that. The realtor in me was impressed, and that was hard to do considering the properties I sold.

Shaking my head, I tried my best to refocus. I couldn't turn my brain off when I was looking at property. This one would sell for a pretty penny. Especially in these times when much of the wealth was moving out of the city and further into the suburbs.

Enough. For some reason, I felt the best place for me to check would be the basement. Wasn't that where the trauma always occurred in horror movies? That was where I would guess a scream would come from. Doing a quick round on the ground floor to look for blood stains or bodies, I headed toward the basement, feeling better each second that passed without finding something awful. Perhaps this had been a false alarm?

Just as I was about to head down, I heard the sound of the front door opening. I had no time to escape out the back, I would have to pass right in front of whoever just came in. Shit!

Petra

Someone else just came in? Seriously? What was this, a party? I had to get out of here. Seeing my window, I snuck back down the staircase, hoping to God I wouldn't run into whoever had come in the back way. From the sound of the footsteps I had observed, my guess was they were all the way on the other side of the house. That left me with just a few spare seconds before whoever came in through the front would see me near the back door.

I thanked the Lord that this back staircase was carpeted, giving me my chance to escape. It would probably be wise to stay and try and eavesdrop on the two people who were now in the house, but this was starting to feel like the wrong time to do it. Now my chances of being discovered had doubled. This was not what I needed right now. I couldn't help but think of Paul's face should I get caught and possibly turned in to the police. I had just broken into someone's home. What was wrong with me?

My heart was pumping through my chest as I looked around, noting there were still no lights on in this back part of the house. But there would be soon. I could hear whoever it was whistling to themselves and setting things down near the front door.

Hoping my legs wouldn't give out, I bolted, keeping my movements as quiet as possible. My hands slipped on the handle of the back door twice because of how sweaty they were. Finally, the knob turned, and somehow, I was outside, doing my best to close it without making a sound. I tiptoed down the back stairs, desperately wanting to get home and close the door behind me. I needed the safety of my house, the warmth of my kids, the confidence of Paul, circled around me.

I wasn't cut out for this private detective nonsense. I was a doctor, for God's sakes. I was a doctor with heavy PTSD, making up stories in my head about my neighbor. I had to get some help. This wasn't normal.

Suddenly, I was down on the ground, sprawled out in the snow. I was in such a panic to get back that I'd slipped on a patch of ice and hit my head. Oww, that hurt. Groaning, I pushed myself up, but not before noting a drop of blood in the snow. What? Whose blood was that?

It took a second to put two and two together that it was actually my blood. My mouth was bleeding. I'd landed on my mouth and it was bleeding. Running my tongue around my mouth, to my dismay, I felt that one of my front teeth had chipped. Oh no.

I stood up, determined to make it home without any more drama. What the hell was I going to do about this tooth? I didn't have time for this.

By the time I reached my driveway, I was out of breath, panting like a hyena. So much for my morning runs keeping me in great shape. I logged in the code for the garage, ran inside, and immediately pressed the button to close the door behind me.

I leaned against the wall, trying to put my story together. Looking down, I took in the damage. I was soaking wet from falling in the snow and there was blood on me from my mouth injury. I needed a mirror immediately. My guess was that I'd also cut my lip based on the amount of blood. I'd probably have to give myself stiches tonight.

When I pulled my hand up to check out my lip, it finally registered that there was something in it. The key to Carrie's house! In my rush to get out of there, I'd forgotten to put her key back. And I hadn't turned the security camera by the back door to the angle it was supposed to be.

Wait! AND I'd left my car down the block instead of pulling it back into the garage like I intended to do after I'd searched Carrie's house.

Just when I thought it couldn't get worse, I heard the rumble of the garage door opening. Paul was home.

Before I could figure out a story, our eyes met over the dashboard. He had the girls in the car, having picked them up from school. His eyes locked in on mine and widened in shock. I stood stock still like a deer in the headlights. How was I going to explain this to him? From the backseat, I heard the muffled sound of the kids yelling excitedly, "Mommy!"

Lisa

"Of course, I will do that favor for you. I'd be happy to take the kids for you," Rick the Dick cooed into the phone in a tone I knew he considered to be his sexy voice. I threw up a little bit in my mouth but managed to swallow it back down.

This creep still considered spending time with his kids as doing me a favor. God, why didn't I leave him ten years ago? I knew then. I was just so scared. And stupid. Before I could respond, he cut in with a response I should have seen coming.

"I'm just so glad we are getting along so well. If only it could have been like this the whole time, LiLi," he said, using the pet name he used to call me.

Don't engage. Don't engage.

I wasn't able to afford a lot of therapy, but in the couple of sessions I was able to attend, I took notes and studied them as though my life depended on it. And the biggest thing I learned was that the fight was over. There was no hope in trying to win. It was just an unwinnable situation. Best to just accept that there was no reason to engage, don't give him any of my emotion anymore, and limit the conversation to black and white answers. Like when he was going to do me the huge favor of watching his own children.

But he was hitting on me. His ex-wife. There was no doubt in my mind that he was hitting on me. I'd caught him doing this to many women when we were married. I knew the way his voice pitched up to a certain octave that this was happening. Eww. I pictured the way he swayed his body back and forth, a tell I knew too well when he wanted someone's attention. I think he thought it was cute. For the second time in this short conversation, I felt myself swallowing a little puke back down.

This was a mistake. I couldn't leave these kids with Rick. What was I thinking? I had to come up with something better.

Taking a deep breath, I simply ended the call and set my phone down. Janie needed me, but not at the cost of my children's mental health. She wouldn't want this. There had to be another way.

My phone buzzed, most likely Rick the Dick calling me back, but I ignored it. Shit. Now that I wasn't going to have him watch the kids, I knew what would happen. He would chase me down until he got the time with them. Even though he'd been MIA in their lives for the last nine months.

I'd just have to come up with a way to get him off the scent. Could there already be trouble in paradise with his new lady love? His new wife to be? Thinking back to the cheating timeline I put together once I decided to file for divorce, I thought, definitely. Rick tired fast of being monogamous. Very fast.

Well, whatever, it wasn't my problem anymore. When I'd found out he had a serious girlfriend, I was pleasantly surprised by my non-reaction. I simply didn't care. And that said it all.

Now onto the things I really cared about. Pulling out my computer, I googled "Alcoholics who become pregnant." I deleted that then typed in, "How to help alcoholics who are pregnant."

It led me to a few articles and websites that showed disturbing pictures of babies born with fetal alcohol syndrome. I clicked one open and immediately regretted doing so. The images were graphic and disturbing, to say the least, and the statistics listed next to the pictures even more so.

"Mom?" I heard one of the girls say behind me.

I slammed the computer shut and turned around to find Veronica staring at me with her perpetual irritated look on her face.

"What?" I asked, wishing I could erase the last five years from her life and start fresh with her. If she hadn't seen so many fights, would she have been this damaged? This couldn't be normal teenage snottiness. This felt beyond that.

"What were you just looking at?" she snarled.

"Just schoolwork," I said, trying to come up with a diversion. "What do you guys want for dinner?"

"Anything. I'm starving. You never cook anymore," she complained, opening the pantry and sighing. She pulled at the sleeve of her pumpkin-colored fleece shirt and hunched over in a pout.

Veronica took any shot she could when it came to tearing me down. It seemed to be her life's mission. She had it out for me and there was nothing I could do. "Stay strong," the therapist had said. "Remember, she's just testing you to see if you will leave her."

That sounded tempting right now. But I never would. I knew I only had a few short years with her before she would be off to college, and this would all be over. I had wasted all my precious kid time. All that time I could have been forming happy, healthy children. I knew why I did it. I didn't want to share them. I didn't trust that Rick would take care of them during his court-appointed time, which I knew he would get, despite what a shit he was. All the women I knew who got divorced had experienced just that. It had scared me into staying. I had heard endless stories of how their kids were neglected or even abused once they got turned over to the other parent for their time. Whoever the bad parent was-the mom or the dad-once left with all that alone time, had blown it. Bad shit went down.

"You can start cooking more dinners?" I volunteered. "I would love it if you were more involved," I smiled back, trying my best to entice Veronica into some of the decisions and operations of the house. That was what the therapist had suggested.

She just grunted and closed the pantry.

"Maybe," she said, turning to leave the room.

I watched her slumped-over pumpkin-colored form sulk out of the room, tossing around names in my head of who could possibly watch them while I went with Janie and Petra to the spa. The idea of that much luxury almost made me laugh. It seemed impossible.

Maybe one of my sisters would come watch them?

"Bahahaha," I laughed aloud, allowing myself to register how ridiculous the thought of my self-absorbed twin sisters doing anything for me or offering any help was. No, that wasn't going to happen. They'd joined forces a number of years ago when things were clearly not well and told me either

I left my marriage or they didn't want a relationship with me anymore. No matter how much I tried to explain my reasons for staying, they'd made up their minds. They weren't going to "enable me" anymore. And they'd stuck to their words. I hadn't seen or heard from them in about seven years.

I was on my own. But not really. I had my friends.

"I forgot to tell you, Mom," Veronica said, sticking her head back into the room. "Dad called me. He's on his way."

I put my head down in my hands and groaned.

Janie

I was in so much trouble. What the hell was I thinking coming over here? I'd really screwed myself now. Here I was, hiding in someone's basement, someone I didn't even know, hoping I was going to find something that was going to solve some kind of mystery that I didn't really understand. How was I going to explain this to whoever found me? Maybe there would be no explaining. Maybe I would just be shot on the spot, which I deserved, quite frankly.

My eyes scanned the darkness, desperately looking for somewhere to hide. I turned on the flashlight on my phone, keeping it low to the ground, hoping that whoever was here wouldn't spot my light bouncing around. My eyes fell on an oversized bar at the far end of the room. Perfect. I tiptoed my way over there and ducked behind it, feeling like my heart was beating so fast I would hyperventilate. I listened to the sound of heels clicking around upstairs, praying they would leave soon.

Somehow, I'd allowed myself to get sucked into Petra's story about Carrie, probably desperate to distract myself from my own problems. No more. If I got out of this, which I prayed for now, I swore I would go straight home and call my sponsor and book an appointment with my therapist. It was time.

And I would take that spa trip with my friends. Sam was right. I needed to get out and break the obsession I'd developed at work. So what if I wasn't number one? The need to succeed was killing me. Look where I was right now. Look what I was doing.

Just as I was starting to feel comfort looking into the future, the overhead lights in the basement turned on. My mouth dropped to the floor and my heart stopped. This was it. I was caught. What was I going to say? I needed a story and fast.

Before I could think of anything, I heard a familiar female voice say, "Here it is. Isn't it amazing?"

The silence that followed made me wonder if I was supposed to reply. Was she talking to me? Did she know I was here and was waiting for me to respond? I could just stand up and say yes and make up some bullshit about checking on the house for Carrie. If I was going to go that route, this would be the moment to do that. Any more time hiding would blow that to pieces.

Just as I was about to jump up from behind the bar and go the "fake it till I make it" route, I heard another muted voice respond, "Oh, it's amazing. You'll sell that in a heartbeat. Now why are they moving again?"

It was clear now that whoever was in the house was talking to someone on the phone, probably a FaceTime situation. I held my breath and crouched lower. She had to be a realtor based on what she just said, and if she was, that meant that she would be leaving, not staying. Unless, of course, she was hosting an open house, which would make my nightmare even worse.

"I'm not really sure. But if you ask me, there's trouble in paradise," the mystery woman said.

"Why do you say that?" the recipient of the FaceTime call said in response.

"Because I haven't talked to the wife in a few weeks. We did at the beginning but now … I don't know," the realtor said. Her voice was getting closer, making me fear that she was coming over to get herself a drink. Oh no.

"I mean, isn't that strange? It's normally the wife who I work with on all the details," realtor voice said.

She was super close now, just steps away from me. I closed my eyes, somehow feeling and wishing that it would make me invisible.

"It is weird. Maybe you pissed her off?" the other person laughed.

"Please. Everyone loves me," she chuckled in a not-so-nice way.

All of a sudden it hit me who this was. They chose Heather Platt over me to sell their house? I couldn't believe it. I mean, I didn't really know them that well either, but Heather was not someone I would do business with, nor would anyone who lived in the community. She didn't have a great reputation locally, even though she would beg to differ. From what I knew of her, she was new to getting back into the business, and her area of focus was high-rise condos in the city through her husband's connections. I didn't know her to do a lot of local deals.

"Are they coming back?" the recipient of the FaceTime call asked.

"I hope not. Hopefully, I list this tomorrow and then it sells in a day and I'm done. To be honest, I get the creeps here," Heather said, her voice taking a turn and sounding a bit shaky.

"What do you mean?" asked her friend.

"I don't know. I just feel funny here. Everything about this place feels like they left in a hurry," Heather said.

A shiver ran down my spine at those words, making me think of Petra's theory. Maybe she was right. Perhaps we should have listened. Something was wrong here.

"Well, everyone is fleeing Illinois in a hurry. That's the pandemic. So many people have cleared out quickly. I've seen it here in California, too. Don't let it bother you," her friend said.

"I know. It's just, I don't know, something," she said, sounding like a human for the first time. Heather was always so confident, in your face, asking too many questions, ballsy. To hear her a little rocked was nice. Made me like her just a bit. A very little bit.

"Anyway, I have to take these pics and head out. I get the creeps being here after dark," she said.

"Why are you taking pictures this late?" her friend asked her.

"I did the rest of the house yesterday and was about to list it but then completely forgot to do the basement. I'm just going to grab a few with my phone and then head out of here," she said. "Okay, call you later tonight after I list it. I want to see what you think."

"Like if I spot a ghost or a dead body in one of the pics?" her friend callously laughed.

I cringed, thinking that was exactly what I was scared of.

"You're hilarious. Bye, babe," Heather sang before disconnecting.

I heard her click a few pictures on her phone and mumble to herself, "dead body," before diving into a little video. As she walked the room recording herself talking about the can lighting, fully stocked bar and tray ceilings, I let my eyes wander around me. The bar was immaculate except for a pair of very expensive, black, high-heeled shoes discarded on the floor behind me.

Strange. I knew the brand well. I owned two pairs myself and knew them to be in the ballpark of three thousand a pop. Weird that they would just be lying here.

"Like they left in a hurry," Heather had said. Based on this, I couldn't agree more. Was Carrie even allowed to properly pack before she was whisked out of this house? If she ever left this house?

Before I could inspect any further, I heard Heather talking to herself more.

"I have to get the hell out of here. I'm ready to be done with this creepy house," she said before hitting something on the wall and killing all the light in the room.

As she went on her way, I remained crouched in the darkness, happy to have not been discovered but now very anxious to get out. I officially had the creeps.

Petra

"Hi, guys," I said, meekly, trying my best not to let myself cry. That was what I wanted to do right now, but I had to pull it together.

Paul said something to the kids and jumped out of the car. He must have told them to stay because they sat staring at me wide-eyed, making me feel even worse. He quickly made his way over to me, his dress shoes clicking on the concrete. Suddenly, his hands were all over me, checking me out.

"Are you hurt? What happened, baby. There's blood," he said. "Were you in an accident?

He had no idea.

"I just fell, honey, I'm fine," I said, doing my best to stay calm. This was never going to work. Paul could see right through me. I had no game when it came to stretching the truth for him.

"It's not from the hospital?' he asked.

"No, I would never come home like this from the hospital," I said, getting defensive.

"Your tooth is chipped," he said, putting his hands on my face to get a closer look.

"I know. I have to go in and call the doctor," I said, waving his hands away.

"And your lip," he said, grabbing for one of the towels I kept stashed in the garage. "Where did you fall?"

"Babe, I'm fine," I said, feeling like he would crawl into my mouth if I let him keep going.

The irritation in my voice must have registered with him because he dropped his hands and looked deeply into my eyes. I looked away, unable to withstand the scrutiny.

"You fell?" he asked softly.

I nodded my head, unable to meet his eyes.

"Petra, what is going on?" he asked. He started to cup my face with both hands, but then pulled away probably because I stepped back. He clasped his hands together and put them up to his mouth and breathed a heavy sigh out.

"Look at me," he said, not in a command but a loving request.

I was trying to come up with a story in my head, a simple explanation for why I was standing here with blood all over me.

"Did you get in a fight?" Paul asked, raising an eyebrow.

"No," I said, chuckling a bit and finally looking at him.

He stared back at me, allowing a small smile to form on his lips. Thank God. I was going to tell him the truth. That was the plan, but I didn't want to hear any lectures. I wasn't crazy, I wasn't imagining things, but perhaps I was in a little over my head. I just wanted that to remain unspoken between us. I really didn't need any mansplaining on how I needed to stop obsessing about the neighbor. And that was how any feedback from him would feel right now.

"Where is the car?" he asked calmly.

"It's parked down the street," I said.

He nodded.

"Do you want to tell me why?" he asked, a look of hope flitting across his face that broke my heart.

"Maybe later?" I extended as my peace offering.

"How about this. Let's get the kids inside. Let's get you inside, and let's call the dentist," he said. "And we'll talk later?"

"Definitely," I said, wiping my face with the towel. I wanted to blot as much blood as possible, so when the kids jumped out of the car, they wouldn't freak out.

"I'm going to pull in and then go get your car," Paul said, releasing me and turning back in the direction of his car. Suddenly he whipped around and walked back to me.

"One more thing," Paul said, holding up his pointer finger and coming close.

I looked up at him, waiting for him to lower the boom. More therapy, more couples counseling, a commitment to explore anti-anxiety medication. Something big was coming. I could feel it.

"I need you to promise me something," he said, exhaling.

I nodded my head, holding my towel to my mouth and forming my defense. I was not crazy. I'd experienced trauma, I worked in trauma, I was having a bit of an obsession with a neighbor, that I might add had turned out to be true. But I proved my theory today. No one was supposed to be in that house, and there were definitely people there.

Before I could say anything, he interrupted with a request I had not seen coming.

"Sam called me today. Janie has won an all-expenses-paid trip for three to a spa in Wisconsin. I want you to go with her. Lisa is going to go as well," he said, flooring me.

This was not what I saw coming.

"But, what about work and the kids?" I said.

"I will take care of everything here and use a mental health day at work, for the love of God. You deserve it. The last thing the hospital needs is to burn you out. They need you," he said. "And so do we. But we need you refreshed and not," he waved his hands over me, "this."

The words could be construed as insulting, but it only made me feel relieved. He was looking at me as though I had work burnout, a mental burnout. Good. Let him think that. It was true.

"Then I agree to it. It sounds great," I said, smiling back. "When?"

"Details," he said, turning back to the car. "We'll figure it all out."

"Can I at least get my tooth fixed first?" I called out to him, chuckling a bit.

"Oh, hell yes, as soon as possible please. I need my hot wife back. Not this WWF, boxing ring version of her," he laughed, jumping in the car.

My kids must have calmed after seeing their dad get back in the car with a good attitude because they waved and called out to me excitedly.

Watching them made me feel guilty and lucky at the same time. What if I would have been shot in Carrie's house? What if someone thought I was an intruder and shot me? My kids could have lost their mom. I had to get a grip. I waved back and vowed to be more careful. No more crazy adventures. There had to be a better way to go about this sleuthing. And standing there with a towel up to my lip, a chipped tooth and a freaked-out family in the car, I knew that I had no choice. If I was going to solve this mystery, if there even was one, I was going to do it right. And not in a way where I put everything at risk. That was crazy. And there was one thing that I knew for sure in my heart of hearts, deep down in my strong, successful, female soul.

I was not crazy.

Lisa

"So, we do wear the masks during the service, but not when we're in the therapy pools? Is that what she said?" I asked, peeling back the uncomfortable disposable mask I wore for the tour of the spa. "And we put them on when we order? Is that right? Or just the server?"

Janie pulled her mask off and scanned the menu. "I think we keep it on when we order. But that's Chicago. The rules may be totally different here in Wisconsin. I can already tell that there are a lot fewer masks on here than back home."

"I'm going to keep mine on until after I order. Just to be respectful. We're very lucky to all have been vaccinated already, so I feel good, but I just want to be respectful," Petra said.

I watched Janie closely as she scanned the order. I could tell already that she was in a better place having some time away from home, but still, she checked her phone constantly. She had her assistant at work set up to do her showings today, so she had disconnected a little bit, but still, the way her eyes bounced from the menu to the phone screen told me she had not completely turned off.

My eyes focused in on the drink list. Man, would I love a cocktail right now. Thank God this wasn't one of those spas that only served water and salad. This was a genuine, indulge yourself however you like, paradise-like spa. I loved the soft, coaxing music, super-high ceilings, waterfalls and pools everywhere. It almost felt dreamlike. I ran through the list of services we were all set to have and smiled to myself. Multiple massages, facials, body wraps, and saunas were something I had been dreaming of for a while but never thought I would experience again.

"I'm getting a margarita," Janie said, pulling me back to reality.

"What?" Petra asked softly.

I sat their mute, not knowing what to say. I was still playing around with the idea that Janie might be pregnant.

Before I had left, Sam had come up with the idea that my girls could come stay with him. We could sell it as a "job." We would pay them to help watch the girls, and they would in turn be housed, fed and trained as future babysitters. Win. Win. He'd even made a comment like, "This is good. We're training our future babysitters, and I promise to spoil them with ordering whatever food they want or cooking. Whatever they want to do."

The future babysitter comment made me think that their crew was in expansion mode. Good for them. As long as Janie could handle the stress.

Also, the plan that the girls would be earning money had even turned them off from the idea of maybe staying with their dad. They had straight up turned him down, which in my opinion was for the best.

Needless to say, he had not done well with the rejection, and we were all still dealing with his harassing phone calls. I so badly wanted to text him, "Taste of your own medicine. Rejection hurts, doesn't it?" But, so far, I was holding strong and sticking with my mantra: do not engage.

"A virgin," Janie cut in quickly. "The strawberry one I always get."

She set the menu down and put her hands out to both of us.

"I'm sorry," she said.

"About what?" I asked, grabbing her extended hand.

"That I'm putting you both through this. Again," she said. "Thank you so much for coming here with me. I know how hard it was to leave your families, your jobs, etc.

"You do not have to apologize," Petra said, squeezing Janie's hand with both of hers. "This is what we do. You guys dropped everything for me when I went through my hard time."

"Oh yeah, this is just so tough to come here to this horrible place," I laughed sarcastically, waving my hand over the beautiful dining room of the spa. Everything about it-the high ceilings, the exposed wood beams, the elegant music, and the comfortable leather chairs screamed luxury. So different than my life back at home.

"My kids are being taken care of, I have a little break from work and school, and I'm going to spend the next eight hours being pampered. Yes, indeed, I've made quite a sacrifice," I laughed.

Janie laughed and released our hands, sitting back in her chair.

"Seriously though, Janie, fill us in. What can we do next?" Petra asked.

Janie's face turned serious and she released a sigh. "I wish I knew. I'll be honest with you guys. I haven't found a meeting to attend yet. I have a one-on-one meeting booked with my therapist via Zoom, and I've been working with Susanna. That's it," she said.

I could tell she was being honest. At least she wasn't saying things like, "I'm fine" or "It was just a blip." Then I would be really worried.

"I'll be honest. It's a terrible time to have mental health issues. The psychiatrists and therapists are booked solid. Everyone is losing their shit in this season of the pandemic with the holidays just passed, all of us cooped up at home," Janie said, picking up her menu again but not looking at it.

"Honey, you have no idea," Petra said.

She could be referring to the status of her patients or she could be talking about herself. I worried suddenly that I had been so distracted by Janie that I may have dropped the ball on watching Petra.

"Have you at least given yourself a little more grace at work?" I asked Janie.

"What do you mean?" she asked.

"Like given up on this crazy 'I need to be number one' mentality?" I asked.

Janie just sighed and looked down at her phone, allowing her blond bob to fall over her face. Her non-answer was her answer. When I looked over to Petra, I was surprised that instead of meeting my gaze, she too was looking at her phone with her eyebrows down. Thinking I had missed something, I glanced over at my phone that sat next to me on the table.

It was lit up with a text message. Oh no. What had I missed?

There were two messages from two different men that caught my attention. The first was from Rick:

Call me immediately. I need to talk to you about the girls.

I passed over that, knowing that there was really no emergency there. Sam would have called me if there was one. I knew him to be working from home today and watching over the girls-his and mine. The only emergency was Rick's ego needed saving, which was no longer my job and never should have been.

The second message was from Erik and it blew me away:

Want to grab dinner before class on Monday night?

My heart started beating very fast. This little idea that I had been dancing around with was now a full-blown real thing. He was asking me out on a date. A real date! Did people even go out to dinner right now? Were restaurants even open? Of course, they were. I was sitting in one. But this was Wisconsin. Ugh, I hated Covid.

I looked up and noticed two sets of eyes staring back at me with puzzled looks on their faces. I did my best to tuck my smile away but knew it was too late. It was time to fill the girls in, but was it appropriate to even talk about right now?

Janie

"Janie," a soft, quiet voice called to me from across the room, waking me from a nap I didn't even remember falling into. "Wake up. You have a call."

Petra was crashed out asleep across from me on the lounge chairs we'd camped out on in the designated Quiet Room. We'd both migrated to this after our massages and had been chatting with each other in between sessions. We didn't feel it was inappropriate, considering we were the only ones in the Quiet Room and quite possibly the entire spa. The last thing I remember discussing was how a quiet room wasn't necessary, considering the whole place looked like a ghost town. We both agreed it would be a miracle if this place survived the pandemic.

"I have a call?" I asked the staff member who had opened the door. My heart was pumping wildly now. A complete 180 from the peaceful state I was just in. I took the phone from her hand and swallowed, anticipating bad news.

As she opened the door of the Quiet Room to leave, I was shocked to see a completely naked man showering in the Rain Room across from us. Warm water poured down in a steady stream from jets on the ceiling, making you feel as though you were caught in a pleasant summer rainfall. We'd enjoyed it earlier, though we had worn swimsuits, unlike this rebel. Weird.

The worst thing was that the spa employee had left the Quiet Room door open, so now I had to turn my body to avoid watching this strange scene.

"Hello?"

Before the other person on the line could respond, the hallway between our Quiet Room and Rain Room started to sparkle with water. It looked as though the drains on the floor of the Rain Room were not working correctly because water poured from its floor into the hallway. This couldn't be right. I stood up, intent on finding the spa employee to notify her of this impending crisis. The last thing this spa needed was a flood.

"Hello? Janie?" I heard Sam say on the other side of the phone line.

"Yes?" I said, halting in my tracks and immediately forgetting about the water. He wouldn't call me unless something was really wrong. He was adamant about me disconnecting this weekend.

"Janie," he whimpered. I could tell now that he was crying.

"What is it?" I demanded, desperate now. My feet splashed through water on the floor of the Quiet Room. The hallway was now overflowing with so much water that it was piling over the tile in here.

"They're dead, Janie. They're all dead. They didn't have the vaccines, and we went out to dinner and somehow, they just...all died," he said through broken text. I was able to understand him, but the words came so fast, I asked him to repeat them.

While my brain was trying to absorb and edit the news, my eyes stayed locked in the Rain Room, past the staff member that had finally seemed to take notice of the water, to the naked man. He was turning around now. He was looking at me. And he wasn't a stranger.

The gray, mesmerizing eyes of my ex-husband stared back at me, his rock-hard body just as sexy and intriguing as it was in the years I had been married to him. How many times had I told my girlfriends: His body kept me and his heart broke me?

He smiled back at me as though he were laughing at my news. I watched, stunned, as he pulled a finger up and crooked it at me as though he were calling me to the Rain Room with him.

"Janie," I heard Petra say sharply.

I sat up, awoken from my dream. We were alone in the Quiet Room. There was a wall where the Rain Room had just been a few moments earlier, and my ex-husband had vanished. Thank God.

I was shocked to find myself a bit flustered and even, could the right term be, excited? In my clarity now, I knew that I had been passed out, probably super relaxed from the massage I had, and dreamed of my ex. How I could possibly still be physically attracted to him after what I had gone through was beyond me. This was just another clear signal that I had to get myself back in therapy NOW.

"Everyone is okay?" I mumbled, wiping at my eyes.

"No," Petra said, moving across the room and sitting down next to me. "Everyone and everything is not okay. We have to go home."

"What?" I said, swinging my legs around and grabbing for my phone and water bottle. "What is happening. Is it Sam?"

Petra grabbed my arm and kept me sitting, a confusing motion based on the panic I had just heard in her voice.

"Our families are fine. Sorry. I didn't mean to scare you like that," Petra said, taking me in for a hug. "Take a second to wake up and I'll explain everything."

Maybe it was the confusing dream, or the aftereffects of the massage, but something in me broke. I started crying, feeling completely and utterly overwhelmed suddenly.

"Please just tell me," I said, pulling away from Petra.

"It's Carrie," Petra said, reaching out and grabbing my shoulders to steady me.

I looked back to the door expecting to see the rain shower and the spa employee reappear again. Surely, I was still dreaming. Why was Carrie coming up now? Again, with this crazy Carrie story? I promised myself I was done with all of that after I'd escaped the house I'd broken into the other day.

"What?" I said very loudly. I needed to hear my own voice. Possibly wake myself up if I was still dreaming. No such luck.

"Carrie's husband is on the news right now claiming she has gone missing," Petra said, shocking me. The look in her eye was determined, not panicked.

I pulled my hand up to my mouth, knowing one hundred percent now that I was no longer dreaming.

Petra

I ran my tongue over my newly bonded front tooth, asking myself for the hundredth time if I should tell them. I should. No wait, I shouldn't. It was going to get out anyway, right? Better if I was just upfront about it? Would I lose my job? Surely, I would lose my reputation. But my girls would back me. They would tell the police that I had been suspicious. That I had reasons for what I had done. Oh my God, what had I done?

"They're interviewing him now. It's live on CNN. He said that she left last week and just vanished," Janie said, sitting in the back seat.

Lisa sat shotgun with her face also glued to her phone. "I see the same thing."

"Turn up the volume, so I can hear it, too," I said, my eyes bouncing between the dashboard to check how fast I was driving and the rearview mirror. The last thing I needed was to get pulled over right now. I cringed at my reflection. My long, dark hair was greasy and slicked to my head from the oils the massage therapist had used during my scalp massage. I looked terrible. Zero make-up, under-eye circles and a small, red pimple on my chin probably from the intense facial I'd had.

"If anyone has any information about Carrie, please come forward. We are hoping she will return to us safely. Her three children love her, I love her, and we need her here with us," a male voice I assumed to be her husband said.

I scrunched my eyebrows down, puzzled by what I was hearing.

"Bullshit," I mumbled to myself.

"Is he saying that someone took her?" I called out, barreling down the highway.

"Hold on. They are listing a hotline right now to call," Janie said.

"Are they back home in Chicago?" I asked.

"No way. When he spoke, I could see palm trees in the background. They must still be in Florida or wherever. Wait, what was his story again?" Lisa asked.

"They were supposed to be in Disney," Janie said emphatically.

I looked up in the rearview mirror and caught her eye. Had I told her that? I didn't remember telling her that. I thought I had just said Florida.

"I saw it on her Facebook a few days ago," Janie said, shrugging her shoulders in answer to my questioning look.

"So, wait, if they are there in Florida and the police are involved and working on this, why are we leaving the spa again? Why can't we wait to go home until tomorrow night like we had originally planned?" Lisa asked from the passenger seat.

I didn't answer her, just kept my eyes straight ahead because I didn't really have an answer for her. What if the police found my blood in the snow next to the house from when I fell? I should have done a better job cleaning it up. They were going to find it. It's not like I went back to cover it up like a seasoned criminal. I had messed up and I'd given up. I thought that I had put it in the past and had overthought something. I was wrong.

Maybe there was still time to do some damage control.

My phone rang and we all seemed to freeze.

"It's Paul," I said, looking down at my cell.

"Petra," I heard Paul's strong, commanding voice say on the other line. I'd answered the call on speaker and before I could switch over to my earpiece, he said the words I was dreading. The ones I had feared the most.

"The police are here. They are all over the place. But they are here and they want to speak to both of us," he said gravely.

"Okay," I answered in my calm, confident, doctor voice. Behind me, my friends had gone silent. I snuck a peek to the backseat and noticed Janie's eyes were on the ground.

"About what?" I asked, not knowing what else to say.

"Carrie is missing," he said.

Shit. I had meant to call him as soon as I got in the car but somehow, I had forgotten. I'd been so determined to get home and get ahead of things that I had completely forgotten to call Paul. It seemed ridiculous now. What was I going to do? Hide snow? Pick up the entire backyard and move it? As though it was that easy?

"Yes, I heard," I said in a clipped tone. I didn't know what else to say.

"First off, I'm sorry I didn't believe you. I think you must have known something was going on. You sensed it," he said quietly into the phone. My guess was he was not alone and trying to not be overheard.

I turned and looked quickly at Lisa, who just stared back at me.

"Yes," I said.

"And second," Paul sighed. "I think we should get an attorney. They are here to question us. I'm going to call my friend, Jacob. They said they have us on tape, both you and I, crossing our yard to visit Carrie's house multiple times in the past couple of days."

I picked up the phone and put it up to my ear before my friends could hear anymore.

"I'll be home in about an hour," I said as calmly as I could manage.

"Hurry up," my tougher than nails, or so I thought, husband replied. His voice, normally so calm and collected, sounded shaky and scared.

I disconnected without offering any comfort or counsel. I just didn't know what to say. What could I say? What I had done had been risky, stupid, and possibly condemning. And I had dragged him into it.

"What the hell is going on, Petra?" Lisa asked next to me. Her steel gray eyes were crinkled up in confusion and fear. I hated the way she was looking at me right now. I was only trying to help, but I'd managed to terrify my friends and possibly pull us all into a mess that had just blown up like a firecracker right in my face.

Lisa

By the time I got home with my kids, I was more stressed out than I had been when I left for the spa. I thought it was supposed to be the opposite way around. This whole thing had been a disaster.

"Hi, beautiful," I heard a familiar voice call out to me from my kitchen. No freakin' way.

"Rick, what are you doing here?" I demanded, dropping my bags to the floor and putting my hands on my hips. I was not in the mood for any niceties. Rick the Dick was in my house? Why? How?

"The girls told me what was going on, that you were coming back early from your getaway due to some unfortunate circumstances. I thought I would swing by to pick up the girls to help you out. It sounds like something might be going on at the neighbor's house, huh?" He cooed, standing up from the stool next to my kitchen counter he'd been parked at for who knew how long.

How did he even get in? Had he gone through my stuff? Had he looked around? Not that I had anything to hide, but geez, talk about stepping over boundaries.

I snuck a look over to my girls to gauge their reaction. They both looked just as shocked as I was, but Brenda looked especially frazzled.

"Dad, I told you we were babysitting," she said meekly. "I thought we said we would meet up next week?"

"I know, sweetheart, and we definitely still can, but I wanted to surprise all of you. I miss you," he said, pulling her and Veronica in for a bear hug. The stiff way they held their arms at their sides made me sick to my stomach. This bastard.

They both glanced over at me as though looking for some kind of instruction on what to do.

"Rick, this is so inappropriate," I said sternly. I knew I had to set a line here. This was not going to be tolerated. He was not allowed to enter on my turf like this whenever he wanted. It made me feel violated and just downright gross.

Rick released the girls and looked at me as though he'd just received the shock of his life. He ran a hand over his gelled hair, which appeared a darker shade than what I remember him having last time I saw him. Had he had it colored? I wouldn't be surprised. He probably didn't want his young lady to see all his gray.

"Girls, I left something for each of you in your rooms. Why don't you run up and check it out?" he suggested, recovering quickly and plastering his fake smile on his face. He pulled up the sleeves of his expensive-looking light blue, cashmere sweater, that matched the color of his eyes. That detail, I was sure, had been on purpose.

He'd been upstairs.

My girls stood frozen where they were and didn't even look at him. They just kept their eyes locked on mine.

"I have to talk to your dad a minute," I said, refusing to acknowledge the gifts he had left the girls. Whatever it was, I had no interest. They had been looking for his presence for endless months now, not his presents.

In true teenage fashion though, they looked at each other and started upstairs. There was no mistaking the gleam I saw in their eyes. No one could fault them. They were still kids, after all. Who didn't like a surprise present?

"Rick, this is not going to happen. I need you to leave right now," I said, taking him by the elbow and leading him to the front door once the girls were gone.

"Babe, wait, I just want to talk to you quick," he said, trying to reach for my hand and hold it in his. I pulled away as though I'd just been zapped. His touch disgusted me.

"Nope. The only reason you are here is because you were told no. The girls wanted to be somewhere else besides your house and you couldn't handle that. Once again, your ego leads all," I said, putting my hands on my hips, far away from his grasp.

"No, babe," he said, his voice contrite. "That's not it at all."

"Do not call me babe," I said, feeling my body flail in disgust a bit at the use of my old nickname. It did nothing for me now.

"I'm here because that woke me up. You're right. Hearing them tell me 'No' rocked me a bit. It had an effect on me. Just kind of made me see how silly I was acting. They're growing up so fast. They'll be gone in a few years. I need to reconnect with them before they fly the coop," he said, shooting me a dazzling smile.

What the hell did he think he was doing? The overwhelming feeling that he was flirting with me sent my head spinning. Did he really think I was going to fall for this? Did he ever respect me? Obviously not if he thought I was that dumb.

I could see right through him. He wanted something being here. I just wasn't sure what. But I knew for certain it wasn't the girls. That I would bet my life on.

I heard a cheer from upstairs and knew I had to make this brief. He'd obviously gifted something pretty good, and I wanted no part in the hugs and thank yous.

"You have to leave now," I said, walking to the front door. If he didn't follow, I would threaten police. I was in no mood for his bullshit. All I had on my mind right now was Petra. I had to wrap this up and figure out how to help my friend.

"Call me later, will you? I want to talk," Rick said, following me to the door.

"No," I said, sticking to my guns.

He ignored my rejection and leaned in conspiratorially.

"What's going on with our old neighbor?" he asked, leaning down and putting his face way too close to mine. I backed up, as much as I didn't want to. It was just instinct.

"She's missing?" he said.

"How do you know?" I asked, the hairs on the back of my neck going up.

"It's all over the news. And the girls told me over the phone. That's why you were coming home early?" he said, setting his 'I'm ready to discuss serious news with you' look on his face. "Did you know her?"

"Did you?" I asked, finally figuring out why he was here.

He shook his head no and broke eye contact. "No, but I hope she is okay. Listen, I understand you don't want me here," he said, sauntering out the door like he was leaving after a nice, normal visit. "But I'm here, whenever you need to talk. I'm going to be the best ex-husband and father from here on out. I heard you guys and I am awake. Goodnight, babe," he said, waving goodbye as though all was good between us. Like he hadn't had multiple affairs outside of our marriage, ran our finances into the ground, and hid from all responsibilities, as though he had the right to.

"Sure," I said to myself and shut the door quickly. "Whatever you say."

I watched him walk to his large, black SUV, all confidence and swag. Same old Rick. Nothing had changed. As he clicked the door open with his key fob, I tilted my head, a thought running through it that I couldn't avoid.

Why did he care so much about the Carrie story? Had he known her? And, good Lord, had he slept with her?

I turned and started to head up the stairs when my final thought stopped me in my tracks.

Had he killed her?

Janie

"Do they need a lawyer?" I asked my husband, my eyes bouncing back to the television. I strained to hear what Carrie's husband was saying over the constant chatter of my two girls who were competing to get my attention.

"Girls, give your mom a break and go down in the playroom for a few minutes," Sam said, trying to intervene.

"But she just got home and we missed her," Nola whined, grabbing at my leg.

"Mommy, you were gone forever," Zoe said, matching the whiney tone of her sister.

I had been gone for under twenty-four hours, but enough to have my entire life blow up. God forbid we moms cut loose a bit and get away.

"And we don't want to go downstairs. We're scared that the Lady of the Lake is going to get us," Nola said, putting her mouth right up to my ear and shouting into it. These girls were unhinged. They were probably picking up on my nervous energy and channeling it into bad behavior.

There that was again. That silly story about the Lady of the Lake. Now that Carrie was actually deemed missing, it freaked me out even more. Was there something to it?

"Quiet," I said, straining to hear what Tom was saying at the news conference I was trying, but failing, to watch.

"Girls, go to your rooms right now," I barked, much harsher than I normally spoke to them. I needed to hear this. I needed to know if Petra needed an attorney, but even more than that, I wanted to know if I needed one.

The girls both looked at me like I had just killed their pet bunny then joined hands and walked upstairs together like they were on their way to a funeral.

"My wife left our rental home in Orlando on the 9th of this month to go home and prep our home to sell. She just seems to have disappeared. She had planned to be home for a bit, so at first, we didn't suspect anything. But it's been too long with no word from her. We are asking for anyone,"

Tom paused before going on. He looked down and touched a point on his tie, visibly struggling to continue. I hadn't noticed this before, but there was something about him that resembled Paul. Probably the bulging muscles.

I could hear the cameras clicking away as though everyone knew this was the moment. Tom was breaking. "I know I took too long to call. I thought," Tom paused and tears started to pour down his face. They looked genuine to me. "I'm begging anyone who has seen her to come forward. Anyone who knows something. Please. We love her and want her to come back home. Her children miss her and need their mother."

I watched in horror as the camera zoomed in on Tom's defeated-looking face. He seemed to force himself to look directly into the camera. I couldn't imagine how hard this was, if he were truly innocent. He had to know he was going to be the number one suspect in most peoples' minds. And there was something about him that was too put together. Too slick. Perfect suit, well spoken, appearing anxious at all the right times. But those tears? I just couldn't tell.

Maybe I was being too judgmental. What if Sam went missing and I had to speak on a very public platform? Perhaps slicking up in this suit and tie costume was the way Tom was protecting himself from his emotions so that he could speak clearly? I would be a blabbering mess and what good would that be?

My mind raced to the camera that I spotted outside the back door I had entered. Surely, they had me on camera entering the house. It was time to fess up and tell Sam what had happened. I didn't do anything. I hadn't taken anything. But I had heard Heather enter the house. I had to tell the police what I had done. If it could help Carrie, they needed to know. But I didn't see Carrie in the house. And they obviously had searched the house and had not found her. Where had she gone?

I thought about the shoes I had found by the bar.

My God, I wanted a drink. I was losing my mind. I took a deep breath and grabbed Sam's hand.

"Sam, I have to tell you something," I said.

Petra

"They have you on camera multiple times going over there. What were you thinking?" Paul asked, his eyes popping out at me. The muscles in his neck looked like they were going to explode as he angry whispered in my direction.

"It's not just me. They have you on camera going over there as well," I countered, a little bit fed up with having to defend myself. I thought my neighbor was in trouble, I tried to help her out, and it backfired. That was it. I didn't hurt anyone. I was only trying to help. Hell, I'd spent the last ten months of my life putting myself at risk just to try and help other people stay alive. I was in the business of saving lives not taking them. I felt like the police in my kitchen were basically accusing me of having something to do with the disappearance of Carrie. When really, I was trying to make the reappearance of Carrie happen.

"Yes, I was going over there to look for you," he said, spittle blasting out of his mouth. "I was worried about you. You were obsessed."

"For the last time, I'm not obsessed," I said, louder than I should have. I put my hands on my hips and looked over in the direction of the kitchen where the two detectives sat at our kitchen island, blatantly staring at us and watching our argument through the glass doors of Paul's office.

"I thought I heard a scream and I was worried. Turns out I should be worried," I said, moving out of the doorway so that the police officers could not see me.

"And by the way, how many times do they have you on camera walking over there?" I asked, an idea popping into my head.

I thought back to how distracted Paul had been when my brother Danny had been struggling. How I'd called Paul multiple times from the hospital, asking him to walk over to Danny's when I had been unable to come home or was just too wiped out from a heartbreaking shift at the hospital. There were more than a few times he'd been MIA or just took very long to get back to me. Often, he seemed hesitant to go over there. I had chalked it up to him being too busy balancing work and the kids, which he had more of due to my increased hours at the hospital when the number of sick patients were climbing. But maybe the police were interested in talking to him because they had him on tape multiple times going over there, even before I had my own personal worries about Carrie. Was there something funny going on?

I sat down on Paul's office chair and stared up at him. The extra time he was putting in working on his physique. The teeth whitening. The general guilt I'd seen in his eyes. Could I have been so blind? So overwhelmed that I'd missed the signs? Could he have been seeing Carrie more than I realized? Maybe that was why she had fled to Florida with her husband? Maybe Tom had found out and forced the family to get out of town while they worked things out? Maybe Tom had killed her in a jealous rage and was now going to try and pin this on Paul.

Wait. Maybe perhaps Paul had killed her to keep her from telling me?

Paul was talking, but the room was spinning.

"Everything okay in here?" one of the police officers asked, opening the glass door to the office and sticking his head in. He looked like a hunter who had just sniffed out the scent of his next victim. His eyes glowed with excitement that made me want to throw something at him.

"We're fine," Paul said.

"Okay, if you're ready, let me just grab my partner and we'll chat," the officer said.

Paul stood up, nodded his head, rounding back his shoulders while putting his hands on his hips. I looked up at him and caught his raised eyebrows, his clenched lips and hardened chest.

I watched him closely. Had my soul, my gut, whatever it was, known that something was wrong, really wrong next door and pulled me there? Was it more tied to me than I had realized? Was I allowing the loss of my brother to muddy my thoughts? Was I allowing the loss of countless patients over the last few months cloud my judgment? I had seen more death over the past year than I'd seen in all of my medical career. Surely, I was not going to walk away from that unscathed. There had to be some collateral damage going on here. There was no way I was thinking clearly, right? Paul was a good man, right?

"Paul," I managed; my head still spinning.

"We're not saying another word until we get an attorney," he said, his hard eyes turning from me and onto the police officers in our kitchen.

This couldn't be real. This wasn't happening.

Lisa

I put the phone down on my counter, feeling an overwhelming sense of guilt, while at the same time trying to justify my actions. She would want me to do it, I know she would.

No, she would not want you to invite your hot, way-too-young boyfriend over while she was being questioned by the police. And I should be doing more research on my new theory that maybe Carrie was linked to Rick the Dick. I mean, they did live in the same neighborhood for a while. She was a wealthy woman. And he seemed to love wealthy women. And, specifically the wealthy women in our old neighborhood, considering he was trying to get back over there now. So far, my research had shown that the two were friends on Facebook. I clicked off quickly, suddenly freaked out that somehow, they would both be able to tell that I had looked them up.

"I should head over there," I said to myself, grabbing my keys.

My plan was to just drive over to the neighborhood and see who was home. After we got home from the spa, Petra had dropped me at home and said she would text me as soon as she had an update. That was over two hours ago. I'd been texting back and forth with Janie, but now her texts had gone dead as well. Now I was just sitting like a lame duck, waiting. Were the police going to question me, as well? Of course, they were. I was sure that Heather the nosy realtor had turned Petra and I in for being on her property when supposedly she was missing.

The news blared on and on in the other room, awful stories about the pandemic filling the majority of the time. I waited anxiously for another update, but the stories of Covid and political upheaval left me feeling so anxious that I ended up plopping down on the couch and shutting it off. It would be better for me to just look up what I wanted to find online. Online reporting was probably faster anyway.

I was about to text Erik not to come when the doorbell rang, making me sit up straight and cover my mouth. He didn't say it was going to be this fast. I thought I still had some time.

Erik had sent a text ten minutes ago telling me he could drop off some extra study sheets he'd picked up from the library. In our last class, our teacher had referenced an anatomy book that she thought would help for an upcoming clinical session. I'd thought it was overkill, but when Erik had mentioned that he found it and really liked it, I'd said sure, I would take it. I just thought he meant later.

I ran to the bathroom, checking my reflection. Since I'd been home from the spa, the house had remained fairly intact, having been cleaned by both myself and my girls before we all left. That part I wasn't worried about. I was still in my post-facial, post massage, no-make-up glow. At least what little glow I had left after getting ripped out of there and subjected to a very stressful two-hour car ride home.

Taking in a deep breath, I grabbed the jar of Vaseline I kept in the downstairs bathroom, rubbed a bit on my lips and shrugged my shoulders. That was about the only thing I could do unless I freaked out and bolted upstairs to apply make-up, which seemed too much right now.

What could I do? This was me. My finances were in shambles, my friends were being questioned by the police as we speak, and my kids hated me. But my house was clean and my kids were out for a few blessed hours. I wasn't sure if there really was going to be a better time to allow this in my life. Now or never. He'd been vaccinated, I'd been vaccinated. We were good, right?

On the way to the door, I quickly leaned over and lit a candle I kept on a little table near the entryway. There. Now I was ready.

Smiling, I swung the door open without checking to see who it was. Nothing could prepare me for the huge serving of hotness that stood in my doorway. Erik was dressed in a large, down coat with aviator sunglasses, reflecting the sun that seemed to shine directly on him. When I opened the door, he flashed me an adorable grin that made him look bashful and sexy as hell at the same time.

"Hey," he said, sweetly.

"Hey," I swooned, feeling like I could fall straight into his arms. I held back the urge of asking him for an ID. Seriously, I had to find out how old he was. Right now, he could be anywhere between 25-35. Wait a minute. No, I can't believe I had not put this together yet. He was into men. That was why he seemed so relaxed around me, not cocky like most men I met who looked like him.

But then, he motioned with his hand if he should bring the folder in and suddenly, I was engulfed in his smell as he moved past me. The way he turned and smiled back at me, taking his sunglasses off and running his hands through his gorgeous tumble of waves on top of his head at the same time dazzled me back to my first assumption. This hotty totty was interested in me. He wouldn't be here if he wasn't.

And even though I had kids due home in a few hours, my friend a possible suspect in a missing neighbor case, an ex-husband sniffing around, and a house ten times too small for guests, I found myself gesturing for him to come sit down and join me for a coffee.

"I thought you said in class the other day that you were going to be gone all weekend," Erik said, making his way to the back of the house where my kitchen and family room were located. I followed closely behind him, blatantly staring at his butt. After he had set the folder down and agreed to a coffee, I had taken his coat and hung it on the rack near the door. He had on a pair of Levi's and a tight black sweater, allowing me to evaluate his long, lean form. He was so different than my ex, who had been short and stocky. Erik had to be at least ten inches taller than me. And possibly ten years younger than me.

"Yes, my friends and I had a little getaway to a spa. That's right. I forgot I told you about that," I said, doing my best to follow the conversation and not just the butt.

"Yes, it sounded amazing. You guys are all vaccinated, so why not, right?" he said, smiling at me and helping himself to a seat at my kitchen counter.

"I think so," I said, walking over to my Keurig and firing it up. "I feel like the CDC changes their minds every day. One day I feel completely safe and the next I don't," I said, pulling a mug down from my cabinet.

"I think it's going to take a long time for this country to get past a lot of things we went through this year. Fear is going to be something we deal with for a long time, I'm afraid," he said.

Erik had a way of speaking that was very calming. Even though he was talking about fear and vaccines, you still felt like life was okay. I felt safe with him. Like it was okay to talk. I wasn't going to be interrupted, misinterpreted, judged or criticized. All things that I felt with Rick. In fact, being with Erik now, I found myself thinking about how much I had simply stopped speaking in the last few years with Rick. I had simply turned myself off and functioned. Kept taking care of the kids. Kept cleaning the house. Kept cooking. But stopped trying to have a voice. Until I had said one day, enough.

"Are you okay?" Erik asked.

I blinked my eyes a few times and refocused on Erik. He was staring at me with his waves askew, his kind brown eyes wrinkled in concern and both hands on my kitchen counter as though he were about to launch over it.

"Huh?" I said.

Erik just laughed, relaxing a bit.

"You looked like you were gone there for a second. Like your mind had gone somewhere else. You on a tropical island or something?" Erik laughed.

"No, I was just thinking of … my kids," I said, scrambling a bit. "I have so many schedules running in my brain right now. Sorry," I said, turning to put the mug under the Keurig. How long had I spaced out?

"So, you didn't answer me. Do you want to go?" he asked behind me.

"To a tropical island?" I asked, turning back to him.

"Well, we could do that," he laughed and smiled, looking down at his hands. His expression had turned shy, which was so adorable and enduring that I actually blushed.

"But how about we start with dinner?" he said, finding my eyes with a confidence and hope that I found insanely attractive.

How could I say no?

Janie

Sam was on the phone upstairs in his office, probably calling divorce attorneys, when he told me he was actually calling one of his criminal attorney friends to see how we should proceed. I wouldn't blame him. I was an addict. At this point, probably a substance and work addict, a double whammy. And now I was breaking into homes. I was pretty sure he was questioning what he had gotten himself into when he married me, and I would not blame him. I was doubting myself as well.

I sat in the playroom with my girls, listening to them ramble on about their current Barbie adventures. They begged me to play with them and join in on the imaginary play, but at the moment, I was too burnt out mentally and emotionally to partake. I told them that "Mommy has to rest" but promised to stay in the room with them as long as they let me be. The most I could do was sit in their beanbag chair and scroll through my phone, checking for the latest news on Carrie.

I felt like a sitting duck, waiting for the police to ring my doorbell. It was only a matter of time until they found some evidence of me in the home. That was why I had to tell Sam what I had done. I wanted us to get ahead of this.

But my intentions were to help. I wasn't sure how I was going to explain myself except to tell them the absolute truth. I went over to go find a body. But I didn't "make" that body. In fact, I had found nothing but an immaculate home and a mysterious pair of heels. That was it.

I didn't understand why they were questioning Petra but not me? Had Petra done more investigating than I had?

There must be something more on Petra that I didn't know. Something incriminating.

Ugh. I stood up and walked toward the window, feeling like I could peel out of my skin, my anxiety was so high. So much for our relaxing spa weekend. I couldn't help but laugh, thinking of all the calls, showings, stagings, and closings I had done in order to win that weekend getaway. Ha! What a waste. Oh well, maybe, just maybe we would get to a place where we would all be laughing about this someday. But that seemed impossible right now. I knew that one way or another, a very sad end was going to come to Carrie's story. That was just the reality.

As my kids laughed and played in the background, I let my eyes scan the horizon and my brain float. I allowed myself to fly above the neighborhood and look over all the houses, using my realtor brain and the knowledge I had on all the surrounding neighbors. Who could have known more? Who knew Carrie? Who was friends with her? Try as I might, I couldn't think of anyone. That made me feel awful. Why hadn't I tried more with her? Gotten her more involved in school functions, social gatherings, etc.

What about her kids? Why hadn't they played with mine? The easy answer was that she had three boys, fairly close in age to mine, but not a match to my very girly, frilly, Barbie-playing females.

What struck me as odd now is that for having three boys, I saw her driving a lot, but I never really saw her garage door open. You would think with three boys, there would be more playing in the driveway. More soccer nets and baseball throwing and basketball in the driveway. I couldn't gather a memory from my mind of them doing that. Of course, my house was a few down from her and when I did leave, often times I was pulling out in the other direction.

But in general, my gut feel on them was that they were a very closed family. Closed garage doors, closed socially, closed to friends, just all in all, closed.

I went back to my phone, scrolling for more info. She had very few friends on Facebook, too. Though I knew that didn't really mean anything. She didn't seem to have any other social media pages or any information when I Googled her except for the articles that came up on her now about her being MIA. Who was this woman that lived a few doors down? And what kind of narcissist was I that I hadn't welcomed or done any effort to get to know her?

A text came in, pulling me back into my work world.

Ten competing offers for the Sanders house. This is unbelievable.

My assistant's text reminded me that I had not told her yet that I was back in town. I was really hoping to check out this weekend. She seemed like she was handling things just fine, so I made the decision to hold off for now on letting her know.

Great job!

I responded but still kept quiet about being back. God, I wanted a drink. I should probably call Susanna right now.

As I was dialing her number, a thought popped into my head, halting me in my place.

Heather the realtor. That's probably who Carrie spoke to the most. I spoke to my sellers all the time. All the time. It was insane all the things I knew about them. And I was amazing about keeping secrets and confidences. The personal things that come up during buying and selling a home could sink a ship. Finances, goals, things about relationships, conflicts. Once I helped a couple find a home with bedrooms on the opposite ends of the home because they were in an open relationship and wanted to be "respectful" to each other when they had other lovers over. I didn't judge, I just helped them find what they needed. It was shocking what buyers would share with their realtors just to make sure their wishes would be granted.

Heather was the key to figuring out what happened to Carrie. I know I overheard her say she wasn't talking to Carrie, mainly the husband, but I'm sure she got more from Carrie than she realized. Maybe it was all clicking together now in her brain. I had to connect with her.

I smiled, thinking that I had a plan, an idea to help. I kept my face staring out the window, out toward the pond, knowing that if the girls sniffed out a smile, they would be all over me. "Oh good, Mom is happy and ready to play with us."

A sudden gust of wind blew across the pond, causing the water to ripple and the long wheat like grass surrounding it to blow and swish, revealing a fresh mound of dirt on the edge of Petra and Carrie's property. I'd never noticed that before. Wait a minute. What the hell was that? A grave?

Petra

"So, you think she was abused by her husband?" the detective, who I referred to in my head as ex-jock, asked. His muscles strained against his shirt, and though he tried to contain his enthusiasm, I could tell he was feeling a rush from this.

"I can't say who the abuser was, but the marks on her arms and neck were similar to those I've seen in the past on multiple domestic abuse victims I've treated," I said, looking over at Paul, who sat with me in an interrogation room, along with the attorney we'd quickly hired when we realized things were about to get heavy.

"Why didn't you tell me?" Paul asked, leaning in closer to me and trying to take my hand.

Because now I'm wondering if they were from you.

I couldn't stop the suspicious thoughts in my head. It was like my mind was spinning out of control suddenly. I thought I was in a panic before, but now the whitewater rafting excursion my brain was desperately paddling through just got knocked up to a Class 5. My therapist told me that grief often times threw you into a whirlwind of paranoia, jealousy, and doubt. The thing they'd said about having him on camera multiple times going over to Carrie's house had rocked me. I needed to know how many times and when?

Had it really only been when he'd been looking for me? Or had he been looking for her? Looking for her to console him and help him while I was away at the hospital so much. Maybe even looking for a sexual partner when I had checked out completely after my body had been left with burn marks that made me feel undesirable and scared of sex? Had Carrie filled a place in Paul's life when I had been so checked out? And maybe, she had asked him to leave me and he said no. Then he killed her because she was going to tell me? Or hurt her when she threatened to tell me? And that's when she had sought me out in the hospital to treat her. She had wanted me to see those bruises. She wanted me to know what was going on right under my roof.

"Petra," Paul said, grabbing my hand. I pulled it away as though he were burning me with his grasp. "What is going on?"

I turned and looked at the two detectives across the table, who were both looking at me with expectant gazes. Their brows were raised, and the ex-jock actually had a bit of a smirk on his face.

"Can we have a minute alone?" our attorney, Barry Hines, requested in a quiet but firm voice.

"Certainly," the older and slicker of the two detectives said, rising from the table. He was softer spoken, less energetic, but clearly the sharper of the two when it came to interrogation. Even though the younger jock was outwardly friendly and enthusiastic, I didn't feel great around him. I got the vibe that he'd watched a bunch of cop shows and decided one day this was his calling. He kept posing as though he thought he were on some unforeseen camera. This wasn't a game or an opportunity at stardom. This was a woman's life.

As they walked out of the room, Paul kept his eyes glued on me the whole time but said nothing. It felt exactly the way I had been feeling at home for the past ten months. He was always watching me, studying me. I used to think it was because he was concerned for me, for my mental state. Now I was thinking maybe he was trying to gauge if I'd figured it out yet.

"Are you okay, Petra?" Barry asked.

"Of course, I am," I said defensively. "Why are you asking that?"

"They are asking you questions; I'm nodding at you that it is okay to answer them, and you're continuing to stare off into space," he said.

I almost said, "No, I'm not," but stayed silent. Barry wouldn't be making that up. I guess I was spacing out a bit.

"Barry, can I have a minute alone with Paul?" I asked.

"You can have ten," he said, smiling at me and getting up from the table. "I'm going to go grab a coffee."

He walked out of the room as though it were just another day and we were sitting together at a casual lunch. I really liked his style. When we'd hired him this afternoon, we knew he came highly recommended and had a great track record, but his "bed-side" manner was the icing on the cake.

I loved his no-nonsense, calm in the storm take on things. It really put me at ease.

"Petra, I..." Paul started, moving very close to me as soon as the door closed behind Barry.

"Paul, were you having an affair?" I asked bluntly, looking him square in the eye.

His mouth dropped open and his eyes widened. The veins in his neck were like tight, bulging ropes, and he blinked rapidly at me. For a second, I thought he was going to go into shock or have a heart attack, he was so jacked by my question. His shoulders locked up near his ears, and he grabbed onto the chair and the table.

"No," he whispered. "I would never."

He didn't say anything else, just stared at me like I had just killed his parents.

"Why were you going over there?" I asked.

"I told you, I was looking for you. And I'm sorry I didn't believe you. I didn't know you had seen bruising," he said.

He turned and put his head in his hands and rubbed at his eyes.

"Petra, how could you think that? I've never been anything but faithful and committed to you," he kept his eyes turned from me as my head swirled-guilt, regret, anger, grief. The storm raged on.

"How many times did you go over there?" I asked.

"As many times as you did," he said, his hulk-like form standing up and walking toward the door. My mind raced to images of The Rock when he was a professional wrestler. How he used to flex and yell in the camera. I felt like Paul was that angry right now. If he turned and did that, I wouldn't be shocked.

"Check the tapes," he said, exhaling. "I need a break."

He ripped the door open so hard, I thought the hinges would break off and suddenly he was gone.

Lisa

"You, um ... yeah. I mean, yeah," I said, stumbling all over myself. The way he smiled at me was so encouraging and hopeful that I didn't really care if I looked overly excited or awkward. The way he was looking at me made me feel like he thought I was beautiful and amazing. It gave me confidence. That was how I wished my ex had looked at me all those years.

"So, it's a yes. You'll go out to dinner with me?" he said, his smile beaming even brighter.

"Yeah, I mean, yeah," I laughed.

Now. Now is the moment. Do it, Lisa.

Instead of going right for it, I danced a bit. I just couldn't get myself to do it.

"Erik, you know I'm a mom, right?" I said, gesturing around me.

Sometimes I wondered if my super petite body passed me for being younger than I actually was. Maybe that was it. Maybe he wasn't seeing this situation clearly or me clearly. But how much clearer could it get? There was evidence of teenagers all around us-soccer cleats, a volleyball, pictures of my girls, multiple notes up on the refrigerator of schedules and games and life in general. He was here in the madness-right in the midst of it. There was no denying it.

And, I was essentially make-up free right now from the facial I'd received this morning. There was no hiding my crow's feet and my well-earned wrinkles. He had to see them, right?

Erik laughed and got up from the counter, grabbing his mug.

"Can we go sit?" he asked, gesturing toward the couches in my TV room. This was good. I had taken my furniture with me from the old home, the one thing I was adamant on. So, ironically, I had all of this really high-end furniture in this teeny-tiny older house. It didn't really fit, most of it being oversized and luxurious, but all of it was paid off and helped create a nice ambiance.

We chose to sit on the same couch, setting our mugs down on the coffee table in front of us.

"Yes, I know you have kids, and I love kids," Erik finally said, running his hands through his hair. "I've always wanted kids but just have not been presented the opportunity yet. Tell me more about yours. I know so little about them."

I paused, trying to figure out the right thing to say. I thought to myself, *"You know so little about them because most of the time, I feel like they hate me. And when I'm with you, I get to escape that world for a little bit."*

I wanted to tell him about them, but there was a selfish part of me that wanted to keep Erik for myself. I'd been enjoying having my Erik experience as mine and mine alone. The reality was if Erik became part of my life, he'd have to be a part of all of it. And that meant all the drama with having to mesh him with them. Would they like him? Would they be open to him? Would they be jealous of him getting time with me?

All of a sudden, it all seemed like so much. It was fun to daydream and fantasize about Erik but the thought of the big picture and how many hoops I would have to jump through to make everyone happy and comfortable seemed like too much. Couldn't I just keep him to myself?

As though Erik was reading my mind, he scooted over closer to me on the couch.

"Hey. Where did you go?" he asked softly.

I breathed out and focused back on him, not the whole picture. I tried to look only at his sexy, soft eyes, his moist lips, and the way his hair made him look a bit wild but also young, vibrant and healthy.

"I'm sorry. I just got distracted," I said, admitting the truth. "I have so much going on in my life, Erik. I don't even know where to start."

This didn't seem to scare him off. Instead, he moved a bit closer.

"I'm looking forward to getting to know you," Erik said. "I know your life is complicated. I'll be honest. Covid was so dull and isolating, I'm ready for a little complication. I like you, Lisa. I don't see any reason to not put that out there. Life is too short."

I found that statement very endearing coming from those young, innocent lips. Maybe he had experienced more of life than I thought. I envisioned one of those machines that spun the BINGO numbers around, the balls all reading different ages. Which one would pop up when I finally got the courage to ask him?

"I think the pandemic taught all of us that," he said, reaching out and grabbing one of my hands. "Life is short, and if you want something, you have to go after it, because opportunities can be lost. But we can go as slow as you want. I know that you have a lot here on your plate."

Before he could say anything more, like an out-of-body experience, I saw myself take a little leap forward on the couch and suddenly my lips were on his. He froze for just a quick second in surprise, then wrapped both of his hands in my hair, responding to my kiss. His soft lips parted slightly, smiling into our kiss, before diving deeper in. His breath smelled like a good combination of mint and a bit of the coffee we'd just shared, and his lips were as soft as butter.

Suddenly, we were interrupted by the loud sound of my cellphone ringing on the coffee table next to me. He was the first one to freeze and pull away slightly. I would have had no trouble ignoring it. He laughed a bit, not pulling his face away from mine and keeping his hands roaming through my hair.

"Do you have to get that?" he asked quietly.

"No," I said in an immediate response then groaned and said, "Shit. Yes."

As much as I wanted to stay in this make-out bubble for the rest of the afternoon, I knew I couldn't. Kids were going to come blasting through the door, studying was necessary, and, oh yeah, my friends were possibly involved in a missing persons case.

Reluctantly, I pulled away from Erik. His swollen lips and glazed-over bedroom eyes made him only more attractive. So much so, that I considered throwing everything away and taking him upstairs.

Slow down, Lisa! Nothing this rushed lasts long. Slow down.

I smiled back at him and detached, hoping I looked half as good to him as he did to me. Kissing him made me feel like a wild, horny, teenager. My God, that had gone from zero to sixty.

I grabbed my phone, vowing to keep my hormones in check. I liked Erik. I knew that our personalities had clicked. Spending time with him, talking to him, made me forget about some of my other problems. I didn't want to blow it. And now that I knew that we had chemistry? I mean WOW, that kiss. I had to stay cool and not rush it.

Glancing down at my phone, I saw a new text had come in from Janie.

"Everything okay?" Erik asked, watching me from his spot on the couch.

I grabbed my phone and clicked on the text, so I could read the whole thing. At first, I thought I had read it wrong. But no, it said what I thought.

I stood up from the couch, jolted back to my crazy reality.

Can you come over tonight? I need your help. I think we need to dig up a body.

I stopped breathing and put my hand over my mouth.

"Are you okay?" Erik asked, standing up next to me. His warm, tall presence was comforting, but I couldn't let him see this. I put the phone down back on the table and swallowed, trying to come up with a polite way to ask him to leave, as much as I wanted him to stay.

Right now, I had to focus on my friend. This was an emergency.

Janie

That night as I put the girls down, I ran through the list in my head of things I would need. Shovel, check. Bags to hold evidence, check. Partner in crime, check. Lisa was coming over. I was actually surprised how quickly she'd agreed to the whole thing. But Lisa was definitely a no-questions-asked, bury the body, or in this case, unbury the body, kind of friend. She was extremely loyal and non-judgmental. I should have known she would handle the info of me selling her ex's home as well as she did. I think I was just so rattled lately, feeling like everything I did was going to upset someone.

Was it really possible that we might be unburying a body tonight? If there really was a body, wouldn't cadaver dogs had sniffed that out? Did the police bring in the dogs? I'm assuming they would have. I shook my head, flabbergasted by my thoughts. How were we going to do this without Sam knowing? He was watching me like a hawk. So far, the police had not contacted me to answer any questions. Perhaps somehow, they had not seen me on the cameras breaking into the house? Surely by now they would have questioned me. Was I just pressing my luck now by going over there and risking being recorded on camera again? Of course, I was.

"Mom, when is it going to be light out again at night?" Nola asked me in her sweet, little girl voice.

"In the summer," I said, smiling down at her.

She stared at me with her light blue eyes, so similar to Sam's. I could only imagine what innocent thoughts swam deep in those blue waters. I leaned down to kiss her forehead, doing my best to really tune in and be in the moment. My mind was always running a million miles an hour. Their childhoods were roaring past me like a speeding train. Once this Carrie thing was behind us, I vowed to set up a special outing with the girls. Just the three of us. The pandemic robbed us of so many of our annual outings: Christmas shopping in the city, our annual fancy high tea I do every summer with the girls, vacation in MI, so much. We had been following the rules and staying in lockdown for so long now that it felt like the fun in our lives had been completely sucked out. The spa trip with the girls was my first attempt at having fun again and look what had happened.

"Hey, let's do something fun. Just you and me," I said.

"Okay," she said, smiling up at me with her tiny teeth. "Like what?"

"A nice meal out. Or a trip to the city. Or shopping?" I said, listing some of the things we have done in the past that have been a hit.

"Has everything opened back up yet?" she asked naively. "Is Covid over?"

I shook my head no, wondering if I had made a mistake by bringing this up.

"But it will eventually, right?" she asked, a questioning look on her face. She pulled her eyebrows up and watched me closely.

"Of course," I said, knowing that was the right answer. I still had a lot of questions myself, but it had to be the right thing to do, give these kids hope. If I thought Covid was scary, I couldn't even imagine what these little kids would think of it. Mine had rolled with it well, but there was no way these kids were going to walk away completely unscathed. The masks alone were going to haunt their dreams for a long time.

"Will the holidays come back?" Nola asked.

"Nothing can stop the holidays," I said, flashing her a huge smile. This answer I knew I could deliver with confidence.

"Good," Nola said, "Because this year I'm dressing up as The Lady of the Lake for Halloween."

"Tell me more about her," I said, trying my best to sound casual and not look directly at her. That might scare her off. Thinking of the mound I had spotted earlier today; her silly stories now had my full attention.

"The lady who walks around the lake every night looking for her lost child," Nola said, picking at her Cinderella nightgown and releasing a huge yawn.

"How do you know she is looking for a lost child," I asked, an overwhelming feeling of dread filling me.

"Because she calls her name over and over. She yells, 'Pommie,'" Nola said, her hands going up to her mouth in imitation of her version of The Lady of the Lake.

With that, she rolled over and mumbled, "Good night, Mommy." Within seconds, I could hear her breathing switch over to sleep mode.

I lay there next to her, unable to move. Where had I heard that name, "Pommie" before? Now I was the one truly haunted.

Petra

Once we got home from the police station, the kids flocked to me and madness ensued. Everyone wanted something, or wanted to be heard, so for a short time, I was almost numb to all of my worries about next door. Paul went out to run errands. In reality, I think he was just taking a break from me. My accusations at the police station really pushed him over the edge. And the maddening thing was I had to answer their questions, but they didn't answer any of mine. How many times did they have us on film? Did they actually see Carrie come home after she left Orlando? When was the last time they saw her on camera? Had they found any evidence in the house of foul play? They gave us nothing. Clearly, they didn't have enough evidence to accuse us of anything solid. I wanted to help them, so I pushed to answer their questions, but Barry monitored what he thought was okay for them to ask me and when we would answer. I was so glad to have him there.

After we finished with our questions, Paul had driven us home in silence. There were a few times I started a conversation, but he clipped his answers or simply gave none. This was Paul mad. Really mad.

After a few attempts, I'd just given up and turned myself over to the kids once we got home. There was no time to think when I was around them. I was like a short order cook, filling request after request, which actually felt really good.

I couldn't wait to go into work in the morning. When I was there, most of the time I was so consumed by what was going on right in front of me that I didn't obsess about anything else. It was good for me. I think that's why I chose to become an ER doctor. I needed the constant, fast stimulation to keep me motivated. It had worked. Even in Covid, I got through it because I was in the minute. Checked out of all other worries.

But then my brother happened, and I started to see that I could no longer do that. And then Carrie happened, and I let it take control of me. But I had been right. Something had been wrong. And now she was missing, and the police were giving me funny looks. I was the lunatic they recorded walking around the outside of her house a few times. What had I been thinking?

"Mom, can we watch another movie?" my oldest, Shane, asked from the corner of our wrap-around couch.

A few hours earlier, I had us all change into pajamas and said "uncle" to the day. We weren't going to accomplish anything else. It was time to just watch movies and fend off the Sunday night creeps. Monday was coming.

"We can start one, but we won't finish it," I said.

It was very late, much later than our normal routine, and my kids were zoned out. Normally I put all three to bed at the same time and let my older ones read for a bit. I was stalling because Paul liked to be a part of the whole nighttime routine. Tonight, I was so exhausted, I was really hoping he would be here to help out. Where was he? He had been gone for over two hours now. He'd skipped dinner completely and said he'd pick something up while doing errands. Normally, we made a big deal of doing a Sunday night meal together, but this just did not seem like the right time to push that. I'd made grilled cheese for the kids and myself and let them munch on popcorn.

What if the police came back tonight? I'm sure they were crawling through phone records and emails and such. I'd given them a legit reason as to why I would be concerned about her. There would be record of her going to the hospital on the dates I had stated. And we'd never had contact over the phone or email, so I wasn't worried about them tracing anything down on me. Hopefully, they would find threatening texts from her husband, Tom. If he truly was abusive, as I suspected he was, it would show up somewhere.

Just as long as those threatening texts aren't from Paul.

My body jolted up at that thought.

"What's wrong, Mom?" my youngest son, Devin, asked. He'd been sitting on my lap and felt the vibration of my body.

"Nothing," I said, recovering. "Mom just has to go to the bathroom. When I get back, we really have to talk about heading to bed."

I snuck out of my spot on the couch and headed to the bathroom. Peeking back at my kids, I made sure they were still zoned out and quietly tiptoed up the stairs. I had maybe five minutes before they came after me. Probably more like three. Enough time to do some investigating.

On the main floor, I looked around, making sure that Paul had not come home and made my way quickly to his office. Sitting down in front of the computer, I tapped on his keys and typed the password in that we normally used. He had the password to mine. I had the password to his. I thought we had that relationship where there was nothing to hide, so I'd never given it a second thought. Sure enough, it worked and his computer opened.

I stood up, feeling foolish. He would have changed the password if he had something to hide. Nope. I wasn't going to do this. Not going down this path.

I stood up and started to walk back downstairs. In the morning, I was going to call my grief therapist and set up an appointment, this was going too far. We had explored so many things in therapy. She'd really helped me dive deeper and learn so much about myself. She told me to expect jealousy and suspicion. She'd seen it in so many of her patients. I thought I'd already experienced it. When Danny died and I held the majority of the grief, I had been jealous of Paul. He didn't have to carry as heavy of a weight. I thought that was what my grief counselor was talking about. Now, I felt differently. I was suspicious that Paul was having an affair. Jealous.

This was nuts.

Just as I was about to step down the stairs to go back to the basement, my mind stopped me. Upstairs. I had to check out something upstairs. Paul had a safe in his closet.

Lisa

"This is insanity," I whispered to Janie in her three-car garage. We were huddled next to a display of shovels neatly displayed on some sort of cork board at the far end of the garage.

"Melatonin is not harmful. He knew he was taking it. It's not like I poisoned him or tricked him," Janie said in response.

"Janie, I'm not talking about Sam's melatonin. I'm talking about this whole thing. What we are about to do," I said, wanting to take my friend and shake her.

"Lisa, I need your help. I can't do this alone. I am sober. I am clear-headed. So clear headed that I know I can't ask Petra to do this with me, and I can't ask Sam. Both of them can't take anymore. You seem to be unflappable in all of this, so it has to be you. I saw something buried out there this afternoon. Don't you think that if we actually find something, we'll be able to clear Petra's name and settle this whole thing?" Janie asked, looking up at the shovels and putting a finger up to her mouth as though she were contemplating the best choice.

"But, why can't we ask the police to do it?" I suggested for a third time.

"Because," Janie said, putting her head back and sighing.

"Because, what?" I asked, grabbing her arm and shaking her. "Just say it. I'm not partnering up with you in this insanity unless you are totally honest with me."

Janie straightened her head back up and swallowed.

"Because if we get the police involved and they don't find anything, I just look even more unstable to Sam. He'll be on me to go away again to one of those sober programs," she said, speaking very quickly.

I chose to stay quiet, wondering what to say. Truthfully, that didn't seem like a bad idea. It worked last time. She came home and she had years of sobriety after her last trip.

"Lisa, it's so hard. I can't go that raw again," Janie said, begging me with her eyes.

"But, it worked," I said, not wanting to upset her, but knowing I had to be honest with her. What kind of friend would I be without honesty?

"It's the time away, and the therapy, and the food, and the restrictions. Lisa, you don't understand how hard it is. I swear the threat of having to do it is enough to keep me clean. I just need to get back in my group. I know I can do it. Please, please, just believe me. I know I can do it," she said, her eyes tearing up and her hands grabbing at my sleeves.

Last time I had helped her, I went to Al-Anon for a short period of time to better learn how to support my friend. It helped a lot. And taught me how to not be an enabler. I was caught in this moment right now where I did believe Janie. But she was going to have to show me that she would make her meetings a priority again. And, I was also still feeling bad that we didn't believe Petra. She knew something was off next door, and we didn't listen. And now we were about to go looking for bodies. Legit digging for bodies. I didn't want to make Janie feel like we didn't believe her.

"Okay, let's do this," I agreed. "But we need a story. What is our story if we get caught? And what about cameras?"

"It sounds like they have a camera on the back door, front door, and garage. Where we are going won't be recorded."

"Holy shit, you've really thought this through," I said, grateful for Janie's heads-up to wear all black. I reached up and pulled down the most heavy-duty looking shovel I could find.

"So, where are we digging?" I asked, watching Janie yank down another large shovel.

"Follow me. I know exactly where. The Lady of the Lake has already led us to where we need to go," she said, walking in the direction of the side door off the garage.

"Of course, she has," I laughed sarcastically.

I shook my head and hesitantly followed Janie, wondering how in the world we'd gotten mixed up in this mess.

Janie

I was pretty sure I knew what we were going to find and who put it there. There was a part of me that felt a bit relieved by my theory. Just a small part. In the end, a woman was still dead and her kids were going to be without a mom. That was awful.

But if Heather, the high-strung realtor, had killed her, like I had hypothesized she had, then I wouldn't feel as bad about my competitive streak. I thought I was bad trying to beat Frederick for the number one spot. At least I didn't go around killing people to get it. And that was basically what I came up with. I think that Carrie had driven home, like her husband had told the media, in order to break the news to Heather that they were no longer planning on selling. And when she did, Heather didn't take it well and killed her. That was most likely the scream Petra had heard on the morning we were out for the run with the girls. The scream that we had mistaken for a coyote cry.

There were plenty of holes in my theory, of course. The main one being, why hadn't Heather been arrested? Why hadn't Tom contacted the police to tell them what Carrie was doing and that Heather was the last one to speak to her? We would know that by now, right? Maybe. Or maybe not. She could be behind bars right now for all I knew.

Also, why bury the body so close to the house? That seemed odd. Like you were begging to get caught. My guess was that Heather was the "Lady of the Lake" my girls had seen wandering around the pond, looking for a good burial spot. It was so stupid to put it right there. I'd spotted the large mound as soon as a high enough gust of wind had set in.

Who knew? People did a lot of stupid things when committing a crime, and my guess was Heather wasn't a seasoned criminal. She was probably just someone who let the Covid crazy get the best of her and she went a little mad. I could certainly understand that. Not to the extent to where she took her crazy, I would never defend that. But I did see where and how this pandemic had made us all a little nuts.

"Holy shit, you were right," Lisa said once we had reached the mound, and I pulled the high grass back to show her.

I nodded my head, looking at her and then back to the mound. It was smaller up close than what I thought it would be.

I aimed my flashlight all around it, trying to see which section would be the best to start on. Now that we were out here in the freezing cold, this didn't seem like a very good idea. Perhaps we should get the police to do this.

"I mean, holy shit, right?" Lisa said.

I could tell by her high-pitched tone of her voice that she was starting to freak out a bit. I didn't blame her. My grandiose idea to do this seemed great from back inside my warm house, but now that we were out here with the wind howling all around us, it felt like an even better idea to back out.

"Holy shit," was all I could say.

"You think it's Carrie?" Lisa asked, reaching out and linking her arm in mine.

"I don't know. Wouldn't the police have found her?" I guessed.

"I don't know. Why haven't we heard anything about this?" Lisa said.

"Doesn't this seem a little small to be a person in there?" I asked, looking back at my house to see if by chance Sam had woken from his melatonin slumber to look for me. There was a part of me that wished he had.

No such luck. My house was dark, not even a flicker of light. At that moment, my flashlight went out, and we both jumped closer to each other. I smacked it a couple of times, swearing under my breath. Finally, it came back on.

"What if he cut her up?" Lisa said, whispering.

"Who cut her up?" I asked, stunned by this response. Apparently, Lisa had a theory of her own and it didn't sound like it matched mine.

Again, my flashlight went out. Dammit. Why hadn't I thought to check the batteries?

"Cut who up?" An angry, masculine voice barked from behind us through the darkness, causing both Lisa and I to scream.

Petra

I had under a minute to get this done. That's how tight of a leash my kids had on me. I was actually shocked that they hadn't hunted me down already.

Racing up the stairs two at a time, I paused momentarily when I caught the reflection of myself in the mirror at the base of the stairs. My hair looked like a black hornet's nest, my eyes looked red and glassy, and my lips were puffier than normal. This was awful, but my immediate comparison was that I looked like many of the psych patients I treated. Putting my hands on my face, I approached the mirror slowly in disbelief. Could this really be me? "Powerful Petra" my mother had nicknamed me years ago. I was always a great kid-fantastic grades, followed the rules, made my parents proud. My parents were first-generation immigrants from India. They worked so hard for us to do well in this country. Made so many sacrifices. And now their son was dead and their daughter had gone mad. How had this happened?

I pulled my lip out delicately, checking the wound I still had from falling in my yard on the way home from Carrie's. It was just a matter of time until the police asked for a DNA sample to match the blood they surely had found by now. In fact, why hadn't they asked yet? I wasn't a detective or a lawyer, but in my opinion, they were dragging their feet a bit. If this were my husband, or my kid, I would have pushed for more action. Why wasn't Tom, her husband, here? Wouldn't he have raced back to the scene to help look for her? If this was the scene? Maybe they knew she wasn't here. They certainly weren't sharing much. Probably waiting for someone to trip up and say something they hadn't shared.

What had the police said? The cameras were over the garage, the front door, and the back door. All had been malfunctioning for the last few days (the back one probably because of me) but the one over the garage had recorded her pulling in and out at one point. That was all they had shared. They didn't tell me that was the last time she was recorded, even when I pressed them. They just said that they could confirm she had been home at one point. Maybe they had her somewhere else far away at some point after that garage recording. Maybe? All I knew was that I was not arrested and neither was Paul.

So, where had she gone? Where did you go, Carrie? I was in the house and you were not there. But had I really looked everywhere? No, I had to rush out the door because someone was coming in the front door. Who?

Whoever it was must have taken you out then and taken you somewhere because that was the only chance. The question was, were you dead or alive when they did?

And if Tom was in Florida the whole time, who did it?

I pulled back from the mirror and looked up the stairs I still needed to climb. Taking a deep breath, I worked my courage into my core, a process I started back in medical school. I imagined all of my strength gathering in my chest. Powerful Petra. She was still there, right?

I propelled myself up the stairs, hearing the first call come from the basement.

"Mom?" someone had called out. My time was limited.

I ran to Paul's closet and opened the small cabinet to his safe. We each had our own closet, complete with sitting areas and multiple mirrors for outfit evaluations. Within each of the closets, we had a personalized safe. Mine held jewelry, some cash, and a few important papers. We had always shared the same code so that either one of us would be able to get into the other's if something were to happen.

I punched Paul's 4-digit code into the number pad and stepped back. The red button that turned green continued to stay red and a buzzing sound alerted me I had used the wrong code. I had three chances to do it before Paul's phone would be called, alerting him that someone was trying to get in the safe.

I tried it again, shocked when it again stayed red and buzzed.

"What the hell, Paul?" I said, feeling scared and betrayed. We kept a lot of money and valuables in these safes. Why would he change it up on me?

I stepped back, my breathing coming in at an unsteady pace. I grabbed onto one of his shelves, feeling like I was going to faint. Like my world was collapsing all around me. What was he trying to hide? And where the hell was he?

I stepped away, hearing footsteps coming up the stairs. They were coming.

I walked away from the safe and to the stairs as quick as I could.

"Do you guys want more popcorn?" I asked, doing my best to divert and distract.

"I thought it was time for bed?" my oldest said, looking at me with round eyes. He looked so much like his father.

"How about thirty more minutes?" I said, grabbing Shane's hand and leading the kids back down. I needed a minute to catch my breath. Maybe if I got them settled, I could sneak away again and try the code. I couldn't remember how much time had to pass for my attempt to not start as a third attempt on the safe. Maybe if a few minutes passed, I could get more chances with figuring out the code.

"Thirty minutes and popcorn?" Shane confirmed, looking stunned. It was late. Really late for these kids to still be up. But I knew if I tried to put them to bed, they would just keep getting up and asking for me. The best chance I had of some uninterrupted time right now was to feed them and distract them with television.

"Yes," I said, heading down the stairs.

Once we were in the kitchen, I made fast work of getting the microwave popcorn going. I stared out the big bay window onto the pond at the back of the house, wondering what the hell could be in that safe. Phones. It had to be phones that he used to communicate with Carrie. Maybe gifts for her?

I was sick to my stomach thinking about this. It couldn't be real. How had this happened?

"I hate Covid," I said to myself, thinking back to how good things were before our lives had gone to shit.

"Are you okay, Mom?" Shane asked, pulling at my hand.

"I'm fine, honey. Mom is just tired and …" I stopped talking and gasped. There were flashlights. On the pond. Multiple flashes of lights from different sources moving around the side of the pond by Carrie's house. There were people out there.

Lisa

"Paul, you scared the hell out of us," I said, letting go of the death grip I had on Janie's arm. I'd dropped my shovel and raised one hand up in the air and the other was holding tight to Janie. My first instinct was that it was the police coming to do the dig themselves. My second guess was that it was Rick the Dick making sure no one messed with his burial site. Only Rick would be stupid and sociopathic enough to think that he could kill a woman and bury her a few feet from her home and no one would find it.

When it finally registered that it was Paul, all of my theories were put on pause. What was he doing out here?

"Sorry. I saw the flashes of light and I thought for sure it was my wife out here," Paul said, kneeling down to pick up my discarded shovel. "We're not exactly on great terms right now. She's very upset, and then I got upset thinking it was her out here. She's already got us knee deep in this Carrie thing."

"Is she okay, Paul? She hasn't said much on our text string," Janie said, finally speaking up.

She had frozen into a statue when Paul arrived, and I was worried she wasn't going to thaw. It was time to abandon this insane plan and retreat to our homes.

"Honestly, I don't know," Paul said quietly. "She's not herself. And she hasn't been for quite some time. I'm not telling you anything you don't know," Paul said.

It was very dark, the only light coming from our flashlights and a distant streetlight, but I didn't need illumination to know that Paul was at a bottom.

"I'm sorry, Paul," I said quickly.

"Me, too," Janie said.

"Do you guys think…" Paul stopped short, seeming to rethink what he was about to say.

There was an awkward silence as Janie and I both snuck a look at each other. My guess was she was thinking the same thing I was. We need to cut him in on this.

"Paul, we're gonna dig something up here. It should give all of us the answers we need," I said, making the decision to go for it. I trusted Paul. To me, he seemed like a pretty open book. He was always where he was supposed to be, came through on all of his promises to Petra, and was honorable in every situation I'd seen him in over the last five years.

Yes, Petra was still upset with him and very verbal about him not doing enough for her brother when he passed, but to be honest, and I would never say this to Petra or Paul, I didn't blame him. Danny was very intimidating for many reasons. Probably not to Petra, but to everyone else, he was. He was extremely successful, handsome, motivated, and bigger than life. But his history with substance abuse and his reputation for wild parties, I mean, over the top should be featured on a reality show, wild parties, was something that set him apart and made him a little scary. And you just never knew when he was going to flip back to that. If Paul was intimidated to go over to the house to check on him, I didn't blame him. I certainly was. I'd done my best for Petra when I could, but checking on her wild, notorious brother was certainly not a job that I wanted.

Janie stayed silent next to me, but nodded her head.

"Are you serious?" Paul asked, his eyes bulging out.

I pulled the long grass aside, allowing him to see the mound we were talking about. He stepped forward and his mouth dropped open.

"Oh, my God," he said. "Petra," he stopped again.

I was a bit confused on what Paul's take on all of this was, but the shock of it certainly registered with me.

"Is that?" he stammered again.

He stayed quiet and looked over at Janie.

"Do you think she's in there?" Janie asked him, her voice quiet but firm.

"I think we should find out," he said. "And just for clarity, because this day can't get any more messed up, we're all on the same page that we're talking about Carrie, right?"

Janie

Just as we started to dig, my cellphone rang. Since we only had two shovels, I passed mine over to Lisa, who had given hers to Paul. It was Sam. Shit.

Trying to sound as casual as I could, I hit the button and pulled it up to my face. Just in the past few seconds, the wind had picked up, making it hard to hear. The panic in Sam's voice was unmistakable though, even with the distraction of the howling wind.

"Where are you?" he asked. "I woke up and you're gone."

"I'm here. I'm just outside talking to Lisa," I said, keeping my voice casual.

"In the driveway? I don't see you," Sam said. He sounded freaked out and that broke my heart.

Lisa and Paul had stopped digging and were looking at me with raised brows.

"No, I'm in the backyard," I said, my heart beating fast.

"Honey, why aren't you inside? We don't know what happened to Carrie. There could be a killer out there. Can you come in?" he begged.

"Of course. I'll be right in," I said, shaking my head and internally scolding myself for being such an ass.

I hung up and grabbed Lisa's arm.

"I'm so sorry, but I have to go back in there. Sam is looking for me and he sounds scared," I said. "Can we do this later?"

"Girl, go back in. We got this," Lisa said.

"No, I can't leave you guys to do this," I said. "This was my crazy idea. Give me another hour and I'll make sure he is settled then slip out."

"Sam has been through enough. We can't risk him getting wind of this," Lisa said.

I winced and put the phone back in my pocket. That hurt. I knew what she was really saying in the kindest way possible was, "He's been through enough with your drinking and possible relapse."

"I'm sorry, that was a stupid thing to say," Lisa said. "I meant the Carrie thing not ..."

Lisa paused and moved her shovel around with her hand in awkward movements.

"No, it's okay," I said, pulling her in for a hug. "You're right. You're a good friend. The best."

Lisa squeezed me tight and said, "No, you're the best. We got this. Go back to that lovely man and show him you are okay, because I know you are and will always be."

"Yes, go, Janie. We can do this. We'll text you with an update. Sam needs you. We don't normally like to ask of you ladies unless, it's absolutely necessary. Our egos are too big," Paul said with an encouraging smile.

"Thanks, Paul," I said, releasing a sigh. In my gut, it didn't feel right to leave them out here but what could I do?

"Text me," I said, handing my flashlight over and turning to go.

"We will," Lisa said.

I stumbled a little bit, slowing me down. I managed to hear the last bit of conversation before they began the dig.

"You ready?" I heard Paul ask Lisa.

"Born ready," I heard Lisa laugh back to him.

Petra

Just as I was zipping up my coat, I heard the garage door open.

"Shit," I mumbled, slipping into the bathroom next to the garage to buy some time.

What should I do? Should I take my coat off and hide it? But what about the people by the pond? I couldn't possibly tell Paul what I was doing. And what the hell was I doing? I was going to leave the kids alone in the house to go see what was going on. Dammit. He was right. I was slipping. That would have been a terrible mistake. I had just rushed them upstairs and put them all in bed. There was no way any of them were sleeping. What if I had left and they were wandering all over the house while I was in the back hunting random people with flashlights? Worse: what if the people I just saw with the flashlights were the ones that attacked and killed Carrie? What if they did it to me, and I was lying dead in the yard while the kids wandered around the house alone?

I shook my head and scrambled to take my coat off. Rolling it into a ball, I shoved it into the cabinet under the sink. I didn't feel like explaining to Paul why I was in my coat. After we had left the police station, I had promised him I would stay clear of Carrie's house.

Taking a deep breath, I put my hand on the door handle and allowed myself to feel the cold of the knob. I said my name quietly to stimulate my hearing, felt the cold of the knob, and leaned over to grab the soap dispenser, so I could smell the fruitiness of the soap.

"Stimulate all the senses," my therapist had told me. "It will calm the panic attack and trick the mind."

I set the soap down and opened the door to my entire family standing just outside the bathroom door.

"What are you guys doing out of bed?" I asked my kids, meeting Paul's eyes for just a quick second before reaching down to pick up our youngest, Devin.

"We heard Dad come home and wanted to see him," my oldest, Shane, said quickly.

"I'm hungry," Ellie whined.

"Everyone back upstairs," I demanded. "You are not hungry. You just had a million snacks with the movie. Go now," I said, sharper than I normally spoke to them.

This had been such a long day and the last thing I wanted to do was fight with my kids about bedtime. We were pretty strict about bedtime rules, which had paid off, but I'm sure they sensed that we were fried and wanted to take advantage of it.

"I'll take them up," Paul said, sounding completely wiped out. He reached over and took Devin from my arms.

I wanted to ask him a million questions. "Where have you been for the past few hours? And by the way, what the hell is in that safe? You know, the one that you intentionally changed the code for?"

The dark circles under his eyes kept me from going forward. He looked tired, worn, and his body felt cold. Freezing cold, in fact. I felt it on his arm when he pulled Devin from me. Had he been standing outside for the last few hours?

My mind churned constantly as he dragged the crew upstairs. Instead of following them, I ran back to the kitchen to look for the flashlights by the pond. Nothing.

I sighed and put my hands down on the cold granite. I had a basil plant growing next to the sink, so I grabbed it quickly and stuck my nose in it.

Making up my mind, I put it down and headed upstairs.

When I got to our master bedroom, I plopped down on the bed and waited for Paul. He came in a little bit later, with a smile on his face, which quickly disappeared when he saw me sitting there.

"Paul, where have you been?" I asked in a short and angry voice. It wasn't like him to go so off the radar. We were always on track of where each other were and who would be in charge of the kids. We had too many. We had to be in constant communication. For him to just go off the grid for a few hours was so out of character.

He didn't answer me right away, just stood there looking at me and rubbing his hands together. This pissed me off even more.

"Paul, why did you change the safe code?" I asked, tired of hiding my suspicions.

"Oh," he said.

"Oh?" I mimicked, feeling my stomach drop and anger rise. This was not the response I was looking for.

Lisa

Just as I was about to turn into my driveway, I had an idea. A scandalous, risky idea. So unlike the old Lisa. The Lisa that did everything right-raised the kids, ran the house, made the dinners, allowed the husband to do whatever he wanted and kept a dazzling smile on for the public. Maybe a little bit of her, or a lot of her, died when the marriage died. Good riddance to that Lisa. Would it be so terrible if I started making some irresponsible decisions?

I guess while the kids were still living at home it would be. I had to set an example for the girls. But it was late, and it wasn't like they were looking for me. My phone would be blowing up. I had even left a note on the kitchen table that said, "Be right back. Running out for milk," in case they were worried.

"Hmmm," I said, pulling up my phone and rolling through my texts.

After our unproductive dig, I'd shot Janie a text, telling her that all was good, and I'd call her in the morning. Keeping it brief, I'd said simply, "It wasn't what we thought." I wanted the text to be vague but get the point across that there was no body without saying there was no body. Maybe I was being paranoid, but what if the police suspected her, or even me at this point, and were somehow reading my texts or want to read them in the future?

Coming down from the raging paranoia of our search for Carrie, I had the intense need to do something fun, something light.

I shot Erik a text.

Are you up?

I was surprised when the three lights popped up immediately, signaling me that he was writing me back. This was pretty late for him to be up. I personally had to start a shift in the morning at seven, but the pulse of a new crush kept me going. I could make up for the lost sleep later.

I am. Everything okay?

I'd rushed him out the door when Janie had called me earlier about going to look for Carrie's body. My reaction to her news was so drastic that

I thought for sure he would write me off as a lunatic. I kind of felt like one after tonight. Did we really think we were going to find her?

> **I'm fine. Sorry for being such a crazy lady earlier. My friend was having a little emergency.**

I looked up at my house, checking to make sure no lights were on. It was still pitch black. My needy girls were maybe not as needy as they used to be.

Looking back at my phone, I noticed the dots had not yet appeared. Where was he? Maybe he just rolled over and went back to sleep. I wouldn't blame him.

> **So, you're sure you didn't rush me out because of my bad breath?**

The words appeared on my screen, and my heart flew. Good, he was still there.

> **Hahahaha, no, your breath was just fine. Delightful, in fact.**

I waited, wondering what was next. I should just go in and go to bed. Ask him to grab a drink after class tomorrow, something easy and fun. Take it slow. I was starting to feel like I really liked this guy. Or maybe, I had just not been properly kissed in way too long. Either way, I didn't want to scare him off.

> **This is really random, but since you are up, there is an all-night breakfast place right around the corner from me. You want to meet me there for some pancakes in fifteen minutes? I can't sleep.**

My mouth dropped open at his invitation. This was perfect. Innocent. A mutual ground where we couldn't get into any trouble. I wasn't ready for him to ask me over to his place. If he even had one. Holy crap, maybe he still lived with his parents. No, no way.

Tonight. I had to ask him his age tonight. This couldn't go on any longer like this without me knowing. And I had to come up with a number in my head that would be a deal breaker.

Or did I? I mean, as long as he was at least twenty-fiveish, which he had to be. He just had to be. He said this was his second career. And twenty-five would still make me a good ten years older than him. But I was just having fun, right? Being irresponsible? Wasn't that okay?

Look at what being responsible had taken me to? A big fat struggle. That's where the road of responsibility ended for me.

I thought briefly of Carrie and what we had done tonight. She seemed like a woman who took her responsibilities seriously. She had a family, a home, a husband. Everything that was supposed to qualify for the American dream. And where was she tonight? Who knew? Possibly in some shallow grave like we had thought?

I looked up one more time at the house and typed furiously on my phone.

I'm on my way.

Janie

Lying in my bed, I couldn't shake the feeling that something was wrong. I'd received the text from Lisa that the dig had not turned up anything, but it didn't satisfy me. I still felt shaky and unsettled. Sam snored lightly next to me, a high little whistle coming from his mouth as he breathed in and out. It had taken him a little while to fall asleep once I had returned home. I'd made up a story about taking a quick walk to calm my anxiety, which I was sure he hadn't bought. But the fact that I clearly wasn't high or drunk seemed to calm him.

I really wish I never would have had that episode at Petra's house on "Gaga Night." Now everyone doubted me. I could stay sober. I had the skills. But now everyone doubted me.

I sighed aloud, wondering what I could do to gain back their trust.

I guess that wasn't the right way to look at it. Wasn't that the story of every addict? They underestimated their addiction and overestimated their abilities to fight it off. And then they fell hard.

No, it was fine that my husband and close friends knew I was struggling. I had to admit it and own it. My career was gangbusters, my anxiety and stress were through the roof, my kids were trying to go to school during Covid and now, I was digging up random mud hills looking for my neighbor's body. Who wouldn't struggle in this time?

Grabbing my phone, I pulled up my realtor website to scroll through my listings in order to get my mind off of everything. The mental "to do" list was actually something that normally relaxed me and energized me. I truly did love my job. The feel of being successful and self-sufficient was the greatest high I could ever experience. More than anything I could get from pills or alcohol.

Tonight, while checking the website, the thing that grabbed me was how few listings I had up. Nearly everything was sold or under contract. Uh oh. I had to get more listings ASAP.

That was the biggest issue in the market right now. So many buyers moving out to the suburbs and fleeing the city, very few homes to sell. My home prices were up nearly 30% from just twelve months ago. Unbelievable. I needed to get more ads going, more social media, just more presence. That would be the first thing I went after in the morning.

I had hired a company to run more social media ads for me and that had worked pretty well, but everyone was doing that. I had my reputation, which definitely drew my locals, but perhaps I was going to have to branch out a bit.

This thought made my mind circle back to Heather. Why in the world had Carrie and Tom chosen Heather as their realtor? That seemed so odd to me.

I Googled her name quick and went into a deep dive for a few minutes. Just as I thought, she didn't have one other listing in the area. All of her sales focused on downtown Chicago high-rises and even some corporate locations for businesses. Well, we all knew that was dead in the water right now due to Covid. Maybe she was desperate.

But how desperate? I circled back to my previous theory of Carrie putting the kibosh on the sale of the house. Did Heather have it in her to kill over something like that? She seemed like an ass, but not necessarily a killer. She certainly didn't sound like a killer when I was hiding behind the bar and overhearing her filming and talking to her friend. She sounded scared and a little freaked out. She wouldn't be scared and suspicious like that if she had killed her. She would just be cold and matter of fact. Getting the film and getting out of there.

Unless she was setting up her story and making herself look naïve and unknowing as to what happened? What if she even knew I was there behind the bar and was playing me the whole time?

My head was spinning with all of my theories. All I knew for sure was that there was a lot of pressure on realtors right now. It had done enough of a number on me that I had almost started drinking again.

The sound of Sam's cell ringing startled me out of my thoughts. I sat up and shook his arm softly to try and wake him from his slumber. Apparently, he was in a deep sleep because the ringing of his phone had not been enough to wake him. He finally stirred and looked at me while rubbing at his eyes.

"What?" he whispered, in a hoarse tone.

"Your phone," I said, pointing to the bedside table. "It's ringing."

I leaned over and turned my light on to better stir him.

Who would be calling Sam in the middle of the night? His parents had passed long ago, and he was an only child, so it wasn't like there was a large extended family to think about.

"Hello," Sam finally said into the phone.

I sat up and watched him intently, grabbing for my phone to see if I had missed something. Maybe one of my siblings had tried calling me and I'd missed it earlier today.

No, nothing. No missed calls or texts.

"Oh, I see," Sam said calmly.

"Who is it?" I begged, desperate for something.

"It's Lisa's daughter, Veronica," Sam said.

"What's wrong?" I asked, interrupting his conversation. "Give me the phone," I demanded, trying to grab it from him.

I was so scared now that I didn't care if I was being rude or not. The last time I saw Lisa, I'd talked her into doing something she wasn't comfortable doing. Digging for a body.

Sam simply turned and held up his pointer finger.

"Hold on one second, sweetie," Sam said, pulling the phone away to finally speak to me.

"Veronica said she found a note from her mom on the counter saying she ran out to get milk. That was hours ago. Veronica said she just woke up and realized she hasn't come home, and she isn't responding to text or calls," Sam said. "Do you know where she is?"

I swallowed hard and let that sink in. Then, slowly shook my head no.

Lisa said that they hadn't found anything on the dig and that it, "wasn't what we thought it was." So, why wasn't she home? She would never have them worry like this. And she had an early morning shift. We'd talked about it.

I retraced my steps and reread her texts. I'd left her alone with Paul. Wait a minute.

Paul.

Petra had been having trouble with Paul. She'd been upset with him. Angry with him. Had she also been suspicious of him? Had it been right to trust Paul alone with Lisa? It had to be. Paul had been a close friend of our family for years, salt of the earth. He volunteered at school events, was always at his kids' games, seemed to work like a dog at his career but also put his family first.

But, did Paul have something to hide? And had Lisa found it? How did I even know that it was Lisa that had sent the last message? Maybe it was Paul sending the message from Lisa's phone.

I jumped up from my bed and started pacing the room.

Petra

"So, you are hiding something?" I said, knowing now that I was right to listen to my racing thoughts and my upset gut. I stood next to the safe with my hands on my hips, determined to get to the bottom of what was going on. I could take it. It would be so much better for me to know and go forward than to be hiding in the dark anymore.

At the same time, looking at my husband, I had a sinking feeling that what we had would forever be gone now. Our beautiful family, our bonds with our children, our elegant and much-loved home we worked so hard for. How could this be happening? Would I lose it all just like Janie had? Of course, I would. There was no way I could stay with him.

Paul stared at me, his mouth turned down in worry and his eyes refusing to leave mine. He slowly approached the safe.

"I am," he said, reaching out to me.

I pulled away from his grasp, feeling too hurt and repulsed by this moment to allow him to touch me.

He plugged on.

"I changed the safe because I was worried about you getting in there and seeing..." Paul stalled and ran his hand over his chin. Still in his dress clothes from the day, I had the sudden urge to throw a glass of red wine all over his perfectly pressed white shirt. I wanted to stain him just like he was about to put a stain on our marriage. Forget about me, how were our kids ever going to get past this betrayal? How would they ever be able to develop healthy relationships of their own when their own father was a scumbag? My mind raced and raced, twenty years into the future. I couldn't stop it.

"The kids. I couldn't risk it," he said finally.

The kids? What did he have in there? Underwear from his mistress? Or inappropriate sexual toys for their time together?

I didn't get it. I'd worked so hard for so long to keep our marriage strong, to keep us on the same page, to keep us a priority. Yes, I was more absent during Covid. Yes, my job was more stressful and made me very distracted. He got put on the back burner for a bit but, come on. There had been times in our marriage that I had also been placed at a lower priority, especially when he was first building his business. I had hunkered down and been strong. Why couldn't he have given me that in return?

I shut my eyes and shook my head, feeling a deep anger growing inside of me. I was a doctor in the middle of a worldwide pandemic. With three young kids to worry about at home. This was probably ground zero, the absolute bottom I would hit in my life and what had Paul done? Cheat on me. I hated him in this moment.

"Please don't judge me. I'm embarrassed and confused by what I did, but I was scared," Paul said, leaning past me and punching in the code to the safe.

The door made a clicking sound and popped open. Paul stepped aside and motioned for me to take a look. I was confused by what he had just said. I felt like the roaring sound in between my ears halted for a second.

"Go ahead, take a look. I know you hate them and forbid them. Under normal circumstances, I agree, but the Black Lives Matter movement was on fire and the world was getting ransacked. I was scared for us, and there were so many rumors floating around. I didn't know what was true anymore. And, since we're being completely honest, I didn't like some of the people your brother was hanging around with. I got scared," he said, watching me closely. His hands were on his hips now, but he didn't look defensive.

If anything, he looked relieved. The muscles in his face were relaxed, and he spoke easy and soft. Peeking into the safe, I jumped back, seeing the gun tucked in between papers and other familiar boxes that held his expensive watches.

"Paul," I whispered, not knowing what else to say.

"Petra, I'm really sorry. I just kept thinking that if something were to happen, if riots spread to the suburbs, and I didn't do anything to protect my family, I would regret it. What kind of father would I be?" he said, stepping closer to me.

My eyes filled with tears, overwhelmed by his betrayal of our agreement to not keep any guns in the house but also understanding how the mania of 2020 could have forced him there.

"I thought ..." I said, trying to form the words.

"You thought we agreed not to have guns? We did. I did this behind your back, and I'm so sorry. I've been trying to figure out a way to tell you for the last few months, but I just couldn't. You were going through so much with your brother and COVID and, just, all of it," he said, reaching out again to touch my arm. This time I let him.

"I'm so ashamed that as a black man, I sheltered in my home and bought a gun because I was anxious about the movement getting out of control. What does that say about me?" Paul asked, looking past me. His mouth was turned down again and his eyes darkened with stress.

"Oh, Paul," I said, coming forward to take him into my arms. "I've been so checked out."

Paul pulled me in tight to him and put his head down into my hair.

"I've missed you so much. I felt like you were gone, and I had to hold down the fort and make the decision," he said, his voice shaky and broken.

"I was gone," I said, giving him my honest answer. My guilt and my grief had swallowed me whole. Paul's fears hadn't even registered with me.

"But now I'm not gone. I promise," I said, tearing up and holding onto him tighter.

"But I want that gun gone," I said, pulling away and looking up into his eyes that glistened with hope, relief, and love.

"Done," he said, looking down at me and pulling my face up to his to kiss me.

Lisa

I am living my best life. Seriously. My best life. In a pancake house, shoving fluffy, buttery cakes into my mouth in the middle of the night with the most attractive man I've ever laid eyes on. This could not be happening to me. This was just not the way things went down for me normally.

"More syrup," Erik asked, passing me the little bowl of amber liquid we were sharing.

He winked at me and nodded, while shoving a huge forkful of pancakes through his perfect teeth. I loved watching him chew. There was something so sexy about watching the way he attacked his food without hesitation. I pictured him being the same way in bed: confident and aggressive, yet joyful and smiling the whole time. Good Lord, slow your horses, Lisa.

"Tell me again how you found this place," I said, accepting his offer of syrup.

It wasn't until we'd sat down that it kicked in how hungry I really was. I'd been going a million miles an hour in all ways at all times. I couldn't remember the last time I'd sat down and actually enjoyed a meal. I was always shoving something in my mouth while I was working, studying, racing kids to events. Apparently, the only way I was ever going to enjoy food again was to eat in the middle of the night.

"If I tell you, do you promise not to laugh?" he asked.

"I swear," I said, watching his cheeks flush a bit. We sat in an orange leatherette booth; straight out of the classic diners I'd gone to as a kid with my parents. There was something very nostalgic and comforting about the plump seats that made noise when you moved around in them.

"My high school buddies and I used to come here for late night eats after partying," he said, releasing a laugh.

"Oh," was all I managed.

"What?" he smiled.

"I was just wondering how long ago that was?" I asked, trying to sound casual but failing miserably. I choked a little bit on my question and pulled a napkin quickly to my face to keep me from spewing pancake crumbs all over the table. So much for my laid-back cougar cover.

"Are you trying to find out how old I am? My baby face scaring you a bit?" he laughed, patting my back a little bit as my coughing continued.

Good. We were finally going to talk about this. It had to happen sometime. Might as well be in the middle of the night at The Pancake Joint before I made more of a fool of myself.

I nodded and reached for my water, my eyes tearing up.

"You okay?" Erik asked kindly, grabbing for more napkins. "I promise you it's not as bad as you think."

Gulping down my water, I finally felt ready to speak again.

"Sorry. Went down the wrong pipe. I'm ready," I said, smiling back at him.

Erik scooted over in the booth closer to me, setting his fork down on the table. Feeling a bit insecure and unsure about exposing our relationship to the public, I looked around, making sure no one was watching us. We were still the only ones in the restaurant, besides the lone waitress who busied herself behind the counter.

Turning back to him, Erik smiled down at me, his body now touching mine. He leaned down and kissed me, taking me by surprise. His soft lips tasted like syrup and butter. I didn't want to stop. Who would see us anyways?

"I'm twenty-nine," he said, pulling away from me just a bit and staring into his eyes.

I nodded my head, taking this in and trying my best to hide my freak out. Twenty-nine. Holy shit, eight years difference. Could I handle that? It was better than I thought. But almost worse because now it was not totally unrealistic for us to be together. When I thought he was twenty, that made the whole thing laughable. Almost like a joke. A stupid, really, really stupid crush. Inappropriate even. But now, there was a possibility.

Hell, if I was a man, there wouldn't even be a question. I could go for it without society even batting an eye. But a woman would be judged.

And even though this was way, way off in the future kind of conversation, would he want kids? I was thirty-seven. Would I be able to give him children?

"So, are you going to say anything?" Erik spoke softly, rubbing my face with his right hand while his left arm snuck behind me in the booth and pulled me closer.

"I'm not sure what to say, honestly," I said, smiling up at him.

"I guess you only have to answer one question right now," Erik said, watching me closely and flashing me a sexy smile.

"What is that?" I asked.

My mind raced to a million things. What was he going to ask? Would I spend the night? Could we date exclusively? Would I like more pancakes? Could he move in with me because his mom was kicking him out? I knew so little about him. I needed to know more. How did a man this sexy, this put together, or so it seemed, manage to stay single until twenty-nine? Maybe he wasn't? Maybe he was married? There had to be more to this story. That was the only certainty. I had to learn more.

"Can I keep kissing you?" he asked, running his hand up to my hair and pulling me close to his lips.

He kept his parted lips inches from mine until I responded. I looked into his warm, kind eyes, and nodded my head yes. That was the other certainty. I was certain I enjoyed kissing him.

Janie

I had to get back out there. Now. What if Paul had done something to Lisa and left her there? What if he had hurt her? Or worse, what if he had killed her? And Carrie?

Had I really left my friend Lisa out there to face a killer alone?

"Sam, I have to go," I said, racing around the room, looking for clothes to put on. What had I done with the sweatpants I had on earlier? I put my hand up to my head, feeling like I had a tornado in there. My mind was spinning.

"What? Go where?" Sam asked, still holding the phone up to his ear. His normally slicked, gray hair was poking out in all different directions from his head, and his open mouth made him look scared to death.

"I'm going to go over to Lisa's house and sit with the girls until she comes home. This isn't like her," I said, thinking quick on my feet. It was a little frightening how quickly the lies came to me. It was too easy.

I motioned with my hand for him to give me the phone, and he immediately appeared to relax. Like he was happy I was making a reasonable choice. Of course, I would go sit with them.

"I'll go, too," he said, pulling the blankets back and swinging his legs over the bed.

"No," I said, a little too forcefully.

I reached over to take the phone from him and said, "We can't leave the girls alone."

"We'll all go," Sam said, putting his feet into the pair of slippers he kept by the bed.

There was something about seeing him place his feet into the slippers that broke my heart. I bought those for him last year. They were meant to keep his feet warm, but I'd spent an exorbitant amount of time researching which slippers would give the best grip. I'd been worrying about him falling since he had slipped on the floors after I'd had them waxed last year. We all had, but there was something about the idea of Sam falling that had sent me into a spiral. He couldn't get hurt. The girls and I were young and healthy, we could withstand an injury. My poor, sweet Sam wouldn't take a break as well.

"Please, keep them here, honey," I begged. I didn't have to fake worry, I had enough of it in me to be able to express fear and worry without having to act. "What if," I trailed off, knowing that the girls were still listening on the other line.

Sam simply met my eyes and nodded his head.

"Veronica, I'm on my way. Tell me everything," I said into the phone. I leaned in to kiss Sam goodbye, grabbed an extra sweatshirt and bolted out the door. "I'll leave this phone downstairs on the kitchen table," I whispered to Sam.

After I'd made it halfway down the stairs, I had a thought. What if Paul tried to hurt me?

No, that was crazy. This was crazy. It was Paul. How had I even gotten to where I was in my mind right now?

Because there were now two women missing from the same neighborhood, the only other real suspect, Tom, Carrie's husband, was in Florida, and Petra had been acting strange about her husband. Suspicious. I knew she knew more than she was telling us. There was a reason for her anger toward her husband. And most importantly, my MIA friend, Lisa, had last been seen with Paul. My first suspect, Heather, was looking less and less likely to be involved. Why would she go after Lisa, too? That didn't make sense.

I thought of the gun we kept in a safe in the closet. How could I possibly get it without Sam seeing? I couldn't let him see that.

As though the universe decided to help me out, I watched as Sam walked slowly out of our room and down the hall. He must have decided to go check on the girls. He seemed so laser focused on doing so, that somehow, he never turned to look at the stairs where I stood completely frozen. I couldn't believe my luck.

As soon as he passed me, I bolted back to our room to the gun safe. In the years post my divorce, I had gone through a stage where self-preservation and self-protection were all I thought about. Though I was never physically harmed by my ex, I was emotionally abused enough, to the point that I wanted protection around me at all times.

Taking shooting lessons had been very rewarding. The lessons made me feel strong, capable, and most importantly, like I was taking some kind of control of my life, which had gone completely off the rails. Sam didn't love that I had a gun, but he'd allowed it because I always kept it locked up. Until tonight.

Grabbing my ammunition and gun, I turned and made a beeline for the stairs, as quietly as I could.

I was so sick of men taking advantage of women. Praying on their weaknesses. This time, if Paul came for me, if he had come for Lisa, I was going to be ready.

Petra

After my shower, I dried off, tucked myself in a robe and approached the mirror over the double sinks with a new confidence. It was time to let some things go. The mental scars I was carrying were eating me from the inside out. How was I ever going to heal?

I opened one of the small drawers next to my sink and pulled out a brochure my therapist had passed onto me. She had recommended I start group grief therapy on top of the individual grief therapy I'd been going to. I'd been reluctant. So reluctant that I had dropped the brochure in a bathroom drawer and had forgotten about it. Sort of. I guess I had not. What I had actually done was make a point to not open this drawer again, so I wouldn't have to face the brochure.

It was time to get serious about taking care of my grief, though. It was taking over me. I thought of Janie. She had been able to experience a lot of healing and help by doing a group therapy session in her addiction groups. Why did I think it was okay to push her to do it but not be willing to explore that route myself? I knew what worked for my patients. Having people around who were going through similar experiences was some of the best mental work you could do. It was proven to be effective and healing. So, why was I above it? Because I was stuck on my title. Doctor Petra was above what she pushed for her patients. She didn't need it.

I stared at my reflection, shaming myself for becoming such a narcissist. No more. It had to stop here. Or I was going to lose everything.

In the reflection of the mirror, through the doorway, I could see Paul's large body, spread out on our bed, fast asleep. After our heated conversation, we'd made love and it had been wonderful. Soul connecting, like it used to be. I still couldn't believe he had gone out and bought a gun, brought it into our house and hid it from me. That was shocking. We used to share everything. The fact that he did that and had kept it from me for so long was a wake-up call. I had to tune back into our marriage. But I had some internal cleanup to do first in order to be able to do that.

In the morning, I was going to contact this group therapy team and get on board. Even if it was just Zoom meetings. Didn't matter. It was time to be an active participant in the recovery of Petra.

Pulling my robe open, I looked at the scars on my legs and lower arms. I shook my head, again shaming myself for allowing these scars to take control of my happiness. Paul didn't care. The kids had seen them, didn't care. Yes, it would be a lifetime of explaining them to strangers who had the balls to ask where I got them.

"I got them from trying to save my brother's life," I said quietly to my reflection.

That would knock out about seventy percent of the nosy questioners. The other thirty percent of really ballsy people would press on. If they did, I could just walk away.

But you should have tried to save his life earlier, then you wouldn't have those scars.

Ugh. My guilty conscience never gave up. There was a solution to that, too, though. Janie had been pushing me to go to Al-Anon, another group therapy-based program that helped family members and loved ones of addicts get through the trauma of having to live with or have a relationship with an addict. Tomorrow I needed to sign up for that one, too. Time for some control.

"It wasn't my fault," I said to my reflection.

I glanced back at Paul's sleeping prone form, wondering if he was hearing his crazy wife talk to herself. I rubbed lotion onto my face and closed my eyes, thinking about my relief that the only thing Paul was hiding was a gun. What a crazy turn life had taken.

This thought made my mind immediately bounce back to Carrie. What was to come of that situation? It was almost too heavy to think about. I'd given the police everything I knew. That burden at least felt a bit lighter. Now they had to do their due diligence. I'd tried to search the house, the surrounding grounds, etc. I didn't think Carrie was there anymore. That was my gut. We'd all searched and come up with nothing. Eventually the truth would come out.

My phone beeped quietly, alerting me to a text coming in. Shoot, I'd forgotten to silence it like I always did unless I was on-call. I'd turned it on when Paul was out tonight because I was anxious to hear from him.

Are you home? Is Paul with you?

The text from Janie struck me as extremely odd. Of course, I was home. And of course, he was with me. What was she talking about?

I picked up the phone and was about to call her when something in me made me glance in the mirror again. That's when I noticed the bed was empty. Paul was no longer there.

Lisa

"I really have to get going," I said, reluctantly.

My stomach was full, my heart was pounding, and my libido was the size of the Empire State Building. Good Lord, he made me hot. And the forbidden, yet not quite totally taboo age gap had me even more turned on. I simply didn't care who was watching us or who saw what. Which meant I had to get out of here.

"Do you have to?" Erik said, moving to my ear and whispering into it before giving it a little nibble.

"Yes, I do," I said, allowing him to nibble. He could have my ear if he wanted it.

I could only imagine what sex would be like with Erik. If he was this good of a kisser, generous and attentive, he was going to be an amazing lover. I could just tell by the way that my body responded to his, how his smell was welcoming and intoxicating to me, that we would have good chemistry. In my experience, you knew right away when you kissed someone if there were going to be fireworks or not.

That being said, my experience was pretty pathetic. I'd married my college sweetheart after getting pregnant. And the sex had been good. For a while at least. That was part of the problem. It had been good and held me in a bad situation for too long. Until I got too disgusted by who I learned Rick to be at his core, and my desire for him plummeted to zero.

I cringed visibly, unable to stop thinking about Rick the Dick. Ugh. An hour with Erik had wiped him completely from my brain. It had been glorious but not reality. Hadn't I just come up with a theory that Rick might be Carrie's killer a few hours ago? Forgot about that. Could he be a killer on top of an adulterer, a swindler, and a deadbeat dad? In my opinion, that was an absolute yes.

"What happened?" Erik asked, pulling back and running his hands through his curls. I loved the way he looked right now with his hair askew, his lips swollen and red, and his cheeks flushed with lust.

"What do you mean?" I asked, reaching around with my hand on the booth. I had to find my phone. Thinking of Rick made me realize that I'd not only blanked him out but all of my other responsibilities. Like my kids!

"Your face just got all scrunched up. You looked mad," he said, reaching out carefully and placing his hand on my face.

"I'm sorry. I'm not mad," I said, leaning in to kiss him quickly. "I'm just overwhelmed all of a sudden by having to get back to the girls. I've been gone for over an hour now, and I'm scared they are going to wake up and wonder where I am."

I kept reaching around but finding nothing.

"And where is my phone? You saw me bring it in, right?" I asked, feeling a little prick of panic start rising up.

"Honestly, I only saw you," Erik said, feeling around as well. "Hey, come on. Let's go. I can see you're worried. Let's go check your car and get you home. I'll go pay the bill at the counter."

I smiled quickly at Erik, grateful for his understanding. Perhaps I had left my phone in the car? I had been in a mad panic to get into the restaurant and see Erik with my own eyes. I was still in complete disbelief that he would want to see me. To meet me for a late-night rendezvous. Up until Erik, I had kind of written myself off as an old, used up hag. Now I felt amazing. Like life was finally giving me a break. Feeling around the bench one more time, I gave up and walked to the front of the restaurant. I noticed that it had started to snow outside, something I had been completely oblivious to during our hot make-out session over pancakes.

Once he had paid the bill, Erik walked over and opened the door for me, steering me out with a light hand on my back.

"Thank you for the pancakes," I said, feeling happy but completely anxious at the same time. I had to get to my phone.

"It was my pleasure. Thank you for the ..." Erik stopped, presumably searching for the right words.

We were in front of my car now, and peering through the window, I could see my cell phone was visible on the passenger seat. Instant relief.

I leaned in and kissed Erik, stopping him from having to find the words.

"I'll see you in class tomorrow?" I asked.

"Can't wait," he said, helping to open my door for me once I had unlocked the car. There was so much left unsaid, so much that we didn't figure out tonight, but it didn't seem to matter. Were we both okay with the age difference? Maybe. Maybe not. What kind of background did he come from? Would he be okay with dating a divorced woman? Did he want to get married in the future? Have kids?

All of these big-ticket items had been left on the table, not addressed. I didn't care. Why did I have to have all of these answers right now? We didn't.

After he slammed the door shut, I started the car up to warm it and quickly reached over and grabbed my phone. The clock on my car dashboard sent my mind reeling. I was going to get so little sleep tonight. How in the world would I function?

Glancing at my phone, my head started buzzing, and I could feel the blood in my veins speed up to a breakneck pace.

"Shit," I mumbled.

Janie

Stumbling along the path that led around my house to the pond, I paused for a second to make sure the gun was properly loaded. This gun had been my little secret. Well, a secret that Sam and I had. I could never hide this from him.

I hadn't felt comfortable telling anyone else. People could be very judgmental, especially in this heightened stress-filled time. Suburban moms could be cruel. And I just didn't want to hear it. The gun made me feel safe, it was the start of my new ass-kicking life after my ex, and it sure as hell was going to come in handy now.

Or was it?

Had I completely misjudged this whole situation? What if my first theory was right and Heather had been behind Carrie's disappearance, not Paul, and Lisa was fine?

But the reality was, the girls had called to say Lisa was missing, and the last time I saw Lisa, she was digging up a grave with Paul. She wasn't answering calls or texts. Lisa, just like Carrie, was now MIA. And they both had a direct link to Paul.

Checking that the safety was on, I stuffed the gun into my coat pocket. The snow was coming down in drifts now, and I was barely able to see a few feet in front of me. But my journey wasn't that far, and I knew exactly where I was going. Nothing was going to stop me.

Wait a minute. I'd just had a major misstep. My plan was to pull the car out of the garage to make Sam think that I'd left to head to Lisa's house and then circle back on foot. I'd completely forgotten to do that because I was so frantic about getting out to the pond.

Now what? Should I go back?

I had to. If not, I would be worrying the whole time that Sam would be out here looking for me. It was hard to keep track of lies. That's why there shouldn't be any in the first place.

This was all Carrie's fault. Or maybe not. Maybe it was all her husband's fault. Tom, if you had been nicer to your wife, she wouldn't have gone missing. Or maybe it was Heather's fault. Maybe she got greedy and killed her. Or, maybe, just maybe, this was Paul's fault. Maybe he had an affair with Carrie because he had been feeling neglected by Petra while she was consumed by her grief and her job.

NO. You know who was really at fault? The pandemic! It had made us all nuts. That was the only theory that I knew to be rock solid. Everything else was a wild goose chase.

Once I made it back to the garage, I jumped in the car and pulled away, inching my way along the street. Geez, it was really bad out here. The snowstorm had come on like a beast. I just hoped wherever Lisa was, she was being careful. If she was alive.

I parked just far enough away that Sam wouldn't be able to spot me, but as close as I could to limit how far I would have to walk to the lake. Cutting in between the houses, I cursed to myself thinking about the whole camera scandal. I'm sure I was coming up on someone's security camera, but at this point, I didn't care. I just needed to get back to where I had last left Lisa.

By the time I made it to the pond, I was freezing, my toes completely frozen. Icicles were starting to form on my eyelashes. I was going to buy better boots tomorrow. For as much as the ones I was wearing cost, they were clearly not working. I wasn't leaving Chicago in the foreseeable future. It was time to invest in a better pair.

Well, I wasn't leaving unless I froze to death out here. Or got killed.

That thought sent me into action. I began waving away the tall grass, trying to find where we had found the mound. Seeing as I was turning into a human snowman, I felt a little disoriented. I'd arrived at the mound area from a completely different direction. I kept trying to look back and use my own home as a marking point, because I knew that what I had spotted had been kiddy corner from my house.

Getting frustrated, I was just about to give up and call Paul. What was I going to say though? Get out here and show me where you killed Lisa?

No. I wouldn't allow myself to go there yet. There had to be another explanation. A safe, reasonable explanation where everyone comes out of this unharmed and alive.

Just as I was about to turn and give up, I spotted it. I'd been nearly on top of it the whole time, but in my delirium from the cold and the stress, I'd walked by.

"Lisa?" I called out, looking around just to see if she was out here. Maybe Paul had been called back home and Lisa had volunteered to finish the dig? Maybe she had fallen and accidentally hit her head? If so, her phone would be out here with her.

I dug into my pocket and pulled out my phone with shaking hands. No calls or messages from Lisa yet. Just a response from Petra that Paul was home with her.

That didn't tell me anything. But it did indicate that she didn't know about Lisa being missing.

I tried calling Lisa's phone, hoping I would hear the ringing over the wind and snow that was swirling around me. After three times calling, I gave up. I'd heard nothing but the howling of the wind. She wasn't out here.

I pulled the grass back again to really take a close look in the area they had done the digging.

My stomach dropped as I took in the details. There was no mistaking that the grave appeared much bigger than when I last saw it with Paul and Lisa. The dirt appeared higher and more spread out. Almost like there was more buried in there now.

Petra

My phone buzzed on the bathroom counter, pulling my attention back. Where could Paul have gone?

Janie was calling now. I had to pick up. Walking over to the bathroom door, I peeked out into the room and sure enough, he had vanished completely now. Maybe he had gone down to his office? We were both famous for getting up in the middle of the night with work worries, especially Paul, being the owner of his own business.

I shut the door completely and took Janie's call.

"Hello?" I said into the phone. My voice was filled with worry and concern. Perhaps she had been taken in for questioning as well? Maybe they had spotted her on the film. But no, that had been Lisa I dragged over to Carrie's house, not Janie.

"Petra," Janie said loudly into the phone.

I could barely make out her words because the connection was garbled and broken. It sounded like she was in some kind of windstorm. Could she be outside?

"Where are you?" I asked, trying to remain calm.

"I'm outside near the pond. I have to talk to you. Can you meet me out here?" she asked.

At first, I didn't respond. I didn't know what to say. She sounded so heightened and on edge, my mind went to a bad place. My guess was Janie had hit her threshold and was drinking. Why else would she sound like this?

"Janie, what are you doing by the pond?" I asked, trying to remain neutral sounding. I remembered how painful it was to feel discredited by friends. When I had tried to tell them and Paul that something was up next door at Carrie's house and no one believed me. That had hurt. And I had been right.

"I'm looking for Carrie, I mean, Lisa," Janie said.

It sounded like her lips were vibrating, like her teeth were chattering. I looked out the window of the bathroom. Was she one of the flashlights I thought I spotted earlier? I'd been so distracted by my argument with Paul,

I'd pushed this out of my mind. To get a better view, I walked across the room and turned the lights off. Sure enough, with the bathroom darkened, the storm was more pronounced and things looked much scarier out there.

What the hell was she doing?

"I'm coming out to find you," I said immediately. "Where exactly are you? Is Sam with you?" I scanned the pond and detected a weak light in between my house and Carrie's.

"I'm alone. Please come … one. I don't … you to … Paul with you," she said.

"What?" I asked, feeling as though I had possibly heard her wrong. The wind was cutting into her words, making her very difficult to understand. Did she just say she didn't want me to bring Paul with me? Why would she say that? Was she so drunk that she was embarrassed to be seen by him? Or was there something else at play here?

My mind raced back to where I had been earlier. I had had my suspicions on Paul, and here they were rising up again.

I flipped the light back on, trying my best to keep myself from spiraling. As soon as I did that, the door popped open and Paul stood there on the other side of it, glaring at me.

I jumped back, shocked by his sudden reappearance.

"What's going on?" he asked, his eyebrows scrunched down as he watched me closely.

I just shook my head, a wave of confusion flowing through my body, knocking me back and forth.

"Hurry … cold … shovel," I heard Janie say before the line went dead.

I looked down at the phone and back at Paul.

"Who was that?" Paul asked, entering the room.

"Janie," I said simply. "She's outside looking for Lisa."

Paul's eyes widened and his hand went immediately up to his mouth. After a moment, he simply shook his head, closing his eyes.

Lisa

"Oh, my God," I mumbled over and over while scrolling through my phone. I had missed over fifteen calls from my kids and my friends. Even Rick the Dick had called me. What the hell had I been thinking?

I should have been honest about where I was. I should have shared my location with my kids on my phone. We'd gotten in a tiff over them not wanting to share theirs a few weeks ago. Like a fool, I had stubbornly stopped sharing my location with them to teach my teenagers a lesson. What an ass I was.

I was acting exactly the way I didn't want my girls to act. What kind of example would I be to them? Not being up front and honest with them? That was exactly what I preached to them all the time. Just tell me. Tell me what is bothering you, what you want, what you don't want. I constantly begged them. Be honest with me and we'll be able to work through anything. I wasn't paying them the same respect, though, and now they were freaking out.

My heart sank thinking about their little faces at home, worrying about me and where I was. Maybe I should call them quick.

Wait.

Maybe this wasn't just about me. Maybe there was something else going on. I hadn't even read the texts. I'd just noticed the missed calls and all the texts and went into a frenzy. Good God. Maybe something was really wrong.

I reached over to grab my phone, and the car started sliding. I put my hands on the wheel and did my best to gain control of the car, pumping the brakes in desperation. The snow was coming down in gusts, and my wipers worked furiously to fight back the icicles on the windshield. The roads were nearly deserted. Only me, the fool blinded by lust, was out here trying to meet up with someone during this storm. What had I been thinking?

My last thought before hitting the lamppost were of the pancakes I'd just eaten. How selfish I had been tonight. Those pancakes and kisses had been sweet but not worth the cost I was going to pay.

Janie

"Crap!" I yelled after dropping my phone into the long grass. I was so cold now that my fingers were numb and clumsy, and my fine motor skills were failing me.

"Petra!" I yelled out just in case the line hadn't disconnected. I was hoping that I could find my phone by listening to the sound of her voice. No such luck. The wind was so loud at this point that even if the connection was still there, I probably wouldn't be able to hear her.

I grabbed frantically at the grass, pushing it side to side and looking around. In my quick movements, I lost my footing and fell on top of the mound, my body clumsy with fatigue and cold. Lying on top of the mound, my only thought was that perhaps I was lying on top of two bodies now, my friend Lisa being one of them.

I scrambled up to my feet, my survival skills kicking in. Time for a change of plan. Forget the phone. It was gone now. I had to get to Petra.

Turning away from the pond, I squinted to try and make out the large mountainous shape that was Petra's home in the distance. There were a few lights burning, enough to guide me in the right direction. Time to move.

I ran through the snow as quick as I could, approaching the side of her house adjacent to Carrie's. As expected, there were no lights on at Carrie's house, a depressing thought. How would we ever move on from this, all of this? A sudden gripping fear took hold of me for Lisa. Up until this point, I'd been running on adrenaline, but the reality of Lisa being in danger, or worse, shot through me like a bolt of lightning. How had it led to this?

I made it to the side of Petra's house and leaned in against the brick wall. I needed a minute to gather myself and put a plan in place. Taking my gloves off, I rubbed my hands together as fast as I could and breathed into them to try and make them come back to life.

I knew how to get into Petra's house without ringing the bell. We'd shared the garage door code with each other for emergencies. But they would hear the garage door opening. That would kill the element of surprise. I had asked Petra to come out here, so maybe she was already on the move. I should have waited for her at the mound. She would have found me. Dammit.

Moving closer to the front of the house, I felt suddenly very confused and turned around. Was this even the right house? Holy shit, I was really losing it. How long had I even been out here? If I had a phone, I could check. If I had a phone, I could call the police instead of trying to solve this on my own like some vigilante.

The sound of Paul's voice made me freeze in place.

"Where are you exactly?" I heard Paul ask someone in an aggressive tone.

He sounded angry and that scared me. But also motivated me at the same time. I had to do something. Men. They all thought they could just do whatever they wanted. Not tonight.

Inching my way closer to the front of the house, I peeked into the open garage. I spotted Paul holding a phone to his ear and walking back into the house. Seeing my window, I seized this opportunity to bolt into the garage and hide behind one of the cars. Pulling my gun out, I prepped it and waited.

"Please, just come back," I heard Paul's voice say, taking on a softer, gentler tone. "This is nuts. We'll figure it out together."

Who was he talking to? Petra? Or someone else?

Paul kept coming in and out of the garage, pacing and appearing very agitated. I waited a few more minutes to try and hear more to understand what was going on.

"No, wait, don't hang up, babe," I heard him plea.

After a second, I heard him curse and hit something very hard.

"Shit," he yelled again, this time much louder.

Before I could adjust my position, Paul was suddenly in front of me on the driveway, dressed in full winter gear, his large form pacing back and forth. He seemed to make a decision and came straight for me, his eyes looking up over my head to the shovels that hung on the wall behind me. I froze, hoping that if I remained still like a statue, he wouldn't see me.

No such luck.

"Janie?" Paul said softly, his eyes wide in shock and his hand frozen in a reach to get the shovel.

I stood quickly, holding the gun out while watching my arms shake in fear.

"Don't come any closer, Paul," I managed, trying my best to gather any courage I could.

Petra

Racing through the snow drifts, I called her name over and over in vain. What was she doing out here? The snow was so heavy at this point, I'd barely been able to see in front of me, let alone all the way to the pond.

I'd assured Paul I would be home as soon as possible, and that I could do this on my own. At this point, I had to ignore his calls for a second and concentrate. I was the one that started this in the first place, so I needed to end it. We all still didn't know where Carrie was, but what I did know for sure was that we had to let the police handle it. This was going too far.

"Janie!" I yelled again, hoping that she would hear me over the whistling, howling wind. Peeking over at her house, I noticed that as the minutes passed, more and more lights popped on. Good. Maybe I did need more help out here. We didn't need any more missing women.

Finally making it to the tall grass, I yelled again in vain. That wasn't working, and I needed to save my energy. I got a gut feeling that Janie wasn't out here. If she had been, it felt like she was no longer. I didn't feel her. And what crazy person would be out here right now?

I turned to head back to the house, determined to take Paul up on his offer to help. Scratch my previous thought; I couldn't do this on my own. Enough of the tough girl act. In fact, I was going to call the police as soon as I got home to help out tonight. This weather was nothing to mess around with. It was freezing.

Oh, God. Wait. What if Janie had fallen and was unable to respond to me?

I grabbed my phone from my pocket thinking if I called it enough, and she was really out here, eventually I would hear it and find her.

Looking down at my screen I was shocked to see that I had two missed calls from the hospital. What was this about?

Making a decision, I turned in the direction of my house and ran. Could this night be any more stressful? Now what was happening at the hospital?

Just as I was closing in on my house, the phone rang again. I stopped and looked down, noticing that this time, the call was coming directly from my office, which usually meant my friend, Maggie, at the hospital.

What the hell?

I fumbled with my gloves, pulling them off with my teeth and doing my best to hit the button to accept the call.

"Maggie?"

"Yes, Petra, it's Maggie," I heard her calm, professional voice say. That frightened me even more. Maggie was always bubbly and fun, even in the darkest of times. To hear her voice turn somber meant the world was ending.

"Maggie, I hear you," I said, trying my best to put my doctor cap on and remain calm.

"Honey, I think you better get to the hospital. Your friend was just checked in," she said warmly. Her voice was shaking, something I hadn't heard in all the years I worked with her.

"I'm on my way," I said, running now to my car.

My mind was racing, trying to figure out how they had found Janie so fast. I had just been speaking to her on the phone. Had she hung up and called the police immediately?

As I rounded the corner to my garage, the phone still up to my ear, I halted in my tracks to the sight of Paul standing in the driveway, his huge form frozen in place and his hands in the air. Though this was shocking to see, what was worse was that my friend, Janie, was holding a gun directed at him.

I dropped my phone and instinctively put my hands up in the air as well. I wasn't scared, just confused. This had to be a misunderstanding that we would figure out.

But if Janie was here, what had Maggie meant?

Janie didn't turn her gaze from Paul, and he wouldn't look away from me. Finally putting it together, I broke the silence.

"Janie, Maggie just called from the hospital. Lisa is there," I said in my calm, doctor voice. "We have to go. Now."

"What?" Janie said, finally looking over at me while keeping her arms raised with the gun pointed at my husband.

Lisa

The pain was unbearable. And then it wasn't.

I was kissing him again and it was amazing. And then I wasn't.

This cycle seemed to go on for a long time. Lights and darkness. Happiness and then pain.

Where was I? Who was I? Who cared? I did. Or I didn't?

Janie

"But who were you just talking to?" I demanded.

"Petra," Paul said calmly, his hands up to the sky. "I was talking to Petra. She was looking for you." He bounced his eyebrows up and held them there.

"But what's out there? What did you find? Why is the mound so big?" I shrieked. "She's out there."

"Janie," I heard Sam's shocked voice say. He appeared suddenly on the driveway and looked at me with big saucer round eyes. "What are you doing?" he asked. His hand grabbed onto the side of the garage as though for support. Seeing my husband's gesture of weakness rocked me.

"He … did something to Lisa." I said, trying my best to sound confident, though now I was just starting to feel crazy.

"No, Janie, I didn't. I promise," Paul said, keeping his hands up in the air still. "We found a dog buried out there. And then she went home. I promise you. I can go show you now."

"A dog?" My head was spinning. "Not Carrie?"

"Oh no," Petra said, finally speaking up. "I'm so sorry. This is all my fault. I got us all spooked. Janie, the hospital just called. Maggie said Lisa is there. I don't know any details, but it does not sound good. We have to go there now."

"Did you hurt her?" I asked, turning on Paul. For some reason, I couldn't give it up. I didn't trust anything or anyone right now.

"I promise you; I didn't touch her. We dug up the dog, we put it back, I saw her go to her car. That's it," Paul said. "I swear, I left her by her car unharmed."

"Janie, we have to go now," Petra said, walking quickly to me and raising her hand in request for the gun. I hesitated and finally relented. She took it and set it down on the ground.

"Paul, will you stay with the kids?" she said.

My eyes looked over to Sam. He was still watching me with sad, desperate eyes. We connected for a moment, but then I registered Paul's huge form moving closer to the gun. I grabbed onto Petra, bracing for what, I didn't know.

Paul reached down quickly and grabbed the gun.

"No," I said, moving forward, prepared to fight him for possession of the gun.

To my surprise, he simply unloaded it, and then motioned for Sam to take it. Sam walked over and put both hands out for Paul to place the gun in them. He did, and Sam stood there, looking at Paul, clearly unsure of what to do with a gun. He was terrified of them. He'd never even seen mine. We'd just had a quiet agreement that it was locked up safe in the house and that was that.

"Sam, I'll call you from the hospital," I said, doing my best to pull my shit together. I still wasn't completely sure of what was happening, but I knew for sure Sam was scared.

"I'm going to call Abby to come over ASAP, and I'll meet you at the hospital," Paul said, referring to their nanny.

"I'll be there in a bit as well," Sam said.

"No," I responded quickly. The last thing I wanted was for Sam to be at the hospital, the epicenter of this pandemic. He was vaccinated, but still, there was no point in exposing him.

"Please stay home, Sam," I said, walking over to him. "I'll call you as soon as I can. I promise. Do you want me to put that away?" I asked, wanting to take the gun back from him and chuck it into the yard. It looked so out of place in his arms, and he looked so uncomfortable.

But part of me also wanted to take it back and reload it. I still felt unsure. Unsafe.

I guess bringing a gun into a hospital, though, was only going to take this situation from bad to worse.

"Wait a minute," I said, patting my coat. "I just remembered I lost my phone by the pond."

"What?" Sam said raising his eyebrows.

I shrugged my shoulders with a sheepish look.

"Never mind, I got this, honey. Just go," he said, nodding his head.

"We have to go," Petra said again. She ran inside, presumably to get her purse, and Paul, Sam and I stood outside in awkward silence waiting for her.

"Janie, are you okay?" Paul asked softly.

For whatever reason, instead of feeling comforted by his concern, it only agitated me. Here I was again in the position of looking like a crazy woman who had overreacted. Probably how Petra had felt when she was trying to tell us about her concern for Carrie. Pushed aside.

"Paul, if you hurt Lisa, you're going down," I growled, surprised by my own intensity. "Sam, go home now. I'm worried about the girls."

Paul raised his hands in the air in a gesture of confusion. Sam simply turned and headed back to the house.

When Petra finally returned holding her giant Louis Vuitton purse, she didn't seem to even notice the tension in the air.

"We'll take the Mercedes," she said, in her no-nonsense doctor voice.

She didn't even turn to say goodbye to Paul, which told me whatever we were about to see at the hospital was going to be bad. Very bad.

Petra

Racing to the hospital, I did my breathing exercises I did when I knew I was about to go into a very stressful situation. I was used to this but didn't normally have a personal attachment to the patient. I desperately wanted to get Maggie back on the phone, but I would rather have her "on the scene." She was our best nurse. She wasn't normally on these late-night shifts, but I did remember that she took on a few extra this week to help out another nurse who needed some time off. Thank God she was there.

I wanted to ask Janie so many questions. There was a lot running through my head right now, but the roads were so bad, I didn't want to take my eyes or my mind off of them.

"Do you think her kids know?" I asked, trying to stick to simple questions.

"I will call them right now," Janie said. "Wait, I don't have my phone."

I immediately passed her mine and kept driving.

The calm quiet in our car was almost comical compared to the shitshow scene we experienced just a few short minutes ago in my driveway. I wanted to ask Janie if she had been drinking. It wasn't out of the realm and wouldn't a good friend ask that question? Especially after what she had told us. I didn't want to insult her, though. Wouldn't that push her to a place where her sobriety was threatened? But she had pulled a gun on my husband just a few short minutes ago.

"They're not answering. They would have been called, right?" Janie questioned.

"Absolutely," I said. "Maggie would have made sure they were called," I said, trying to be confident in that. I knew Maggie would do everything right, but the ER could turn into a madhouse, especially now. And if Lisa were really bad, they would make her life priority over everything.

"Janie, can I ask you something?" I said, feeling the Mercedes slip a little bit on the icy road. I quickly regained control and kept my eyes on the road even though I really wanted to look at her.

"Sure," she said simply.

She sounded nervous. As inappropriate as this was, I felt the overwhelming sensation to laugh. The extremes of this evening were hard not to chuckle at. I was completely overstimulated.

"Have you been drinking?" I asked. "Not judging, just trying to understand what's happening."

Janie's silence next to me scared me. I think she was giving me her answer in her silence.

"We'll figure out what is going on, make sure Lisa is okay, and then we're going to get you straight to detox. I can even make calls once we get to the …"

"I haven't been drinking," Janie said.

She didn't sound angry or defensive, just to the point. Instead of prodding, I stayed silent.

"But I also haven't been sleeping, and I feel like I'm losing my mind right now," she said, starting to cry.

Keeping one hand firmly on the wheel, I took my other hand off to reach out and grab hers.

"Tell me what's going on," I said. "I'm here."

"Petra, the girls called us earlier to say that Lisa was missing. And the thing is, I left Lisa with Paul."

"What?" I asked, feeling my stomach sinking. "What do you mean?"

"I left Lisa by the pond with Paul because we were digging up a mound there that we thought might have been Carrie."

"Oh, boy," I said, just shaking my head. This was all my fault.

We were pulling up to the hospital at this point. I skidded the car into a parking spot, coming inches from slamming into the car in front of me. Luckily, my brakes finally kicked in, and we stopped in time.

"That's where Paul was tonight? This is what you guys were yelling about in the garage. So, how do you know it wasn't Carrie?" I asked.

"I don't," Janie said.

After a minute of silence, I started gathering my purse and mentally preparing myself for going in.

"But I guess the good news is, we know it wasn't Lisa buried out there," Janie said quietly from her seat.

Janie

Petra and I linked arms and ran into the hospital, slipping and sliding all the way. In my hurry, I'd left my mask in the car and there were a few frantic moments where I thought I would have to head back to the car. In the end, Petra came through with a stash of extra ones she had in her purse.

The absurdity of how we quickly switched from intense conversation about possibly accusing her husband of murder to making sure we were following proper Covid protocol was not lost on me. This night couldn't possibly get any stranger.

At the entrance, Petra squeezed my hand.

"Just stay here for a sec," Petra said. "I'm gonna check in and see what's going on."

"Should I wait outside? I'm not going to be able to get in, am I?" I asked, trying to peek into the waiting room to see if I could see Lisa's girls. With the new protocols, normally they allowed family members only, if that.

"Let me see what I can do," Petra said, leaving me in a heated, covered breezeway that was technically still considered "outside." It was tented, similar to what some of the restaurants did to try and keep customers happy. I was sheltered from the inclement weather to a degree, but still felt the intensity of the storm. The angry winds smacked at the sides of the tented walls, making it sway from side to side. This was going to be a long night.

I watched her approach the front desk of the ER, flash her badge and rush behind the table to look at the computer screen. She looked up and met my eyes then looked back down again. She put up her pointer finger in the air, as though to say, "Wait," and disappeared through the doors that led to the ER.

I took a few deep breaths and turned to look outside. I couldn't quite shake off the chill that held my body hostage. It had nothing to do with the actual temperature. It was fear. For my friend, Lisa. For her girls. For Carrie. For Petra.

How would things shake out for Paul? What were we about to discover? I also had fear for my future.

What was to come of me if I couldn't control my own yearnings? How would I keep going if I was unable to manage my stress?

I watched as the snow continued to blanket the outside. How was it possible, in this time of constant communication, to be left in the dark in these moments of trauma and emergency? How long would it take to get answers to my questions. What had happened to Lisa?

I reached into my pocket, fumbling for my phone. I sighed, hanging my head, frustrated with myself for having lost it and knowing I would be even more out of the loop now.

When I looked up, I saw Lisa's girls running in my direction from the parking lot. They must have just arrived themselves. My eyes instantly teared up and my heart stopped. What was I going to tell them?

Lisa

So many lights.

Petra

I furiously scrubbed as fast as I could, determined to get in and see for myself what the update was. I hadn't bothered to update Janie because there was no time and the answers were just not there. There was no time to waste. I trusted the team working on Lisa, but I trusted myself more. I needed to have eyes on her. Just as I was putting the last of my PPP on, Maggie came through the door, shocking me into silence. I stood staring at her, bracing myself for bad news.

"She's okay," Maggie said quickly. "They stopped the bleeding. They're finishing up."

I leaned back against the wall and put my head in my hands, overwhelmed.

"Tell me everything," I said, unable to meet her eyes. I never did this, but I felt like I could burst into tears at any second.

"She hit a light pole. Her car slid off the road in this storm. They got the internal bleeding under control. We'll fill you in later. The important thing is, she's going to be fine. Thank God for seat belts," Maggie said, coming next to me and rubbing my back. "This scared me," Maggie said, allowing me to see her vulnerability. I looked over at her, noticing and appreciating the softness in her chin and the heavy wrinkles around her eyes that made her all the more lovable. I choked back a sob, knowing it must have been bad for Maggie to say that.

"Where are the girls?" I asked, already moving to the next step and doing my best to bury my emotions.

"I haven't seen them yet. I thought you might want to talk to them," she said.

I looked up and rubbed at my face quickly.

"OK, where is Dr. G?" I said, referring to the surgeon who worked on Lisa.

"He's coming in a sec," she said.

At that very moment, Doctor Gerardo, or Dr. G, as we referred to him, walked in.

"She's all good, my friend," he said to me, smiling.

Thank God he was the one on call. Dr. G was by far my favorite. He was close to retirement when the pandemic started. Thank God he had made the hard choice to come back full time and gift this hospital with his skills in order to help the extreme number of cases we were crushed with.

"I'll tell you everything on the way to see her family. You ready?" he asked me. "I heard her girls are here?"

"Yes, they should be here by now," I said, a catch in my throat.

I stood and made my way to the doorway where he was standing, waiting for me. Dr. G was a good seven inches shorter than me. He was compact and fast. Even in his older age, he moved like a cat, quick and decisive. As he cruised down the hall leading to the waiting room, he linked his arm in mine.

"Don't you worry, Petra. Your friend will be fine. Dr. G is quick like a bee," he said, pulling out one of his rhymes he always used to make people comfortable. This made me feel better. I squeezed his arm with my other hand and broke down in tears of relief. I just couldn't hold it in anymore.

Janie

We huddled together in the indoor/outdoor vestibule with our arms linked together. The more time that passed, the more freaked out I felt. Why hadn't Petra come back to update me? If everything was good, we would have heard from her. There would have been immediate news.

My mind was rushing to horrible places. I imagined Petra scanning through body bags, double confirming that Lisa was in one of them. That's all we heard about on the news. How there were so many bags and so many bodies that there had been mix ups.

"When are they going to let us in?" Veronica whined next to me.

"Can I text her again?" Brenda asked, the calmer one of the girls.

I looked at them, noticing for the first time that they both had their long hair in French braids. My heart broke, thinking back to watching Lisa teach them how to do it when they were younger.

"Yes," I said, fighting to hold back tears. It wouldn't matter if I did. Petra would contact us as soon as she could. That I knew for sure.

Suddenly, the door flew open. Paul's large form commanded the entire doorway, his gaze intense and searching. He looked like a lumberjack in his plaid shirt covered by a down vest. I watched as his eyes softened once they fell on the girls standing there. He looked down before stepping in, pulling off his snow cap from his bald head.

"Ladies," he said quietly by way of greeting.

The girls simply stared at him and held tight to each other. They looked like they were waiting for Paul to give an update, being that he was Petra's husband, but I knew immediately from the lost look on his face, he had none.

I was actually surprised it had taken him this long to get to the hospital. I thought he would be right behind us. It must have taken him awhile to get someone over there to watch the kids.

"Is there any news?" he asked, looking around at the three of us with his eyebrows up in question.

We all shook our heads no.

"Petra?" he asked, looking at me.

"She went in almost forty minutes ago, and we haven't heard a peep," I said.

Paul swallowed and nodded his head.

"And we can't go in?" he said, nodding his chin in the direction of the door.

I looked back at the receptionist who was turned away from me. I'd knocked on the door over ten times in the last thirty minutes checking to see if she had an update. After the fifth time getting up to come see me, she started just shaking her head no, or putting her hands up in the air to answer my questions. She wasn't being snotty about it. She just had nothing.

"No, we can't go in," I said, turning back to him.

"And we don't know what brought her here yet?" Paul asked, stepping close to the door as though his presence could will the receptionist to turn around and give him answers.

I didn't answer.

Paul must have sensed my unease, because he turned to look at me and whispered so that the girls couldn't hear.

"Janie," his eyes pleaded with mine.

I didn't break eye contact with him, trying to see into his soul. What was he hiding?

"I saw her leave. She was safe in her car. I would never hurt her," he said, his face up close to mine, so there would be no chance of the girls overhearing.

Paul was a very attractive man. Up close, he smelled like baby powder and lavender. His cocoa skin was smooth, and his brown eyes were attentive and sharp. But what if his well-put-together exterior had been a front this whole time? My ex was like this. Mr. Suave on the outside, dirt on the inside.

"I can prove it if you need me to. It's in the car," Paul said. "Come with me. I'll show you."

"What are you two whispering about?" I heard Veronica bark in a snotty voice. "We're not children. You can tell us. God, I'm so sick of this," she said, kicking the bench.

But that was just it. These were still children. And I feared they were about to be left alone in this world to fend for themselves.

Lisa

Petra

Dr. G and I approached the girls, who though were family members to Lisa, were still considered a risk to the hospital. Not to mention, the risk they would be taking on themselves being here at a hospital that treated Covid patients.

The girls held onto each other, looking as though I were the Grim Reaper himself coming to meet them. I did my best to paste a smile on my face, gathering my wits. Dr. G had been his usual calming presence, talking me down from the little meltdown I'd had in the hallway. He'd seen so many deaths over the years, but he never made you feel like that was to be accepted. The fact that he made sure I felt better, explaining all the intricate details of the surgery, gave me everything I needed to face the girls. I knew now that Lisa would be okay.

The girls took the news well but became very upset when I told them that they were not going to be able to see their mother.

"Are you kidding me?" Veronica said in an exasperated tone. "That's it. I've had enough."

She went so far as to pull the door open and storm out into the night, as though that were going to somehow change my mind.

I smiled at her sister, Brenda, who watched me sheepishly through lowered lashes. "I'm sorry about that," she mumbled.

"I understand," I said simply, feeling good to experience this "normal" behavior. It was to be expected from a teenager. And one facing the mortality of her mother, even more so. I smiled and waited with Brenda, while Dr. G said his goodbyes for now. He had to get back in, but I thought it best to stay out here until Veronica came back.

"Where is Janie?" I asked, looking around. I'd been so laser focused on the girls that it finally hit me that she wasn't here.

"She and your husband said they would be right back. They were going to the car to get something," Brenda said, pointing outside.

I walked closer to the door leading out to the parking lot. This little indoor/outdoor hallway wasn't very warm. Perhaps she had gone back to the car to warm up a bit. I looked down at my watch and was shocked to see a good hour had passed since we'd first arrived. I'd been so wrapped up in getting the details about Lisa that I'd let so much time pass. She must have been terrified, waiting out here for news.

"Paul is here?" I asked, trying to form a plan in my head. The last time those two had been together, Janie was pointing a gun at Paul. And from our car ride over, I knew that Janie wasn't exactly feeling great about Paul. She had essentially accused him of being a killer. I'd been so freaked out to get into the hospital to see how Lisa was that I hadn't even really let that register.

"I left Lisa by the pond with Paul," she had said.

That had scared me at first, but now we knew that Lisa had not been harmed by the lake, she had been hurt in a car accident.

A thought struck me that rocked me so hard, I had to grab onto the back of a small bench set up in this breezeway for people to rest on as they waited for news.

"Petra, are you OK?" Brenda asked, coming closer to me.

I searched for words, unable to find them. This night was breaking me.

"Did they seem upset when they left?" I asked.

She gave me the strangest look. Her left eyebrow raised and her forehead scrunched down like she was scared and confused at the same time.

"They kind of did," she said. "They were whispering over there," she said, pointing to a corner at the far end of the breezeway.

I looked over there as though that small, dark corner would hold the answers to my questions.

"I'll be right back," I said, bolting out the door and into the snowstorm to find Paul and Janie. I was wearing only my scrubs, my feet in flimsy shoes when really, I needed my heavy-duty boots. I stopped in my tracks, seconds before getting hit by a car heading into the hospital parking lot, where I was going as well. I motioned with my hand for the small, white Jeep to keep going after they had slammed on their brakes. In answer to that, the driver shot me the middle finger before continuing on.

I didn't blame him. I'd been careless.

Running now, it felt like an eternity to get under the protection of the garage roof. My eyes scanned frantically, looking for my husband and my friend. There shouldn't be a lot of cars here. This lot was primarily set up for visitors, and there weren't any allowed right now. Yet, here I was, drowning in a sea of cars.

"Look," I heard my husband's voice bark.

He sounded so angry and unlike himself that at first, I thought it to be someone else. But then a second, "look" broke through the silence, confirming that it was indeed a very angry, aggressive Paul. What was going on?

I ran up the ramp to where I thought I heard his voice. The acoustics made it difficult to identify exactly where the voice was coming from. To add to the confusion, suddenly angry, white Jeep man came racing around the corner, nearly striking me for the second time. This time I was the one that flashed the middle finger. The driver continued on as though I weren't even there.

As I made my way up the second ramp, I saw Janie hunched over, her back to me and her hands on her knees. She reached out and grabbed onto the concrete pillar next to her as though reaching for support. She was definitely hurt or not well. I saw Paul come quickly from behind a car, making a beeline for Janie.

"Stop!" I yelled at the top of my lungs.

Janie

I couldn't control the waves of nausea that ripped through me, starting in my stomach and circling up like a tsunami through my body to form a buzzing sound in my head. The smell. It was in my nose, in my mouth, in my ears. As soon as he lifted that black tarp covering it, it released everywhere. Every. Where.

Grabbing onto the cement pillar next to me, I gagged and gagged, doing my best to keep my stomach contents contained. Why would he put that in his car? What was he thinking? It would never be functional again.

I wanted to scream at Paul, but there was no way I could do that at the moment with my body fighting me like this.

"Stop," I heard Petra scream from nearby. Finally. Where had she been? It felt like we had been waiting an eternity for news on Lisa.

Petra wasn't looking at me though. She was staring, her eyes wide with fear and confusion at Paul, who had moved from the other side of the car and was now directly behind me. The look on her face made me stand up straight and try and pull it together. She was dressed in only her scrubs that were soaked at the bottom, as though she had run through a mountain of snow to get to us. When she yelled, "Stop" again, I noticed a cloud of smoke filled the air, the weather condensing her air droplets. She looked so angry, she reminded me of a fiery dragon shooting off smoke. If flames shot out of her mouth next, I wouldn't be shocked.

"What?" Paul asked in a confused tone. "What are you doing out here?"

"I think the better question is what are you doing?" Petra yelled at him.

Petra made a beeline for me, grabbing my arm and pulling me away from Paul.

"I was showing her the dog," Paul said in an exasperated tone. He threw his hands up in the air and stepped away. "No one believes me, so I dug the dog up and here it is," he said, pulling the tarp he'd placed over the carcass of the dog completely off it.

The decayed animal stunk like mold, manure, decay, and dirt. The wave of it nearly knocked me on my feet again. Involuntarily, I stepped back, pulling Petra with me.

"Oh," I said, searching for something to hold onto. "I think I'm going to faint."

Petra held me up, grabbing my arm and setting me against the pillar. When she had me steadied, she turned, anger dripping off her.

"Paul, you brought a dead dog to the hospital. Have you lost your mind?" Petra said, yelling at him in a way I'd never heard her speak to her husband. She looked around, up near the ceiling, as though she was looking for something.

"I think we've all lost our minds. I, for one, am sick and tired of you not believing me. Or everyone not believing me, apparently. So, I brought the dead dog to show you. This, Pommie," he said, pointing at the collar with identification attached.

Pommie? That had been the names that my kids said the Lady of the Lake had been calling out while she roamed the paths at night. This was what she was searching for.

"Lisa and I dug up the grave by the pond," Paul continued. "We found this, then we put it back. End of story. I didn't kill Lisa. I didn't kill Carrie. Hell, I didn't even kill this damned dog. Apparently, when we put it back in the grave, we disturbed the mud enough to make it look like a bigger grave and now y'all think there are more bodies out there. But I'm here to show you, you're wrong. This is it. It's a damned dog," Paul said, spitting through his speech.

He stopped talking, ran a hand over his bald head, letting out a long breath and looking away from us for the first time.

"And I see what you are looking for up there. I get it. I'm embarrassing you because this whole thing is probably being recorded by the security cameras, and you're hating me even more," Paul said, his voice contrite as he addressed Petra.

Petra stood silent next to me.

"Paul, you looked like you were going to hurt Janie," Petra said, making a chill run through me. What exactly had she seen when I had my back turned to him while I was gagging?

Paul said nothing. Just stood there silently watching us with a sad look on his face. After a few seconds, he said, "I would never hurt Janie. I was rushing to her to see if she was okay. As soon as I showed her the dog and she started getting sick, I regretted doing it. I was just so upset that no one believed me. How could you not believe me, Petra? All I've ever done is support and love you," he said.

The way he spoke was so hauntingly calm that I found myself wanting to believe him. Maybe he was right. Maybe we had all lost our damned minds.

We had all been locked up with each other, feeling that an invisible force was out there trying to kill us.

"Lisa?" I asked, finally feeling a little better.

"She's good. She was in a car accident," Petra said. "She hit a pole, had some internal bleeding, but it's all under control now," Petra said, making eye contact with me briefly before turning back to stare at Paul.

Paul put his hands up in the air in a, "See, I told you so," gesture. For a second, my mind raced to the future, six months from now when we would all be together, barbecuing and trying to put this in the past. How would I ever be able to hang out with Paul again without him hating me? How would we ever get past the awkwardness of me having pulled a gun on him at his house and accusing him of being a murderer? If things weren't so dire, we could almost laugh at the ridiculousness of all of this.

But wait.

One more thing.

"Paul," I said, quietly.

He'd turned to cover the poor dead dog up with the tarp he'd dramatically pulled away to show Petra the contents.

"What if Carrie's body was there, too, and you dug up the dog so you could move her? And maybe Lisa saw the body, ran from you, and got in a car accident?"

Paul stopped; his monstrous body frozen in place near the trunk of the car. He didn't or wouldn't turn around.

Lisa

"Kiss me," I whispered.

Erik's long hair tickled my face as he leaned down and put his soft lips on mine. We were in a beautiful field filled with wildflowers of all different colors, my favorite being the purple ones. When he started to pull away, I held his face to mine longer.

"Do we have to go back?" I asked, wanting to stay longer. It was so peaceful here. The light was shimmery and soft, like a sunset that didn't seem to want to end. "Let the moment last," I whispered softly into his lips.

When he pulled away, my body recoiled at the face I saw now staring back at me. My wonderful, sexy, young Erik had somehow morphed into Rick the Dick.

I crawled my body away, gripping the grass under me for support.

Petra

After Janie asked Paul the question I'd been wondering myself, I grabbed onto her arm, afraid of Paul's reaction. He was angry tonight. Probably the angriest I'd ever seen him. He was always very much in control of his emotions and steady. Tonight, he'd seemed different. Rocked a bit.

A ringing sound caught my attention, making me look around to try and decipher where it was coming from. My first instinct was that it was a security alert going off somewhere. Perhaps the security office had been watching our interactions in the garage and were sounding an alarm that Paul was about to blow. I was almost grateful for an extra pair of eyes on this situation because I didn't like where it was going.

"You," Janie said, interrupting my thoughts.

"What?" I asked, looking at her.

"Your pocket. Your phone is ringing in your pocket," she said.

Paul turned around, meeting my eyes briefly before turning back to slam the trunk closed. I couldn't decipher what I saw in those brief seconds on his face. He looked angry to me. But something else.

"Hello?" I said, noting that it was the hospital calling me.

The voice on the other end was grumbled and barely audible, but it sounded like it was Maggie.

"Are you?" were the two words I could make out.

"I'm in the garage," I said. "I'm still here."

"Come back," were the only words I was able to decipher before the connection cut out. This garage was notorious for being a dead zone with cell service.

"We have to go back. Something is wrong," I said, turning to head back into the hospital. As soon as I said this, I remembered that no one else would be able to go back in with me. What were they going to do now? Stand outside in that stupid little vestibule and glare at each other? What choice did we have at this point?

"Let's go," Paul said, quietly, moving quickly. As he moved past me, I was nearly knocked out by the wave of decay carried over from the trunk.

Normally, Paul's scent was appealing, a constant appeal, in fact. Even when he was sweating due to working out or doing projects around the house, he still smelled good to me. Tonight, after lifting the tarp, he stunk of death, a smell I associated only with myself and my job at the hospital. I wonder if he always had to push that aside when I came home from work? He'd never brought it up. I always made an effort to clean up, but death could linger, as it did on him right now.

I slipped a bit on the ice when we made it to the street that separated the parking garage and the hospital. I was shivering now uncontrollably, the cold air and the powerful winter wind aggressively attacking me in my paper-thin scrubs.

Paul caught my arm as I started to slip and steadied me. We locked eyes for a brief second before he quickly turned and looked forward again. He was angry with me. Probably the angriest I'd ever seen him be. Would we ever be able to recover from this? How could we possibly?

"I'll be right back," I said, knowing that I was lying.

Both of Lisa's girls were standing in the vestibule now, smiling and laughing, with their father, Rick the Dick. I'm sure that they were celebrating and relieved that I had passed on good news just a few minutes earlier. I was sick to my stomach, thinking I might have to change course and prepare them for more. This wasn't that shocking. Things like this happened all the time. Just when you thought things were going well in these emergency situations, things could turn.

"What's wrong?" Rick the Dick asked me, probably catching the stricken look on my face.

I so desperately wanted to say to him, "Oh, now you care?" But instead, I held my hands out to the girls and focused in on them.

"I've been called back. I'm not sure what is going on. I want to go make sure your mom is okay," I said as calmly as I could.

"What?" Veronica shrieked. "You said everything was fine."

The girls grabbed onto each other and Rick moved in.

"I'm sure it is. I'm just going to check," I said, still not making eye contact with Rick.

"We really need you to step up here, Petra," Rick said in a condescending voice. As though I was working for him, and I was disappointing him. Piss off.

Ignoring him completely, I looked at the girls and said, "Stay strong. I'm going to do everything I can."

I raced past them and shoved the door open but not before hearing Rick sneer at Paul, "You stink."

Janie

Paul said nothing in response to Rick's comment. Again, if this night wasn't so stressful, it would almost be comical. Rick was so clueless, so self-centered. How dare Paul come in and invade his private breathing space with such a bad odor? It wasn't that bad now that we were away from the car. In fact, I hadn't even noticed it on him until Paul had taken me to the car. Typical pissy pants Rick to have such a sensitive sniffer.

I looked at Paul, who as usual kept his calm and said nothing. He made eye contact with me and for a brief second, I thought we were going to share a quick laugh, as though bonded briefly by our mutual dislike for Rick and his narcissistic ways.

"Come sit down, girls," Paul said kindly, gesturing toward the bench in the vestibule.

Always a gentleman. That's what made my theory so painful to swallow. I had to be wrong. Or maybe I was right? There was such thing as a covert narcissist. Rick was clearly an overt narcissist. We all knew he was in it for himself. We'd only accepted him because he was Lisa's husband and we loved her. We'd tried our best to support her even when things were clearly not going well and she was unhappy. It took a long time for her to admit it, because she was trying to keep her family together. I understood that. I wanted that for her as well. But in the end, Petra and I had rejoiced when she finally had left him. Of course, we had no idea how dire of a situation he would leave her in when it came to the finances.

Paul had been the husband everyone had loved. His calm, charismatic demeanor had won us all over, including my husband, Sam. He was always positive, always supportive of Petra, and going the extra mile for his kids. But isn't this how the covert narcissist cases ended on all those crime shows? Everyone believes that the husband is such a great guy until it's proven that he really isn't? He's actually a murderer or something of that nature.

I blatantly stared at Paul, trying to get into his head.

Petra had vocalized how hard it had been on their marriage when her brother died. How she had felt that Paul had let her down a bit. Not been there for her enough when she needed him to go check on Danny. I'd always supported Petra but felt Paul's side of the story was on key as well. It was simply hard to be around Danny. He was a little neurotic and unpredictable. Petra, as his loving sister, didn't see it as clearly, but I did. I wouldn't want to go check on Danny. His lifestyle and his friends scared me a bit. From one addict to another, I saw the demons in him. He wasn't well.

But.

Maybe Paul had killed Danny, too? Maybe Paul was a complete psychopath on a murderous killing spree at this point. Danny, then Carrie, then Lisa. And maybe even that damned dog.

"Janie, are you alright?" Rick the Dick asked, pulling me out of my thoughts. He was standing very close to me and had the audacity to reach out and touch my arm. I pulled away and gave him a dirty look. He repulsed me.

"I'm fine," I said, curtly. Trying my best to be cool in front of the girls. He was their father, my client, whether I liked it or not, and we were in crisis. I had to put my personal feelings aside here.

"You had a weird look on your face," Rick said, pushing the issue.

For God sakes, Rick. Just shut up. This was all awkward enough.

"I'm just cold," I said quietly. "And scared," I admitted, feeling like it was better for the girls at this point to be honest. Maybe it would help them? If there was one thing I learned over and over as I clung to the edge of the cliff I knew as sobriety, it was never good to hide your true feelings. That got you nowhere. Because in the end, you would give those feelings over to the bottle, or pills, or whatever you chose as your poison. And you would lose all the people who you could have just talked to instead of taking that way.

"I am, too," Brenda said, holding tighter to her sister.

Veronica nodded, all her teenage snottiness she had used as a shield earlier, completely wiped away. "Me, too," she said, crying openly.

"Me, too," said Rick, dramatically, putting his head in his hands in a theatrical way.

Paul and I made eye contact over Rick's head, and this time there was no mistaking our mutual smirk in reaction to Rick's phoniness.

Lisa

Ouch.

Petra

"Where's Maggie?" I asked, frantically searching the boards and checking to see if any of the patients were coding. My heart slowed a little when I noted that there hadn't been one in the last few minutes. Huh. Okay, maybe I could calm down a bit.

Maggie came whipping around the corner, a little frazzled looking but not panicked.

"Oh, thank God you're still here. I think she might be waking up. She's cringing a bit. I just upped her pain meds," Maggie said, taking off her reading glasses and pulling me to the side of the hallway. "I thought you would want to be here if her eyes open."

"Oh, that's great news," I said, smiling under all my PPP gear. I grabbed my phone, ready to text everyone the good news when Maggie grabbed my arm.

"Go ahead and share that good news with Lisa's girls and then come with me to room seven," Maggie said, her laser blue eyes on me. "There's a patient requesting you."

"Me?" I asked. "Like she asked for me to be her specific doctor?" I asked, wondering where this was going. I was only half paying attention because I was setting up a group text to the girls, Paul, and Janie. I didn't bother to include Rick in it, which I'm sure would upset him. I had an old number for him that I wasn't even sure was updated. Let his ego be wounded. I could care less right now.

After I hit the send button on my happy news, I made eye contact with Maggie, waiting for her to give me the rest of the news.

"Petra, she gave another name, but I think it might be someone you know?" she whispered, looking around the hallway to see if anyone else was listening.

"What?" I asked. "What are you talking about?" I raised an eyebrow and looked at her. My mind was only focused on getting to Lisa's room. I wanted to be standing there when she woke up. And, I wanted to check on the meds they were giving her. I didn't want her to be in pain. I knew waking up from her accident would be excruciating if we didn't balance the meds right.

"Your neighbor who went missing. The one you thought was killed. I swear this woman looks like the woman on the news, but her hair is a different color," she said.

"Carrie?" I asked, alarm bells going off in my head.

"Yes," Maggie said.

I allowed my mind to run in a million directions until it settled on just one. Paul. He hadn't killed her.

I moved in a trance to room seven, Maggie still right behind me. As I pulled the curtain back slowly with my hand, I saw a woman with her back to me on the exam table, her hair a dark black. Carrie had been a light blond like Janie.

"Hi," I said quietly, waiting for her to turn. I could barely breathe as I watched her head turn slowly in my direction. Her hesitation and fear were palpable.

"Petra," Carrie said, in her unmistakable high-pitched voice. The same voice I'd heard in this very room a number of months ago. The beautiful blond I knew was gone, replaced by a haunted woman, the bones of her clavicles protruding and dark circles drowning out the beauty of her young face.

"I need your help," she said quietly.

I walked into the room, Maggie still behind me, forever my back-up, and walked over to her, reaching my hand out to her.

"You're alive," I said simply. "We were very worried about you."

"I had to hide. I was scared," she stuttered. "He was. He..."

I noticed she could barely make eye contact with me and kept looking down at the other hand in her lap that didn't hold mine.

"He killed my dog," she said.

Carrie

I shivered, hugging my arms around my body, watching Petra place a hand on the wall and look down before pulling up a chair to come sit closer to me. There was no going back now. I had to end this nightmare. I'd made it this far and had to finish it. I couldn't and wouldn't go backward.

"Carrie," Petra said in a soft voice. "There are a lot of people looking for you right now. Do you know that?"

Ashamed and overwhelmed by this comment, I hung my head and hugged my body tight. Maybe I should have kept running. It was so embarrassing what I was going to have to face. All I would lose. But what was the alternative? Go back to a life where I wasn't even living? Where I was controlled and diminished and beaten and basically treated like an animal? He controlled my relationships, my food, my sleeping, my access to money, my access to a job, my social media accounts. How I was viewed by the rest of the world. No, I would not go back. I did all of this to help push me to my decision.

"Are you hurt, Carrie?" Petra said, inching her chair a little closer. The squeaking sound of the chair as it moved closer struck a nerve, and I backed up instinctively. Once, he hit me because I'd scratched the wood floors. One of the floor protectors had fallen off the bottom of a kitchen chair, unbeknownst to me, leaving a large gash in our new floors after I'd made the mistake of inching closer to the table to help feed the baby. I'd had a ringing sound in my right ear for three weeks after he'd hit me from behind with a closed fist. That ear still didn't seem to function as well. In those times though, I didn't even dream of going to the doctor to get checked out. It was only in the last few years that I'd started to be brave enough to allow doctors to see me damaged. It was a cry for help. Petra had been so close to discovering my dirty secret that time I came here. I knew it and requested her on purpose but chickened out at the last minute.

Petra put a hand softly on my knee.

"Can I take a look at you?" she asked. "Just to see if anything needs immediate attention?"

I nodded my head, yes, very slowly. The herniated disk at the back of my neck made quick movements nearly impossible when it came to moving my head. Once, during sex, he'd slammed my head into a wall so hard that I'd passed out. I'd woken up naked on the floor, discarded like a piece of trash. I should have been visiting a chiropractor but didn't know how I would pay the bills. Besides, I always told myself, what I had self-diagnosed as a herniated disk would hopefully heal on its own. Clearly, I had been wrong. About the neck and a lot of things. If you ignored things, or let more time pass, that didn't mean they would get better. It only meant you were dragging the pain on.

Petra moved around me, touching me with a calm, nurturing hand. I cringed when she felt the right side of my body, near my rib cage. When I'd told Tom I was going to the grocery store and angrily told him I would be back "when I got back," he'd kicked me, a parting gift. In reality, I'd hightailed it back to Chicago, determined to check on my beloved dog, Pommie. I knew he wouldn't hurt the kids, he never had. They were safe with him. He'd told me that he had set up a dog-sitting company to come to the house and take care of Pommie, but something in my gut told me he lied. I had been so focused on getting the kids packed to head to Florida that I'd allowed him to take on the job of setting up Pommie's care. We were supposed to be scouting out new homes in Florida while we were there and didn't feel it right to drag Pommie into it.

The night before we left, he'd said something about, "That dog getting all my attention," and my stomach dropped. He'd been jealous of the dog I'd taken into our home six months ago and let me hear about it every day. I'd been a fool to trust him to find proper care. I knew it but had been so distracted. That kick had woken me up. All of a sudden, I saw his plan so clearly. He was going to allow Pommie to starve to death. We were going to come home, and he'd make up some bullshit story about how the dog-sitting company had dropped the ball.

No. I'd had enough. He was destroying everything. Controlling everything. He couldn't do this anymore.

I'd rushed back to Chicago only to discover I'd been wrong about his plan. He wasn't going to let her starve. He'd just killed her off himself and left her body outside. I'd called for her and called for her, along the pond, in the backyards until my throat was raw. Finally, I'd found her in a place I had initially walked right by. Her normally white, fluffy fur was matted from being outside in the elements, and her eyes were permanently closed.

I could tell her neck had been broken, and she'd been placed under the patio furniture in a way that was too perfect. Too planned. He was probably going to try and play it that she'd been killed by coyotes, but I knew.

By some miracle, I'd come home before any wild animal had carried her away. I was grateful to at least have some closure. To be able to bury her and know where she was. I scooped up her little body and carried her inside to hold her to my chest one last time. Pommie, to me, represented a taste of freedom. Unlike our children, she was all mine. Tom had nothing to do with her. I'd picked her out, I'd nurtured her, I'd loved her. Tom wanted nothing to do with her. He was resentful of her and hated the way I'd poured love on her. He wanted it all the time. For him, for our kids, for our household. He found a solution and executed it, getting his way, just like he always did.

Holding Pommie to my chest, I'd screamed and screamed, mourning the loss of her and my previous life because I knew this was it. I was done. I turned off those damn house cameras, at least the ones I remembered, I never quite knew how to work them as well as he did. They were overkill. The monster was already in the house. I knew he watched my comings and goings on and made my own plan. I was sure he knew I was here and thought I would simply forgive him and come back to Florida when I was ready. He was wrong. And when I wasn't coming back, that's probably when he realized he had to call the police. For a while, I left the house, getting picked up by a cab that took cash and paying cash at a hotel for a bit while trying to figure out what to do. The only thing I could settle on was coming back to Petra. I knew she could help me.

"I think you may have some broken ribs here," Petra said.

"Probably," I said, my voice stronger than just a few moments ago. "He kicked me right before I left Florida," I said boldly, not caring that I was exposing Tom.

"He did stuff like that, a lot," I said, sneering a bit, finally getting angry.

Petra was looking into my right ear with her otoscope.

"Ow, looks like you might have a ruptured eardrum here," she said, putting her hand on my right shoulder. "That has to hurt."

I shook my head no, numb to the pain. I'd had no one to talk to about the pain. I wasn't allowed to have friends. Something about not talking about the pain had weakened its potency. I didn't have connections to my family anymore. All I'd really had left when we'd married was my mother, and I was pretty sure he'd killed her. Her heart attack never seemed legit to me.

"Petra, I did not abandon my kids. I was just going to check on the dog and then go back and get them," I said, reaching out to touch her arm and make her look at me. "I know what people are saying and who is looking for me, but I promise you I was going back for them. I just needed a little more time to figure things out. I had to leave the car and get back to Florida without everyone following me. But, I started to realize, that was impossible."

Petra looked down at me and sent me a sad smile.

"I believe you," she said, saying the words I'd hoped for.

"Can you help me?" I asked, my eyes filling with tears. I didn't even know where to start. How to move forward, which steps to take. This was going to be very hard, but I had to get away from Tom once and for all, with my kids. I wouldn't let him take them from me. He'd taken enough.

Petra surprised me by sitting down on the exam table next to me, taking my hand in hers and looking me in the eye. She held my gaze for a long second, her eyes peeking over her mask and through her face shield. She squeezed my hand softly and said, "Yes, I can help you."

I believed her, and for the first time, in a very, very long time, I felt it blossom up inside of me, wiping away all the injuries I'd sustained over the years both physically and mentally.

I had hope and hope was power.

Janie

The phones dinged at the same time. When Veronica started sobbing, my initial thought was that it was bad news. But when I looked over at Brenda and saw her calm smile beaming back at me, I relaxed. She showed me the message.

Lisa is starting to wake up. All good.

Paul's face beamed with a big smile. I assumed that Petra must have had included all of us in a group text, except Rick who glared back at me, probably angry that she dared to dismiss him.

"She's okay, Dad," Brenda said kindly to him. She seemed to understand instantly that he was going to have a bad reaction to not being included in the celebratory news.

To my disgust, Rick the Dick stood up, nearly knocking Veronica, who had tried to lean in and hug him, off the bench. He stormed past us, announcing, "I need a break," and rushed out toward the direction of the parking garage.

These poor girls. They were raised in this atmosphere where everything revolved around this man's mood swings and temperament. Even in this life-or-death moment, they were trying to make sure he was comfortable and happy. How would they ever know what a healthy relationship looked like? That this was not how life was supposed to be? No wonder why Lisa was so happy to be away from him. Thank God she was getting this second chance at life.

To their credit, the girls simply let him go and moved over to me on my bench. I put both of my arms around them and tugged them close to me. My thoughts went to the huge commission I was going to be getting from the sale of Rick the Dick's girlfriend's house. It was crystal clear now what I'd be doing with that large chunk of money. It would be my honor to sponsor a scholarship fund for these two bright young women. Lisa had broken the cycle, and now she needed some help to make sure these two had bright futures. I was going to make her take the money one way or another. There had to be a way to do it. Petra and I could come up with a plan.

My best angle would be to tell her it was payback for all the help she'd given me. And the only way to make her see that clearly was to get healthy. I smiled, allowing the tears of joy to run freely down my face, seeing, for the first time in a long time, a path. Susanna had been right. It was time to go to meetings locally and let go of the fear of being labeled. I was proud of the mountains I'd climbed. Why not let the world see? I was an addict. I had struggled, I had climbed, and I had overcome. And I still needed help. There was no weakness or shame in admitting that.

And with the skills I'd acquired, the success I'd experienced from digging deep and building myself up to climb those mountains, I was going to help others. Starting with Lisa's girls. The thought of doing that was everything I needed to motivate me to keep going.

Paul walked over to the bench across from us, sat down and flashed me a huge smile, which I returned.

Lisa

"My girls," I struggled to get out, seeing my friend, Petra, across the room. At least I thought it was her. I didn't know where I was, but that long, black ponytail she always wore registered with me immediately. But why was she in her scrubs? Why was she in my house? In my bedroom? Why weren't the girls here? Didn't they have school this morning? Was Petra going to drive them?

I struggled to lift my eyelids, but for some reason they refused to open. Every time I did though, she was in a different place in my room. It was like she was a bee, buzzing everywhere. Was she picking out my clothes for the day? I thought I saw her go into my closet. Didn't she remember that I no longer needed to pick clothes? I was basically in scrubs 24/7.

This little detail was enough to motivate me to get up. I knew I wanted to wear my light pink ones today. They were my favorite.

Ouch.

Wait.

This wasn't my room. The lights were too bright. Were the girls filming one of their TikTok videos? Is that why they had the lights so bright in here?

Ouch.

Suddenly I heard Petra's voice calling out instructions to someone about medications and "get me this."

That was Petra's hospital voice. We were in the hospital. Had I fallen asleep on my shift? How embarrassing.

"Honey, I'm here," I heard Petra say, this time very close to my head.

"Your girls are here. They are waiting outside and very happy that you are okay. You're gonna be just fine. You just relax and sleep if you want. There's no rush."

"What happened?" I asked her, still unable to open my eyes. I gave up and settled my head back on the pillow, calmed by her soft, confident voice. Petra had a reputation for being able to talk patients back from the edge.

Now I understood it from the other side. Her voice was so calming and soothing. Even her smell was appealing. Why wouldn't you be drawn to it?

"You were in a car accident. You had some internal bleeding, but everything turned out great. You'll walk away from this just fine," she said.

Scenes from the accident flashed through my head like images on a big screen. The ice, the snow, my hands gripping tight to the steering wheel, the pole.

"Bleeding?" I managed to say. In the few months I'd been working here, there was nothing that scared me more than the thought of there being internal bleeding for a car accident victim. In my mind, I had referred to them as Titanic victims. Looked good on the outside, but there could be holes internally that could sink the whole thing.

"I promise you, it's all good now," Petra said. "You know I would tell you."

I relaxed, knowing she would. I could tell Petra was telling me the truth, and that put my mind at ease.

I smiled and allowed sleep's gentle hand to rock me back to slumber. I knew I was in good hands.

Petra

FIVE MONTHS LATER

"I don't want to leave," Paul said, putting his magazine down and looking over at me from his lounge chair.

"Neither do I," I said, pulling my glasses down to better see the kids who were lathered in sunblock and having the time of their lives in the large, in-ground pool next to our rental home.

A few months ago, I'd packed the family up, took a leave of absence from my job, got the kids enrolled in online schooling and hired tutors to come daily to the rental. I'd also signed myself up for an intensive 16-week grief recovery program just outside of Destin, Florida that had lived up to its reputation. I felt like myself again. Finally. It felt like life was starting to piece itself back together.

"Can we extend it?" Paul asked.

I looked over at him and smiled. He set his magazine down on his bare chest and reached his hand over to take mine.

"I love you," I said simply.

"I love you, too," he said, smiling.

To say that the events that transpired during Covid had not affected us would be a lie. There were still scars. But somehow, some way, we had used it to make us stronger. Paul had attended many of my grief meetings when spouses were invited. In the individual counseling sessions, he was open and truthful about his feelings about me believing that he was somehow involved in Carrie's disappearance. We were still dealing with all of that, but somehow, we'd been doing well.

As great as this was, I knew that we had to get back to reality at some point. I spoke with Janie and Lisa nearly every day on Zoom calls, texts, and phone. We were in constant contact.

Lisa had made a full recovery and was dating Erik, a younger man I really liked for her. She was killing it in life. She was excelling in school, and her kids were plugging along, looking at schools for their future. They were on fire. Word on the street was that Rick the Dick had been dumped by his young lady, who moved into the grand house with a different man she'd picked up almost immediately after dropping Rick. Rick hadn't been heard from in three months. The last we'd heard he had moved to California, chasing a potential new sugar momma. The rumor was she was almost ninety years old. Lisa, Janie, and I had a good laugh about that one.

Janie had enrolled in an outpatient sober program connected with my hospital. I'd been able to pull some strings because those treatment programs were bursting at the seams. It worked well for Janie because it was close to home, and she was able to continue working long hours in real estate. After her biggest competition, Frederick, had been fired for bringing cocaine to the office, Janie had relaxed a lot. I think the fact that Frederick had been dealing with his own demons had made her step back a little and relax. She didn't seem judgmental of him or angry anymore. In fact, she'd called him to try and get him help, and as far as I knew, it was going well.

Carrie's story finally died down after a few hellish months for her. Unfortunately, the media clung onto it, trying to make it appear as though she were unstable. It took a few painful months, but finally, they had backed off and moved onto other stories. I was set to help her in her upcoming case against her husband. Tom wasn't backing down in his pursuit to gain sole custody of the children, which was heartbreaking for Carrie. It was like everything she'd been afraid of was coming true. Tom moved back into the home in our neighborhood, another reason I was putting off going home, and had split custody of the kids for now. Janie's husband, Sam, had hooked up Carrie with the best divorce attorney in the area. Sam kept telling us not to worry, based on all he knew about the case, so I didn't. He just kept saying, "Just trust me, justice will be served. These kinds of guys always get caught. We have enough documented threats from all the emails, texts, and phone calls he was stupid enough to do. He's crumbling. She's going to be just fine."

I spoke with Carrie at least once a week and each week she sounded better and better. I could tell she was rebuilding her confidence and her self-esteem. She was with her kids more and more, wondering if Tom was releasing his hold just a bit. Perhaps he would take after Rick the Dick and move on to his next pursuit. His next victim. Everything I read and saw for my own eyes about people like Rick and Tom taught me the same thing. When the victim was done and escaped, the narcissist didn't wait around for them after they realized they no longer had a hold. They just found another victim to suck the life from.

"Let's go in and start lunch," I said, looking down at my watch. Sometimes it was hard to face that I had abandoned my team at the hospital during the pandemic. But I had to take this break. I was losing myself, my family, and my sanity. I needed this reset to be effective at the hospital again. I would get back there. I made sure they had fabulous doctors on staff during my leave. I'd pressed for some favors from old colleagues and so far, so good.

"Mac and cheese again," Paul laughed, sitting up, his six-pack flexing in the Florida sun.

"They love it and it's easy," I said, thinking that saying also applied to my life over the last few months.

Paul leaned over and kissed me. I held his head in my hands and kept him close to me, relishing the smell of his aftershave.

I could stay here forever. But Powerful Petra had to go back at some point. And I would. Just not yet.

Acknowledgements

I would like to thank my husband, Brent Hansen, and my family for always supporting me in following my dreams.

Thank you to my editor, J. Scott Wilson, my cover artist, Deborah C. Blanc, and Kevin Moriarty, for all of my formatting and technical work on the book.

I would also like to thank any medical professionals who talked me through what Covid was like for them, especially, Maralee Castiglioni (RN). Maralee walked me through what life was like in the ER during Covid. Hearing first-hand about the fears, anxieties and emotions clinical professionals had to face while treating critically ill patients during this time helped pull the plot of this book together.

A special thank you to my writing accountability partner, Julie Oleszek. Our monthly meetings keep me on track, hold me accountable, and keep me laughing through the time-consuming and sometimes tedious task of writing a book.

And to my Accountability Club (Shannon Gifford, Kathleen Kilburg and Amanda Borre)-you guys are the best! I have so much fun going after our Top Gun goals. There is nothing more powerful than a group of motivated women with dreams and a "to-do" list.

About The Author

Annie Hansen is the co-founder of Hansen Search Group, a staffing firm she launched with her business partner and husband, Brent Hansen, in 2001. She is the author of her cozy mystery series, The Kelly Clark Mystery Series, set in the far western suburbs of Chicago. Annie can be reached through her website: www.anniehansenauthor.com.

Made in the USA
Monee, IL
23 September 2023

43254406R00155